CRAF

D0727399

DELIA'S GIFT

Virginia Andrews® Books

The Dollanganger Family Series
Flowers in the Attic
Petals on the Wind
If There Be Thorns
Seeds of Yesterday
Garden of Shadows

The Casteel Family Series
Heaven
Dark Angel
Fallen Hearts
Gates of Paradise
Web of Dreams

The Cutler Family Series
Dawn
Secrets of the Morning
Twilight's Child
Midnight Whispers
Darkest Hour

The Landry Family Series
Ruby
Pearl in the Mist
All That Glitters
Hidden Jewel
Tarnished Gold

The Logan Family Series
Melody
Heart Song
Unfinished Symphony
Music of the Night
Olivia

The Orphans Miniseries
Butterfly
Crystal
Brooke
Raven
Runaways (full-length novel)

The Wildflowers Miniseries
Misty
Star
Jade
Cat
Into the Garden (full-length novel)

The Hudson Family Series
Rain
Lightning Strikes
Eye of the Storm
The End of the Rainbow

The Shooting Stars Series
Cinnamon
Ice
Rose
Honey
Falling Stars

The De Beers Family Series
Willow
Wicked Forest
Twisted Roots
Into the Woods
Hidden Leaves

The Broken Wings Series
Broken Wings
Midnight Flight

The Gemini Series
Celeste
Black Cat
Child of Darkness

The Shadows Series
April Shadows
Girl in the Shadows

The Early Spring Series
Broken Flower
Scattered Leaves

The Secret Series
Secrets in the Attic
Secrets in the Shadows

The Delia Series
Delia's Crossing
Delia's Heart
Delia's Gift

My Sweet Audrina
(does not belong to a series)

DELIA'S GIFT

Virginia ANDREWS

hi

First published in the US by Pocket Star Books, 2009
A division of Simon & Schuster, Inc.
First published in Great Britain by Simon & Schuster UK Ltd, 2011
A CBS COMPANY

This paperback edition first published, 2012

1 3 5 7 9 10 8 6 4 2

Simon & Schuster UK Ltd
1st Floor
222 Gray's Inn Road
London WC1X 8HB

www.simonandschuster.co.uk

Simon & Schuster Australia Sydney
Simon & Schuster India, New Delhi

A CIP catalogue record for this book
is available from the British Library

ISBN: 978-1-84739-474-3

Printed and bound by CPI Group (UK) Ltd, Croydon CR0 4YY

DELIA'S GIFT

Prologue

My grandmother used to say that too much of anything is not good.

Too much sunshine dries out the flowers.

Too much rain drowns them.

I know there can be too much anger, but can there be such a thing as too much love?

Once, when Father Martínez was conducting Bible lessons in our church back in my Mexican village, Papan García, one of the brightest girls in our class, asked Father Martínez why Adam went and ate of the forbidden fruit after Eve had done so.

"He knew it was wrong and what would happen to her. Why do it?"

Father Martínez smiled and said, "Because he loved her too much, and he didn't want to be without her."

Papan smirked and shook her head.

"I cannot imagine loving anyone that much."

"You will," Father Martínez predicted. "You will."

I thought about Father Martínez's answer when I left with Señor Bovio to live in his house. I was pregnant with his son Adan's child, and I accepted his invitation. I told myself I was doing it for him as well as for myself. I had nothing else to give him but the joy of seeing his grandchild.

But deep in my heart, I hoped Señor Bovio's love for his son was not as great as Adam's love for Eve.

I did not want either of us to do something forbidden, something to lock us out of paradise.

1

A New Home

All of Señor Bovio's estate employees were there to greet me the morning I arrived at his *hacienda*. No one looking at me for the first time since I had left the mental clinic would know I was pregnant, but from the expression on everyone's face, even the way the gardeners stared at me when I stepped out of Señor Bovio's limousine, it was obvious to me that they knew. There was such expectation and reverence on their faces. Anyone would think I was carrying a future king.

Later, I saw that my mere appearance would stop conversations or lower voices and widen eyes, eyes that would quickly shift down either in deep respect or in deep fear. I suspected that the fear came from the remote possibility that he or she might do something to disturb me and that the disturbance would cause an aborted pregnancy.

Although it was difficult for me to be treated as if I were fragile china by the employees, I couldn't be upset with them. I sensed that in the back of everyone's mind, I was ending the hard period of mourning over the death of Señor Bovio's son, Adan, who was killed in an accident on their boat when I was with him. I was defeating death by giving birth to Adan's child. Those who had truly loved Adan looked at me with reverence and gratitude. If I showed any emotion at all in response, it was to reveal my humility and how I did not believe I was worthy of such veneration and respect. I wasn't the new Madonna. I was simply an unwed pregnant young woman. Back in my village in Mexico, it would be I who would lower her head, lower it in shame.

Mi tía Isabela, with whom I had been living, had been preparing to send me back to my poor Mexican village in just such disgrace. But when Señor Bovio learned I was pregnant with Adan's child, he came to the clinic where I had been taken after my nervous breakdown following Adan's death and pleaded with me to live with him until the baby was born. I agreed, because I could see clearly that for him, my pregnancy and impending birthing were bringing back hope and happiness to a world shrouded in black sorrow.

Still, I expected it would be painful living in Adan's home without him. With the memory of his handsome, loving face still so vivid, I was sure I would see him everywhere I looked. These were the same front steps he had climbed all his young life, I thought when I stepped out of the car and gazed up at the portico and the *hacienda*'s grand front entrance. I knew when I entered and looked about, I would see the dining-room table where he had sat with his father and taken his meals. These people looking at me now were the people he had greeted and who had greeted him daily. I felt his absence too deeply and saw the sorrow in all of their faces. My heart turned to stone in my chest. I was afraid I would stop breathing, but Señor Bovio's strong hand was at my back, almost propelling me forward. He kept his head high and his eyes fixed on the front entrance, as if he were truly taking me into a magic castle.

Once we stepped into his *hacienda*, my eyes were immediately drawn to the dome ceiling in the large entryway. It had a skylight at the center through which sunlight streamed and glittered off the white marble tile floors and walls. It was as if I had entered a cathedral, not a palace. Because of the way everyone moved timidly around us, it was church quiet.

"We'll give you a tour of the *hacienda* later," Señor Bovio said. "First things first."

He immediately led me up the curved black marble stairway to show me to my room. When he opened the large mahogany double doors embossed with two beautiful black panthers with ruby eyes, I gasped, overwhelmed. The bedroom suite was larger than *mi tía* Isabela's. The four-poster, bloodred canopy bed was wider and longer than hers and had enough fluffy pillows to serve a family of ten. Hanging above just beyond the foot of the bed was a gilded chandelier with teardrop bulbs raining light.

On the wall to my right was a large framed picture in velvet of the same two panthers that were embossed on the door, and there were black statues of them in crimson-tinted marble on pedestals. The velvet drapes were scarlet, and there was a red tint to the furniture. Even the bedroom carpet was red. Fresh bouquets of red roses were placed in vases on the bedside tables.

"You will stay here, Delia," he said, nodding at the suite.

"It's beautiful, Señor Bovio, but it is so big."

"It was my wife's suite," he said.

"Your wife's? But . . ."

"This is where you will stay," he said more firmly.

As my father used to say about his employer, Señor Lopez, "He is a man used to having his words immediately carved into concrete."

Nevertheless, I was surprised at Señor Bovio insisting so strongly that I stay in his wife's bedroom suite. Surely there were many other rooms, any of which would have been more than adequate for me in this grand *hacienda,* a *hacienda* that was easily a few thousand feet larger than Tía Isabela's.

"I don't mean to sound ungrateful, but it's far more than I require, Señor Bovio," I said softly.

"What you require?" He smiled and looked at the bedroom and the adjoining sitting room as if I had said something quite foolish.

"*Sí, señor.*"

He shook his head. "This is where my wife was pregnant with Adan, where she spent her pregnancy. It's only fitting that you stay here while you're pregnant with Adan's child."

He paused, nodding softly and looking about the suite.

"Yes, you'll be safe here," he said in a voice close to a whisper. "Safer than anywhere else."

The way he looked around that first day, with his eyes almost blazing excitement, actually gave me a little chill. I sensed he believed the room held some magical quality, believed that his wife's spirit was still there, a spirit that he was confident would look after me and the baby growing inside me.

Belief in spirits or ghosts had always been part of our lives in Mexico. I had no doubt that even though Señor Bovio had spent most of his life in America, he still held on strongly to these ideas. I didn't imagine it was something he talked about, especially with his business and political associates, but I could see that his faith in his wife's continual spiritual presence was strong.

I would never criticize anyone for such thoughts. My grandmother had these same beliefs. Holding on to them as primitive and superstitious as they might seem to others, kept Abuela Anabela close to those she had loved and lost. I wanted very much to believe in spirits as strongly as she did. I especially did not want to give up my parents, and, like her, I would often talk to my mother and my father, hoping, praying, that they still heard me. Why not grant the same hope to Señor Bovio, I thought, especially now?

"If this is what you wish, *señor,* I am honored to occupy this bedroom. *Gracias.*"

The head housekeeper, Teresa Donald, who looked every minute of her sixty-three years, brought in my meager possessions, clothing, and shoes. She was about my height but stout, with roller-pin forearms. Yet she had small facial features, including thin, pale lips and very small light-saffron-colored teeth. Her cheeks were full of pockmarks. It was as if she had been caught in a sandstorm when her face was just forming.

"Don't bring that stuff up here," Señor Bovio told her sharply. "Find a place for it in the laundry closet. She will have new things, clean things only."

She nodded and hurried away, avoiding looking at me, which only made me feel more self-conscious. When would they stop treating me like some divinity descended from the clouds?

"But that really is all I have, *señor*," I said. "*Mi tía* Isabela took back what she had bought me."

He ignored me, closed the double doors, and nodded at the sitting room. In it were two sofas, a love seat, two large cushioned chairs, a wide-screen television, a stereo, and what looked like a wine closet. The carpet in the sitting room was the same soft red color and just as thick.

I sat on one of the cushioned chairs and folded my hands on my lap. Señor Bovio did not sit. He paced a little with his hands behind his back and then stopped and looked down at me. I realized this was the first time since we had left the clinic that he actually looked at me when he spoke.

"I have hired a nutritionist, who is also a private-duty maternity-ward nurse, to design your menu," he began. "As you probably know, pregnant women have different needs because of what the forming child requires. Her name is Mrs. Newell, and she is in the kitchen right now giving my chef instructions. She's already purchased much of what we will require, but the preparations are also very important."

He already had a private-duty maternity nurse? That

gave me pause to wonder. Had he been so confident that I would agree to come live here that he could go and hire someone special and have her in the house even before I had arrived? And why did he say "what *we* will require"? Surely, he wasn't going to follow the same diet. But I didn't question him. I could see he didn't want to be interrupted.

"I happen to be close friends with one of the best obstetricians in the Coachella Valley, Dr. Joseph Denardo. I know women who have come from as far away as Los Angeles to have him as their OB. He will be your obstetrician, and as a special favor to me, he will come here to examine you regularly or as he sees necessary."

"Why couldn't I go to his office?" I asked.

He ignored my question and continued, pacing. "I know that pregnant women should exercise, walk regularly, keep busy, and that you are used to doing household chores, but my servants will perform all the necessary duties. Besides Teresa, I have two other maids who handle the downstairs area. However, only Teresa will be up here to attend to your needs. Your room will be cleaned and dusted daily. And oh," he said, pausing and looking at me again, "Dr. Denardo asked me if you had any specific allergies. I haven't had time, of course, to ask your aunt, but . . ."

"No, *señor.* I have no allergies that I know of."

"Good. You always looked like quite a healthy young woman to me, despite what you've just been through. Adan had described some of what you experienced living in your aunt's home. I can assure you, Delia, that cousin of yours, Sophia, will not be permitted within a hundred yards of this property. We will take no risks regarding our baby. The first chance I get, I'll make sure Isabela understands that," he added.

"*Gracias,*" I said. I had no desire to see Sophia. I knew that as soon as she found out what Señor Bovio was doing for me, she would choke on her envy. I had not seen her since I was taken to the clinic after my nervous breakdown at *mi tía* Isabela's *hacienda* following Adan's death. She surely thought that all of the events had soundly defeated and destroyed me, and I had no doubt that once she had learned I was pregnant, she had worn out the telephone gleefully telling her friends how I was to be sent home in disgrace. Now, she would once again be bitterly disappointed.

"From Adan, I understood that you were friends with Fani Cordova," he continued. "Is that so? You know that Fani is a cousin. Her father is my second cousin."

"*Sí, señor,* although I have not spoken to her since . . ."

He spun around, with his eyes widened in anticipation of the possibility of my mentioning Adan's death, but I had another thing in mind.

"Since I returned from Mexico," I added, and he nodded.

Fani had had nothing to do with me after I had been returned from Mexico with my cousin Edward and his companion, Jesse. I had talked them into taking me back to my little village, ostensibly to show them our culture and visit my parents' and my grandparents' graves, especially *mi abuela* Anabela's grave. I was the closest to my grandmother.

However, I really had been there to meet with my

boyfriend, Ignacio, with whom I had fled across the desert after he and his friends had gone after Bradley Whitfield. Sophia's rich boyfriend had taken sexual advantage of me when I accepted a ride from him on my way back from where the bus stopped on my return from school. I was attending public school then. Bradley took me to see a house he and his father were restoring, and there he performed what other girls called a date rape.

Later, while crashing a party for Ignacio's sister at his home, Sophia and her friends deliberately stirred up Ignacio and his friends. Sophia told them Bradley was in that same house with another girl he was seducing. They left the party and went looking for him, and when one of Ignacio's friends threw Bradley through a window, he was cut badly and bled to death before any help arrived.

Ignacio had faked his own death in the desert to throw off the police pursuit, and I had kept the secret, dreaming of us being reunited, even when I was seeing Adan Bovio. I was sure this had angered Fani. She loved being a matchmaker, and I had never revealed my secret correspondence with Ignacio and his existence to her. I thought she was more annoyed about that than anything.

My cousin Sophia had found out about my planned rendezvous with Ignacio in Mexico and secretly had alerted the police, not even warning her own brother. Ignacio was arrested moments after we had met in the village. Despite my emphatic denials, he thought I had been the one to arrange his apprehension in return for some generous reward that would enable me to continue living the rich, high life in America. Afterward, he wouldn't respond to any of the letters I had sent to him in prison.

All of us almost went to prison. Tía Isabela had to get political help from Señor Bovio and some of her own powerful friends to intercede for Edward, Jesse, and me so we could return and not be prosecuted for aiding and abetting a criminal. But in saving us, she had demanded that Edward have nothing more to do with me. She was always jealous of our relationship. Earlier, she had forced me to spy on Edward to confirm that he and Jesse were lovers. It had almost destroyed my relationship with Edward until he discovered what she had done.

Mi tía Isabela had continually threatened to have the authorities prosecute me and his companion, Jesse Butler, if Edward disobeyed. He and Jesse had been very upset with me for not having told them the truth, but Edward could never hold a grudge against me. He had simply wanted to protect me and Jesse, so he obeyed his mother. We hadn't spoken since the day he left to return to college.

I had been returned immediately to a servant's existence in *mi tía* Isabela's *hacienda* and had been sent back to public school instead of the private school. Sophia had soaked up the pleasure of lording things over me again. I had plodded along, just counting the days until my eighteenth birthday, but Adan Bovio had come around to ask me on a date. Once Adan had learned about Ignacio and my involvement, I thought he would not want to see me anymore. His father was running for U.S. senator, and I imagined he was not happy about his son being involved with me.

Of course, I had been surprised and reluctant when he appeared. I had been embarrassed about not telling him the truth about my relationship with Ignacio. However, I couldn't drive him away. Adan had been so sincere and loving, and my aunt had pressured me, telling me this was my final opportunity for a decent life. I knew all she wanted was to continue climbing the social ladder herself.

Adan had invited me on his boat again. That had led to a terrible disaster when we were caught in a windstorm and he was fatally injured. I had thought my life in America was surely over, even when I realized I was pregnant with Adan's child.

Now, after all of this, here I was in Adan's mother's room, listening to his father's plans to make my pregnancy easier.

"*Sí, sí,* I know all about that fiasco in Mexico," Señor Bovio said. He shuffled the air between us as if the words still lingered. "We won't discuss it. What's done is done. I'll see about Fani," he added. "Is there anyone else with whom you are friendly or have been friendly, girls at the public school, perhaps?" He raised his eyebrows. "We should be very careful about whom we invite to this house."

"No one at the moment, *señor.* However, I do want to finish my schooling and get my high school diploma," I said. "Someday I hope to go to school to be a nurse."

"*Sí,* that's a good thought. You should pursue a career. I'll get you into a very good nursing college. A friend of mine is the president of an excellent one on the East Coast."

"East Coast?" I smiled. "With a baby to care for, it

will be some time before I am able to attend a nursing school, *señor,* but there are surely ones not far from here."

"*Sí,* you are right. Let's not put the cart before the horse. As you have said, you still have to get your high school diploma. I told you at the clinic that I would look into home schooling or some tutoring. Don't worry about it. Leave it all up to me. It's nothing for me to arrange someone qualified to come here and get the job done."

"But really, I could attend the public school and . . ."

"No," he said sharply, and then took a breath to simmer down and smile again. "That would be unnecessary and foolish under these circumstances."

"I have only a month of school remaining, and I'm not much more than two months' pregnant, *señor.*"

He shook his head. "I don't want you mixing with so many people, people from much poorer conditions, unsanitary conditions. You know yourself how some of those schoolmates of yours in the public school live. They bring in diseases, flu, and now, with your being pregnant . . . well, it's not necessary to take any of those risks. I'll look into it for you. I'll get you all the books you need, everything. Don't worry. I'm very friendly with the commissioner of education. I can make these things happen. Do not think of them again."

I saw that these, too, were words inscribed in concrete. It was futile to argue about it. Maybe he thought I would find another boyfriend at school, even while I was pregnant, and run off to live far away with my baby.

"Whatever you think best, *señor*."

"*Sí*, good. The doctor will be here this evening after his regular duties," he said. "He'll check you out, and we'll go slowly from there. In the meantime, I'll have them prepare something for you to eat for lunch. You can make yourself comfortable. You can wear anything you find that will fit you until we get you your own new clothes. You will see that much of what is here has barely been used. As Adan used to say, my wife was a clothes junkie, and you're not far from her size. She was about your height, and you have a similar figure. There are pictures . . ." He waved at some of the framed photographs. "I have many more in my office downstairs, her films, her photo shoots. You can see them later."

He smiled and just stared at me as if I were some window through which he could look back at a happier past.

"She wasn't much older than you are when we first met," he said, just above a whisper.

"*Gracias, señor*," I replied, bringing him out of his musing.

His smile dimmed and faded like a light slowly going out. He shook himself as if he had just felt a chill. "*Sí*. Let me see about the lunch. Just rest," he told me, and started out of the suite.

"One more thing, Señor Bovio."

He paused.

"When you came for me back at the clinic this morning, you promised you would take me to my village in Mexico so I could visit my parents' and my grandparents' graves." I smiled. "You even joked about flying me in a helicopter."

He nodded. "*Sí.* I'll look into it, but first, let's be sure the doctor thinks it's okay."

"Why shouldn't it be okay, *señor*? I'm not a fragile person, even though I'm pregnant. *Mi madre* worked in the soybean fields until she was into her ninth month."

He took a step toward me. "That's true, Delia. Women did do that and still do that now back there. They have to in order to put food on the table, but we don't have to do that. And no one ever talks about the miscarriages and the babies born dead or sick. I'm sure you're not fragile, but why not be cautious, Delia? You have to look after the welfare of more than yourself now, no? You wouldn't want to do anything that could result in a disaster, would you? You would never forgive yourself. Besides, it won't be that much longer. What are a few more months in your life? You're young. Am I right, Delia? Well?" he insisted when I didn't immediately acquiesce.

"*Sí, señor.*"

"Good," he said. "Then we agree." He flashed another smile and was gone before I could say another word.

Maybe he was right, I thought. Maybe I was being selfish to think otherwise. And besides, I was certainly not suffering. I laughed at my good fortune. I was sure *mi tía* Isabela wouldn't have sent me home first class. At this moment, if Señor Bovio hadn't come to see me, I would be traveling and bouncing on some smelly, old bus on a dirt road in Mexico, working my way back to who knew what.

Look where you are instead, Delia Yebarra, I told myself.

I gazed about at the beautiful furnishings, the velvet drapes, the thick, soft carpet, and the enormous vanity table with wall mirrors. Actually, there were mirrors everywhere, even on the ceiling. It was the suite of someone who was in love with her own beauty, I thought, keeping in mind that Señor Bovio's wife had been a movie actress.

I rose and looked into the walk-in closet. There was a wall of mirrors in there as well. It looked as if there were acres and acres of clothing hanging on the racks. I could see tags dangling from garments she had never worn. I had never seen so many shoes in one person's possession. Shelves filled with them went up to the ceiling. There was surely double the number that Tía Isabela had, and there were wigs, all lengths and colors and styles, neatly hanging on a wall. Perhaps Adan's mother had needed all of this to attend so many celebrity functions and public-relations events.

Yet there was another consideration. As beautiful as all of this was, and as convenient as Señor Bovio would make everything for me, I couldn't help wondering whether or not I would do more harm than good by staying. In my heart of hearts, I still believed that the evil eye had attached itself to my destiny ever since I had first left Mexico. The *ojo malvado* was always there to work a curse just when things looked good. I remained convinced that everyone who got too close to me suffered. My cousin Edward had lost an eye in a car accident when he rushed out to get Bradley Whitfield for attacking me. Ignacio was now languishing in a prison, sentenced to six years. Adan had been killed on the boat. Perhaps I was better off returning to the poor village in Mexico and accepting my fate. Perhaps it would be better for everyone if I just slipped away and made my way home.

As I gazed out the window at the gardens, the tennis courts, and the pool, I heard my poor Mexican village call to me. I could hear the whispered pleading, *Come back, Delia. Come home, and accept who you are. Stop trying to fight fate. You cannot hold back the tide.*

But then I remembered the terrible pain in Señor Bovio's face at the hospital when he learned that his son had died. He was a shell of a person whose soul had gone off to be with his son's. The realization that his son's child was growing inside me brought his soul back to him and filled him with renewed hope. How could I run off and leave him like some rich fruit dying on the vine? How could I be so cruel? How could I be so selfish, especially when he was doing so much to make me comfortable and to ensure the health and welfare of my baby?

No, Delia, I told myself. *You must learn how to take advantage of good fortune when it comes to you and not dwell on memories of sadness and defeat.*

I thought of heading to the bathroom to take a shower, freshen up, and get into different clothing. Because of all there was to choose from, I was sure I would find something to wear. For a while at least, as I went back to the closet and sifted through some of the garments, my attention was taken off everything else. I felt like a little girl in a candy store told to take whatever she wanted.

But then I heard *mi tía* Isabela's unmistakable voice. She was just at the bottom of the stairway, arguing with Señor Bovio. I stepped out of the closet and moved closer to the double doors that had been left slightly open and heard her say, "Are you mad, Ray? Why would you bring her here? The girl had a nervous breakdown and was in a clinic."

"I am not bringing only her. I am bringing my son's child."

"Oh, that's ridiculous. Let me send her back where she belongs and get her out of everyone's hair once and for all. I should never have sent for her after her parents died. She doesn't belong here."

"My son's child does not belong in some backward Mexican village to grow up uneducated and live like some peon," he countered angrily. "You didn't think you did, and you were willing to defy your father to pull yourself up and out. Should I remind you of the things you told me? How you described this village to which you want me to send my grandchild?"

Those words and his tone obviously took the wind out of her sails. She mumbled something, and the next thing I heard was her coming up the stairway. She was wearing one of her pairs of sharp, high-heeled shoes that gave her the staccato footsteps I knew all too well. They were usually the drumbeats of her anger and rage. I backed away from the door.

Despite quickly feeling as though I had been taken to a fortress because of the walled-in property, the gates, and the security guards, and despite all the ways I was being insulated from the outside world, the arrival of *mi tía* Isabela was still terrifying.

When she had found out from the clinic doctor that I was pregnant, it seemed to please her and to justify her sending me off. Her big threat was that she would not arrange for an abortion. She was surprised when I told her that was fine, that I didn't want one, but she looked happy about that as well. She knew that being an unwed mother would make my life even more miserable back in Mexico.

"Fine. Be pregnant. I'll make arrangements immediately for your return. Get yourself prepared for your life as a peasant. Go back to speaking Spanish," she had told me.

She had started to leave when I stood up and defiantly replied, "The truth in any language is still the truth, and the truth is that you are the one who suffers, Tía Isabela. You have no family. You will suffer all three deaths the same day your body dies, but don't worry, I'll light a candle for you."

I was referring to our belief that we die three times, once when our bodies die, once when we're interred, and finally when we're forgotten.

She had just walked out after that. And then, before she could have me sent away the following morning, Señor Bovio had come to see me and had taken me off to be here with him.

Now she was back, surely frustrated and annoyed, which made her more of a threat, more like a scorpion. She was coming to sting me in whatever way she still could. I could hear it in the clacking of her footsteps on the hallway's marble floor.

I retreated to the chair at the vanity table, and a moment later, she stepped into the bedroom suite. She was dressed as elegantly as ever, wearing one of her favorite wide-brimmed Palm Springs hats and one of her designer suits. As usual, her face was caked in the makeup she took hours to perfect before she set foot out of her house. She looked about the bedroom suite, shaking her head.

"How ironic that he put you in this bedroom," she began. "He never let me in here, never unlocked the door when I came to this *hacienda*."

She paused and stepped farther in so she could continue to drink in everything she could see in the suite.

"I imagine he hasn't changed a thing all these years," she muttered. "And this obsession with black panthers just because she played one in a horror film. Idiotic." She sniffed the air. "I wouldn't be surprised if he sprays her favorite perfume periodically to keep the scent of her alive."

"You are smelling the fresh roses, Tía Isabela."

"Really?" She laughed. "Men and their perverted secrets and weaknesses. They're such fools. She betrayed him, made him look like a cuckold, and he still worships her memory."

She was referring to the stories about Señor Bovio's wife having affairs with actors and directors. Supposedly, she had been killed in an automobile accident in France while she was on some rendezvous with the director of the film she was shooting. The director lived and, of course, denied the stories, but I sensed that even Adan had come to believe they were true.

She turned to me, nodding her head with a look of pity and disgust. "You're such a fool, too, Delia. Can't you see?" she said, raising her hands and spreading her arms. "He's put you in a tomb, a museum. Why has he kept all this? Did he expect his wife to have some miraculous resurrection?" She made a guttural noise that sounded like a growl. "It makes me so damn angry to think he led me to believe he might ask me to marry him when all the while, he was still married to this . . . this illusion. I can tell you this," she said, waving her hands as if she were driving away flies, "if he had married me, I would have torn this room apart and redone it from top to bottom."

She nodded at it all as if she thought the furniture was trembling at her threat. Then she turned her attention back to me and spoke in a softer, almost loving tone.

"I know you don't trust anything I say and especially any advice I might give you, but you had better heed me, Delia Yebarra. You're playing in my world now. Get on the first bus out of here, and go home. Go back to the village in Mexico, where you belong.

"No matter what Señor Bovio tells you, no matter how rich and expensive the gifts he lavishes on you are, make no mistake about it. He still believes his son is dead because of you. He thinks you bewitched him. If Adan hadn't come back for you, he would never have been on that boat that day, and if you hadn't lost control of the steering, he might not have suffered such a terrible accident. In the days following Adan's death, Señor Bovio muttered all these things to me repeatedly.

"And don't think his priest talked him out of them," she added. "There's no forgiveness in him. He has a bloodline that goes back to the Aztecs. He lives for vengeance. I know him through and through, Delia. You," she said, now stabbing her right forefinger at me, "are in for a terrible time. Go home before you suffer some horrible fate."

She opened her purse and took out a wad of bills.

"Here," she said, "is more than enough to get you home and even set you up in some comfort down there. I'll send you something more once you're there," she said. "You'll have what you need to get by. I promise."

"Why are you suddenly so worried about my welfare, Tía Isabela? Why this change of heart since we last spoke? Why is it so important to you that I leave, that I am safe and happy now?" I asked her. "Or is it more important that Señor Bovio be unhappy? You sound angrier at him than worried for me," I told her. "Should I remind you of the terrible things you said to me at the clinic? You were happy to hear I was pregnant. You thought it would make everything even worse for me. No, Tía Isabela, you are here today because you hate to be contradicted, especially by a man. You are not here out of any concern for me."

She pulled her shoulders back and flushed crimson through her cheeks. "You deserve whatever happens to you, Delia. You haven't changed a bit. You're still as insolent, defiant, and stupid as ever." She laughed. "You think you hit some jackpot? You think you are spitting in my face by living here and accepting all this from Señor Bovio?"

"No, Tía Isabela. As hard as it might be for you to believe or even understand, I am not thinking about you. I am thinking only of myself and my baby."

She threw her head back and laughed again. Then she fired a look at me that might stop a charging wild boar. "Your baby? You really are a foolish girl. Maybe you're even more foolish than Sophia after all. Or," she said with a wry smile, "do you think having an anchor baby will ensure your legal status here since I've disowned you? I know how you immigrants think. What, did that family of Mexicans give you this advice?"

"No," I said quickly. "That is not why I'm here. And you are an immigrant, too."

"Right. You're always right. You're just like your mother, stubborn but stupid."

"Believe what you wish. You will, anyway, Tía Isabela. Sophia isn't so different from you. You twist and turn things to make everything seem to be what you want it to be. She learned from a good teacher."

She stood for a moment staring at me, and then her face seemed to soften even more before hardening again. It was as if she were caught between wanting to love me for having such spirit and wanting to hate me.

"Okay, fine. Do what you want, but I'm warning you, Delia. If you stay here, don't come running back to me for help," she said. "I am finally washing my hands of you."

"Wash as much as you want, Tía Isabela. You will never get me or the family you left behind off your conscience by taking showers or baths. Every time you close your eyes at night, we'll be in your dreams."

She fumed. "That is surely something your grandmother would say."

"Then I'm glad I said it," I told her.

She turned and walked out in a fury, but she left the money on the dresser. Something kept me from running after her to throw it back at her. Instead, I rose and put it in a drawer. Then, a moment later, I went to a window and looked out to the front of the *hacienda,* where I saw Señor Garman, her driver, holding the limousine door open for her.

She approached with Señor Bovio at her side. They spoke for a few moments. Despite how she had just behaved with me and the things she had said about

Señor Bovio, she didn't appear to be angry at him. In fact, she leaned over to kiss him on the cheek. He stood watching her get into the limousine and be driven off, then turned, gazed up at my window, closed his eyes, said a short prayer, crossed himself, and walked back into the house.

I watched Tía Isabela's car wind down the driveway and out the gate. Her words of warning echoed around me as her limousine disappeared.

I suddenly realized that my heart was pounding and I was holding my breath.

I was terrified of one thing.

I was terrified that in the end, she would be right.

2

Custom-made

Not long after I showered and changed, Teresa returned with a tray of food for me. Mrs. Newell, the private-duty nurse and nutritionist, walked in right behind her to introduce herself. She was in a nurse's white uniform with an RN's cap and was perhaps in her fifties, although she looked younger. She was an inch or so taller than I was and had a nice figure, bright light-brown eyes, and a firm, straight mouth that would certainly make *mi tía* Isabela envious, although I wouldn't call her pretty.

Anyway, I thought that someone who dictated to others how to eat healthier had better look healthy herself. I was sure it was the same for doctors. It would be hard to take their advice if they smoked or were seriously overweight themselves.

She flashed a smile at me so quickly it was more as

if her face had blinked. Then she nodded at Teresa to serve me my tray on a table in the sitting room.

"I'm Millicent Newell," she said. "I understand Mr. Bovio has already informed you that I will be looking after you during your gestation?"

"Yes, he has told me."

"Good. Then let's start."

"Start?"

"There is much to go over concerning your health and the health of your fetus."

From the way Mrs. Newell continued, I assumed Señor Bovio had told her that I knew nothing about how to take care of myself. She had the tone of a lecturer but also of someone who had been given authority over me.

"I am here to guide you safely through this ordeal," she said.

I thought it was odd to refer to pregnancy as an ordeal, but later I learned that although she was married, she had no children. I would wonder why not. Had she and her husband chosen not to have children, or was she simply unable to conceive? If it was for the latter reason, I couldn't help but wonder if she was jealous of the women she took care of in the maternity ward. It wouldn't be long before I learned more.

"Because of your condition, you have a greater need for nutrients such as calcium, iron, and folic acid. I don't imagine you know what folic acid is."

"Yes, I do," I said, but she acted as if she didn't hear me.

Once she had begun her lecture, she was like an unstoppable robot. "Folic acid is a water-soluble B vitamin that occurs naturally in food. We usually recom-

mend that women take a folic acid supplement prior to
conception and for the first three months of pregnancy
to help reduce the risk of neural-tube defects such as
spina bifida.

"Unfortunately, you conceived without planning
and weren't even aware of it until nearly the third
month, as I understand."

She sounded disapproving, even a little disgusted. I
glanced at Teresa and then back at her, answering with
a slight nod.

"Actually, you're the first patient I've had who's a
prospective unwed mother. Accidentally pregnant, I
guess, is the kindest way to put it. Consequently, there
is a great deal more for me to do, and there is a great
deal more with which we must be concerned, medical
concerns, dangers that can destroy your baby."

Teresa stood by, gaping at me, her eyes widening as
Mrs. Newell proceeded to describe a terrifying sce-
nario.

"For example, I mentioned spina bifida. Spina bifida simply means an incompletely formed spinal cord.
I won't get into all the consequences of that. You can
discuss it with Dr. Denardo later, but we'll do the best
we can to compensate for your poor nutritional preparation."

"I ate well before I came here," I said sharply. She
was making it sound as if I had been living in the
street.

"I'm sure not well enough," she insisted, blinking
that smile again. "For example, pregnancy increases
the need for iron. The developing fetus draws enough
iron from the mother to last it through the first five or
six months after birth, so the need for iron is very sig-

nificant if you want to have a healthy child. As you will see, I will provide red meat and good sources of vitamin C to help absorb the iron. I'm sure that's something you never knew," she added. "Most poor rural people have no idea of—"

"We might not have had formal education, Mrs. Newell, but we knew instinctively what we had to do."

"There is no such thing as instinctive knowledge of nutrition, my dear," she said, this time smiling at me as if I were clearly an idiot. "Did you know that the RDI of iron during pregnancy is ten to twenty milligrams more than for nonpregnant women? I guess not," she sang. "I'm sure Dr. Denardo will do the proper blood analysis to see what your storage of iron is. One side effect of this increased iron intake is constipation, so we'll have to do something about that."

"That's a relief," I said, looking at Teresa to try to lighten the conversation, but she didn't smile. She lowered her eyes quickly.

"To continue," Mrs. Newell said, ignoring me, "the RDI of calcium during pregnancy is eleven hundred milligrams per day, which is about three hundred milligrams more than for nonpregnant women. Don't tell me that rural women living in some poor Mexican village are aware of that."

"I was quite healthy when I was born, Mrs. Newell. I'm sure it wasn't by accident."

"No, not by accident but by luck," she countered without skipping a beat. "We're not going to depend on luck here, Delia. I know that Dr. Denardo is going to keep very good track of your nutritional health, and with the food groups I provide, you should do very well. You shouldn't require any supplements, in fact. I will warn you against eating late at night, and we will prohibit caffeine and alcohol. You could suffer dis- comfort, heartburn, because as the baby grows, there's more pressure on the abdomen. During the later months, I'll keep your portions smaller.

"The reason I wanted Teresa to remain here while I spoke with you is that I don't want her bringing you any snacks or any garbage food from the outside," she said, glaring at the maid, who shook her head to assure her that she had no intention of doing such a thing. It was almost as if she suspected Teresa already had done so.

Mrs. Newell turned back to me. "You don't want to gain too much weight, anyway. Dr. Denardo will tell you about where you should be, but most of the preg- nant women for whom I have worked stay around twenty-two to twenty-eight pounds heavier by the time they come to term. Again, that's not luck. That's good scientific dietary planning," she added. She smiled a little more warmly this time. "Any questions?"

"Yes. Since you've kept Teresa here for this, I'm sure she might like to know what RDI means," I said. I knew what it meant, but I couldn't resist teasing her.

"RDI simply means recommended daily intake," she said, looking at Teresa.

Teresa immediately started to shake her head again. I could see the almost palpable fear in her face, fear that Mrs. Newell might complain about her to Señor Bovio.

"One final thing," Mrs. Newell said. "I am vigilant when it comes to preventing a listeria infection. Again, I'm sure you don't instinctively know what that is."

She had me. I didn't know.

"This bacteria, *Listeria monocytogenes,*" she said pedantically, "can contaminate some foods. There is great danger to an unborn baby, an increased risk of miscarriage, stillbirth, or premature labor. Some foods are more prone to this contamination, and we'll exclude them, but I can't follow you everywhere you go outside this house. Avoid precooked or ready-prepared cold foods that aren't reheated, foods you might get in some fast-food joint you're probably accustomed to eating in, unpasteurized foods, soft-serve ice cream or yogurt, and soft cheeses. Do you understand?"

"Clearly," I said. "And I never ate in dirty fast-food joints."

"Good. Teresa, you can go now," she said, dismissing her. Teresa hurried out. Mrs. Newell waited for her to leave before turning back to me. "This part is more private," she said. "Pregnancy does not mean a woman cannot have sexual relations, but I have seen pregnant women miscarry because they were, how shall I say it, too vigorous or too compliant when their male partners wanted them to be so. Most men don't have the control or care to control themselves to protect a woman carrying a baby. Now, if you go out—"

"Don't be concerned about it. I don't intend to have sexual relations during my pregnancy, Mrs. Newell," I said quickly.

She pulled her shoulders back and pursed her lips for a moment. "Well, I don't imagine you intended to be pregnant, now, did you, dear?" she said, blinking her smile.

I looked away.

"I'm sorry, but I'm just giving you my best professional advice. What you do and don't do is your own business, Delia."

"Good," I said.

"After you give birth, that is. Until then, it is both our businesses."

She waited for my response, but I said nothing.

"Enjoy your lunch."

I looked at the salad, the salmon, and the slice of whole-grain bread. There was a plate of strawberries and some walnuts for dessert.

"I could have just as easily gone down to the dining room for this," I said.

"Mr. Bovio wanted it brought to you."

"Why? Isn't it better for me to walk?"

"I'm not saying you shouldn't walk. Of course, you should walk. I'm simply following Mr. Bovio's orders. You're my patient, but he's employed me," she replied, and finally left. I felt as if a weight had been lifted from my chest.

I ate and thought that the food, although adequate, was basically tasteless. Mrs. Newell was more of a nurse than a cook, I decided. I felt sorry for all the well-to-do married and pregnant women for whom she had served. Like me, they were probably happy to get her out of their homes and get back to eating what they wanted.

I pushed the bedside table aside and sprawled on the love seat in the adjoining sitting room. I was emotionally exhausted and just wanted to calm myself and relax. I know I dozed off for a while, because when I opened my eyes again, my tray was gone. I closed them again.

For a few moments, I tried to forgot all that had happened to me since my parents were killed in the truck accident in Mexico. With my eyes closed, I could pretend I was in my and Abuela Anabela's bedroom back in our little village. Before our family tragedy, I had been a happy young girl who never thought of herself as poor and unfortunate. We had worked hard for the little we had, but we had found ways to be grateful and happy. Nevertheless, I would never deny that I didn't fantasize about living in a palace and having servants and a beautiful bedroom just like the one I was in now. I would imagine that my and Abuela Anabela's little room with its concrete floor was suddenly magically quite different.

There were beautiful velvet curtains over the windows just as there were here. There was a carpet that also seemed like a floor of marshmallows, and my bed was just as big, with pillows as fluffy, and with a canopy and four posters. I had pretended I had a magic wand and could wave it over the old mismatched furniture, the crates and boxes we used for dressers and drawers, the clothes line that served as our closet, and the cracked and pitted walls. I had turned it all into a wonderland for a princess. Imagining that I had enchanting powers, I would travel to places I had seen only in magazines and occasionally on our snowy black-and-white television screen when the electricity worked.

But as soon as I would hear Abuela Anabela's or my mother's voice, I would blink my eyes and come crashing back down to reality. Never did I really believe I would be living in such a luxurious *hacienda* after I blinked. I had immediately felt foolish even dreaming of such things, such a place.

Yet here I was, only not under the circumstances I would have included in my fantasy.

I had been living in a beautiful *hacienda* my aunt owned, but just before Señor Bovio brought me here, I had been sent back to the dingy, dark, and dirty servant's room in a separate building, the room in which I had been placed when I had first arrived from Mexico. That now seemed much farther in the past than it really was. All of the recent events in my life were jumbled and twisted in my mind, anyway. I wished it really had all been a dream, every moment. This wasn't the first time I had made such a wish. Many times, I would have gladly woken to find myself back in that small bedroom I shared with Abuela Anabela. I would trade all the clothes, the glamorous events, the mansions, any and all of it, to return to that simple life, if only my parents were still alive.

Because this bedroom wasn't far from the circular stairway that led up to the second floor of the *hacienda* and because my door was still open, I could hear the voices below echoing up the walls, past the large paintings, and around the drapery. I could hear some joy in Señor Bovio's voice. Someone who pleased him had arrived. At least *mi tía* Isabela hadn't returned, I thought.

I was sure that in these past weeks and months, Señor Bovio did not laugh or smile very much. I recalled when I had first met him at my friend Fani Cordova's home. Her parents were holding a fund-raising dinner for his senatorial campaign. It was there I had first met Adan as well. I remember thinking how alike they were, a father and son who were both handsome and charming. Abuela Anabela would have said, "*De buena fuente, buena corriente.* From a good spring, a good current."

Adan had his father's stature and his elegance. Señor Bovio looked as if he really should be a U.S. senator, someone who could be a protector of the less fortunate and less powerful. He reeked with confidence but not arrogance, and he had a smile that would calm a raging bull. Adan was more than reflection of all this to me. I could see he would grow into such a man himself. Even though he had lost his mother as I had lost mine and Señor Bovio had lost his beautiful wife, they looked solid, successful, and full of promise. Seated between them that night, I had felt safe and honored. How different now was the Señor Bovio who had brought me to his home. Sad and broken by Adan's death, he was a shadow of himself, so any sound of happiness coming from his lips cheered me as well.

I heard footsteps on the stairway and rose from the love seat in anticipation, wondering who could be coming to visit me so soon after *mi tía* Isabela. Could it be Fani?

"*Hola,* Delia," Señor Bovio said. "Did you enjoy your lunch? Isn't Mrs. Newell a terrific and efficient nurse?"

He had changed into a light-blue sports jacket and was now wearing his trademark silk cravat. Seeing this resurrection of light and happiness in him, I didn't want to start off with a complaint about the food or about Mrs. Newell, so I said, "*Sí, señor. Gracias.*"

A short elderly gentleman stood beside him, holding a large, flat briefcase.

"Good. This is Mr. Blumgarten. He has been my personal and my wife's personal tailor for some time now."

"More than twenty years," Mr. Blumgarten proudly added. He had a small nose, beady dark eyes, and ears too large for his small, watermelon-shaped head with its thin, graying hair lying so flat it looked ironed on his skull. I didn't think he was much taller than five feet four, with a slim, almost childlike body.

I nodded and waited to see what they wanted. Señor Bovio indicated that Mr. Blumgarten should enter the suite. They both came in, and Mr. Blumgarten put his large briefcase on the counter by the vanity table.

"I am employing Mr. Blumgarten to design and create some maternity clothing for you personally, Delia," Señor Bovio began.

I looked at them with surprise. Personally designed maternity clothing? I had to smile, thinking about how Señora Díaz, our tailor back in my little Mexican village, would improvise with whatever a pregnant woman had in order to create so-called maternity outfits. Most of the time, it simply meant letting out waists.

"It's a very serious thing," Señor Bovio said sharply, so sharply it chased the smile off my face as quickly as a shout would frighten a sparrow. "Your maternity outfits must be soft to the touch and able to stretch. The outfits have to be light and breezy. A pregnant woman feels heat far more than a woman who is not pregnant. And you don't want to wear anything that cuts into your circulation or binds and draws."

Mr. Blumgarten nodded after every sentence Señor Bovio spoke, as if he were providing the periods.

"I have fabrics that contain Lycra," Mr. Blumgarten said, smiling as proudly as a parent bragging about his children. "So they stretch and move with your body."

"Exactly," Señor Bovio added. "And he has very bright and attractive colors. I want you to look like a flower about to bloom and not like some faded rose. There must always be an air of health and vigor about you. It's something our baby will sense."

He paused to smile at Mr. Blumgarten, who instantly smiled himself, although I could see he had no idea why he should.

"I remember vividly how my wife felt when she was pregnant with Adan," Señor Bovio continued, as if to justify his comments. "She went through a terrible period of depression, worrying that she looked ugly, deformed. There were weeks, months, even in the very beginning, when she wouldn't step out of the house, terrified some paparazzi might snap photos of her and sell them to a magazine. If I didn't start every day telling her how beautiful she still was, she would go into a sulk.

"And, as I said, don't think these emotional and mental downturns have no effect on the baby you're carrying. It's another form of stress, and stress is unhealthy for you and for our baby. Just as people are healthier in a house full of happiness, a baby is surely healthier in the womb of a happy woman."

I thought Mr. Blumgarten's head would never stop bobbing.

"I understand, and I am grateful for your concern, *señor,*" I said.

"*Sí.* Good. Mr. Blumgarten," he said, turning to the tailor, "we need clothing immediately."

"I'll get right on it today, Mr. Bovio. By the end of the day tomorrow, she will have her first outfit."

"Outfits," Señor Bovio corrected.

"Absolutely. Without delay," Mr. Blumgarten said.

Señor Bovio stepped back, and Mr. Blumgarten opened his briefcase and spread the fabric samples out, smiling at me to invite me to come choose what I liked. I glanced at Señor Bovio, who nodded and smiled as well.

"Just feel this material," Mr. Blumgarten said. I did, and I had to admit it was all so soft.

"Don't make her skirts too short," Señor Bovio ordered, and left us.

Mr. Blumgarten showed me some styles and then took measurements. When he grazed my breasts with his knuckles, he immediately blushed and apologized.

"Well, now, I . . . that is," he said, stammering, "I don't think you're going to show too much until your sixth or seventh month, but we'll allow for it, especially . . ." He nodded at my bosom. "Of course, Mr. Bovio wants me back to redo or add to your wardrobe every three weeks."

"Every three weeks!"

"Changes come quickly," he said, although I sensed that even he thought that was extravagant.

I shook my head, imagining the expense.

Afterward, every style and garment he suggested looked fine to me. I really wasn't all that worried about being in style. I was no movie star. He was happy I made his work so easy for him, so he could hurry out to go to his shop. He said he would return before din-

ner the next day. When I told him there was no reason
for such a rush, that the clothing I had available would
be fine for a while, he looked at me as if I had gone
absolutely mad.

"It's what Mr. Bovio wants. It's his first grandchild," he said, as if nothing could be more obvious.

I smiled to myself as he fidgeted with his briefcase
and reconfirmed all of his measurements, taking special
care not to touch my breasts. He checked and double-
checked what he had written. The way he fluttered
about reminded me of the rabbit in *Alice in Wonderland*
chanting, "I'm late. I'm late for a very important
date . . ."

For now, this was amusing, and I was grateful for
Señor Bovio's almost motherly concern for my comfort and welfare. I had been here barely a few hours,
and he was rearranging anything and everything to
make things as easy and pleasant for me as could be. If
he wanted to spoil me with personally designed and
tailored maternity clothes, so be it, I thought, as I ran a
brush through my hair again and started out. I wanted
to take a short walk and get some air. I had been shut
up in the clinic too long, and I was interested in exploring this wonderful estate.

"Wait!" Señor Bovio shouted from the bottom of
the stairway when I appeared and was about to descend. He held up his hand like a traffic officer.

Next to him was a young, light-brown-haired man
in a dark brown suit and matching tie. He carried a
black leather satchel and stood nearly as tall as Señor
Bovio. I imagined him to be in his early thirties at
most. They both stood at the foot of the stairway and
looked up at me.

"I was just going to take a short walk, *señor*," I said.

"In a while," Señor Bovio said.

He and the young man started up the stairway.

"First, there is one more thing I want to get out of the way immediately. Dr. Denardo will be happy we've made these preparations, too."

I had forgotten the doctor was yet to come.

"Please, go back to your bedroom," he said, waving at me.

Curious about what else he wanted done, I returned.

"Delia, this is Mark Corbet from the New Mom Shop on El Paseo," he said when the two followed me into the bedroom suite.

El Paseo was the street of fancy and expensive stores, a street I was told was similar to Rodeo Drive in Beverly Hills or Worth Avenue in Palm Beach. I had been there before, shopping with Tía Isabela.

"Hi there," Mark Corbet said.

I nodded and said hello.

"One of the things they specialize in is maternity shoes," Señor Bovio said.

"There are maternity shoes?" I asked, surprised.

"Well, you may or may not know that pregnancy will cause your feet to get a good half-size bigger," Mark Corbet said. "Your shoes should allow for some swelling. Also, you're better off in low-heeled shoes. Less stress on your spine."

I nodded. In Mexico, we wore sandals, so what he was talking about never mattered.

"However, that doesn't mean you have to wear something ugly," he quickly added, smiling at Señor

Bovio. "We have some pretty fancy styles. I have a few samples here, and I—"

"Mark will measure your foot. I've explained that I'd like the shoes personally made for you."

"Personally? Shoes, too?"

"*Sí.* Mark."

Mark Corbet moved into my room quickly and set his satchel on the floor. He took out his mechanism for measuring foot size. I sat on the chair by the vanity table. I was still quite surprised. Tailored maternity clothing and now shoes? Why was it necessary for everything to be made personally for me?

"I don't want any cheap imitation materials," Señor Bovio emphasized. "Exercise is important. You're going to do a lot of walking, I'm sure, and I don't want to see you get any blisters."

"Oh, we have specially designed walking shoes for pregnant women, too," Mark Corbet said. He looked up at me. "May I?"

I nodded, and he slipped off my shoes and began taking foot measurements.

"No swelling. That's good," he said, smiling at me. He held my foot tenderly.

"Get on with it," Señor Bovio ordered.

"Yes, yes. I'm no obstetrician," he said as he measured, "but wearing maternity support hose helps support tired leg muscles, too. We sell that, of course."

"*Sí,* she'll have that," Señor Bovio said. "You'll bring it all with the pairs of shoes."

"Yes, sir."

It suddenly occurred to me that Señor Bovio was having everyone come to the *hacienda* rather than have me taken to the shops. Even if he didn't intend for it to happen, I was in danger of becoming as spoiled as Tía Isabela and especially my cousin Sophia. Señor Bovio stood by and watched Mark Corbet complete his measurements and then suggest some styles and colors for my maternity shoes. I really didn't believe it mattered very much, but I made choices to get it over with as quickly as possible. He promised, as Mr. Blumgarten had, to put a priority on everything and return quickly.

When Señor Bovio emphasized that cost was no concern and that he was sure we would need different shoes as my pregnancy evolved, Mark Corbet almost fell over himself in his excitement.

"I'll get right on all this, Mr. Bovio," he said, and then turned to me. "Any problems with anything, you just holler."

"She won't have to. I will," Señor Bovio said sternly, and led him out so quickly he barely had time to squeeze in a good-bye.

I sat back to catch my breath. Nutritionist, private maternity nurse, private tailor and shoemaker, doctor who would make house calls—who else would Señor Bovio bring to my room? A hair stylist? Maybe a dentist for an initial checkup? Nothing would surprise me now, I thought, and laughed at how amazed *mi abuela* Anabela would be if she could see all of this.

Once again, I started downstairs, intending to take a short walk around the *hacienda*. When I stepped out, I was surprised at how warm it had gotten. It was difficult to go far. I went around the *hacienda* to look more closely at the pool. It was a bigger pool than Tía Isabela's, and it was oval in shape. The lounges had been set out with towels, as if Señor Bovio had a houseful of guests. A young Mexican man was vacuuming the pool. He wore a wide-brimmed sombrero and was shirtless, in a pair of knee-length white shorts and sandals. He glanced at me but quickly returned to his work as I drew closer.

"*Buenos días,*" I said, and he smiled and nodded.

"*Buenos días,*" he replied, and paused to take a better look at me. "I will have everything ready in a moment, *señorita.*"

"That's all right. I'm not going swimming today. Why are all the lounges prepared? Are there guests expected?"

He looked toward the *hacienda* before replying. "Every day, the lounges are prepared," he said. "For as long as I've been here, I have been told to put them out in the morning and then take them in early in the evening. Most of the time, nothing is used." He smiled and shrugged.

"How long have you worked here?"

"*Tres años* . . . three years. I work with my brother. Sometimes, he comes here and I go somewhere else." He looked back at the *hacienda*. "You are Señor Bovio's guest?"

"*Sí.*"

"I was told he had a guest who was *una muchacha hermosa.* I was told the truth," he said, smiling.

"*Gracias,*" I said, feeling myself blush. I quickly went around to a lounge. Once there, I unbuttoned my blouse a bit. He continued to smile at me and then returned to his work.

I loved hearing the compliment. It had been a while since I could even think of myself as attractive, but I didn't feel like a beautiful young woman. At the moment, I felt like a lost young woman.

I closed my eyes for a few moments and enjoyed the soft breeze that carried the scents coming from the well-manicured gardens. In a day or so, I'd go swimming, I thought. I imagined I could find a bathing suit of Señora Bovio's that would fit. Swimming, like walking, would be good exercise for me now.

Finally relaxing, I casually looked about the enormous property. Trees had been planted to the north and south in front of the high stone walls marking the boundaries of Señor Bovio's estate. There were two tennis courts nearby, and way off toward the western boundary of the property, I saw the horse-training track and the stables.

It all reminded me of that first night at Fani Cordova's house. I closed my eyes again, remembering. Fani had taken Adan and me around her family's property in a golf cart, and she and Adan had had an amusing argument about who was richer, who had more. I recalled Fani's mentioning the horses when Adan pointed out that her father had a helicopter. It seemed like just yesterday. I couldn't help but smile, recalling how happy and optimistic we three were once. It seemed as if the world were opening endless opportunities for all of us to pursue. It was hard not to fall in love with ourselves.

"What are you doing?" I heard, and opened my eyes to see Señor Bovio standing over me. He had shocked me out of my pleasant musing.

He gazed at the young pool man, who immediately began to rush through his work and gather his tools.

"Just resting, *señor*," I replied. "Getting some fresh air and walking, too."

"It's better you're not here at the pool when the help is working," he said.

"*Por qué?*"

"It distracts them, and they don't do their work as well," he said.

He glared again at the pool man.

"You should button up. The sun is right on you. It's too hot already," he continued, wiping his forehead with a handkerchief. "You should go out only in the morning these days. You have to be careful. You don't want too much sun, and you don't want to get dehydrated."

"I haven't been in the sun long, *señor*. I haven't been out in the fresh air and sunshine for some time."

"Yes, yes, but you have to be careful," he muttered.

"I will," I promised. I gazed toward the stables. "Do you still have horses, Señor Bovio?"

"What? Yes, there are two. One was Adan's, and the other was his mother's. But I don't race horses anymore," he added. "I don't know why I bother keeping them. It's expensive, and no one rides them except for the man I have looking after them."

He looked at me, a terrifying thought coming to his mind.

"Don't you go there," he told me quickly. "There are too many flies, and you can't ride, either. Don't even think of such a thing. Not yet."

"No, *señor*. I was just curious."

"*Sí*," he said. He looked at the pool man again, who was now hurrying away. "Did he bother you?"

"No, *señor*."

"He's taking longer than he should. I don't approve of them working without shirts," he said. "I might get rid of him. I told him previously I didn't want him working like that in front of my guests."

"There was no one here until I came, *señor.*"

"That's not the point. Don't stay out too long," he told me, and walked after the young man, who was approaching his pickup truck.

I watched them talking. Señor Bovio waved his arms around. I couldn't make out what he was saying, but he looked very angry. The young man lowered his head and got into his truck. Señor Bovio headed back to the *hacienda*. Not long after, I followed him.

It was quiet when I reentered the house. I made my way up the staircase. I paused at the top, looking down the hallway at the various doors and wondering which one had been Adan's bedroom. Suddenly, one of the doors opened, and Teresa stepped out. She had a vacuum cleaner in hand and some dust rags. She nodded, hurrying by me.

"Teresa?"

"Yes, Miss?"

"Which room was Adan's?"

"The one I was just in, Miss."

"Oh. So, you look after it from time to time?"

"No, Miss. Just like always, I clean and dust and wash the windows every day. I don't mind, and I can see it eases Mr. Bovio's pain."

"Eases his pain? How?"

"Well, Miss, it's like Adan's returning, like he's just on one of his trips."

"Oh. I see." I smiled at her. "How long have you worked for Señor Bovio, Teresa?"

"I'm going on thirty-two years, Miss. This has been my first and only job since I came to America."

"From where?"

"England, Miss," she said.

"So you've been here ever since Adan was born?"

"Yes, Miss. I was quite fond of him. He was a very nice young man. His absence makes the house feel empty. It's nice that you're here," she added.

"Thank you. I'm sorry Mrs. Newell was so stern with you, Teresa. There's no reason to put so much pressure on you. Everyone just has to calm down. I'm not the first woman to have a baby."

"Yes, Miss."

"No, really. I don't need all this special attention, tailors, shoemakers, nurses. I bet you think it's all a bit over the top," I added, imagining all the help were buzzing about the things Señor Bovio was doing.

She nodded but looked at me as if I were totally crazy to suggest it.

"Don't you agree?" I pursued.

She shrugged. "Yes, Miss, but from what I see, nothing is really much different."

"Nothing?" I smiled at her. "What do you mean, nothing's much different, Teresa?"

She didn't look as if she wanted to respond.

"I don't understand," I said.

"It's the way it was when Señora Bovio was pregnant with Adan. She had personally tailored maternity clothing and shoes and a nutritionist, too, only . . ."

"Yes?"

"She expected no less," Teresa said. "I'm sure she would have expected no less for you. I guess Señor Bovio still hears her commands," she added, and then nearly bit down on her own lip. She surprised herself more than she surprised me.

"Still hears? What commands, Teresa?"

"Nothing. I don't know what I'm saying. Sorry, Miss," she said, and continued down the hallway.

Still hears commands? What a strange thing for her to have said, I thought.

In the midst of all of this opulence, luxury, and privilege, some dark cloud hovered, clinging to the ceiling and the corners of the walls around me.

The sounds of Tía Isabela's heels clacking on the tile floor echoed in my mind.

It left me trembling again, defeating the warm sun that had lifted my spirits.

3

A Bargain

"Dr. Denardo has arrived," Mrs. Newell announced after overseeing the delivery of my dinner. It came so quickly I was unable to tell her and Teresa that I would insist on having dinner in the dining room rather than in my suite. I began to wonder if Señor Bovio was simply avoiding ever having to sit at a dinner table with me. Perhaps Tía Isabela was right. He did still blame me for Adan's death and, aside from dealing with my pregnancy, wanted nothing more to do with me.

"Oh," I said, looking toward the doorway and pushing my dinner tray aside.

"No, no. He is in the office with Mr. Bovio and will be up shortly. Don't rush your food," she added. "I'm sure they'll be a while. They both know you have just been given your meal. I have given the doctor my preliminary report."

Earlier, she had checked my pulse and blood pressure and then weighed me.

"Fine. I don't expect it will take me all that long to eat this, anyway," I said, nodding at the tray. The portions were very small.

"Everything is weighed so that the proper amount is given to you. As I explained before, it's too easy for a pregnant woman to gain weight rapidly," she said, "and I don't intend to let that happen on my watch, thank you."

"I don't want that to happen, either, Mrs. Newell."

"Good," she said, and left.

I ate because I was hungry, but again, none of it was particularly tasty. When Teresa came for the tray and dishes, a thought occurred to me.

"Do you know if Señora Bovio often ate in this suite, Teresa?"

"When she was pregnant and began to show, she rarely left the suite. She even gave birth to Adan in the house, which was quite a surprise, I must admit."

"In the house?"

"Yes, Miss. My mother was born in her mother's house," she added, smiling.

"Sí, so was mine. So was I, in fact, but . . ."

"Many women are turning to midwives and more natural birthing, I hear," she added, and left.

With all of the special concern and care Señor Bovio was taking with me, I doubted he would want to take the risk of having me give birth in the *hacienda*, but I couldn't imagine why he had permitted his wife to give birth to Adan in the house or why she would want to do that when she had so much professional care available to her.

When Dr. Denardo finally appeared, Señor Bovio was with him, actually carrying the doctor's satchel. Mrs. Newell was right behind them.

Dr. Denardo was a tall, dark-complexioned, good-looking man, with a well-trimmed coal-black goatee. He wore a light-brown suit and had an open collar and no tie. I imagined him to be in his mid-to-late fifties, although I couldn't see a single gray strand of hair. There was simply something weathered and wise in his gray eyes and his no-nonsense demeanor. He looked at me so intently that I felt he was actually taking medical measurements, evaluating my overall health immediately.

"This is Dr. Denardo," Señor Bovio said. "He will be taking good care of you and our baby."

Dr. Denardo glanced at him when he said "our baby" but quickly turned back to me and smiled. "How are you feeling, Delia?"

"Fine," I said.

"No morning sickness anymore?"

"No, *señor.*"

He tilted his head and nodded. "Good. Did you keep close awareness of when your period was supposed to start?"

"I knew about when, *señor.*"

"So, about when?" he asked, sitting in the chair Señor Bovio had moved over for him beside me.

"Eleven weeks ago."

He made a quick mental calculation. "Normally, we estimate the date of delivery by adding nine months plus seven days to the first day of the last menstrual period. We call it Naegele's Rule," he added, mostly for Señor Bovio's benefit. "So, we'll figure another seven and a half months. We'll get a much more accurate estimate as we go along, of course. Tonight, I would like to take some blood and urine, and we'll do an internal pelvic examination to check the size of your uterus. I will do a Pap smear as well. You know what that is?"

"*Sí, señor,* but why aren't we doing all this in your office?" I asked.

He glanced at Señor Bovio and smiled at me again.

"It's all simple enough, safe enough to do here. No need to drag you out."

"I wouldn't be dragged, *señor.*"

"Well, let's see how it goes. I'm here already. We might as well go forward and not try to fit you into my busy office schedule. You've become one of my patients almost overnight, so we couldn't get you onto the schedule. Last I looked, I was booked up for the next three weeks, in fact. I have two more deliveries to do this week alone and another three next week. And I do have a pretty good nurse here with me," he added, nodding at Mrs. Newell, who looked as though she expected nothing less than such a compliment. "Okay?" he followed, a little tension in his voice.

"This is a special favor Dr. Denardo is doing for us, Delia," Señor Bovio said. "You should be grateful." He fixed his eyes like daggers on me.

"It's all right, Ray," Dr. Denardo said. "Let's not get our little patient more nervous than she already is. Thank you for bringing my bag and introducing us," he added, clearly indicating that Señor Bovio should now leave. "I'll be down shortly to speak with you."

Señor Bovio looked quite disappointed but nodded.

"Of course," he said, and left. He didn't close the door.

Dr. Denardo nodded at it, and Mrs. Newell hurried to close it.

"Okay," he said, returning to me, "let's hear about you. Tell me whatever you can about your medical history, any illnesses you've had." He opened his bag and began to take out what he needed for the examination. "I understand you grew up in a rural area in Mexico and have been here a little less than three years, correct?"

"*Sí.*"

"Any hospitalization, medical problems, while you were here?"

"She was recently in a mental clinic," Mrs. Newell volunteered.

"Yes, I know about that, Millicent. For now, let me have Delia answer," he told her. She snapped her shoulders back instantly, pursing her lips and nodding. He looked at me again. "I mean, any diseases, operations, things of that sort?"

"No, *señor,* but I have had routine physical examinations for school."

"Remember the doctor's name?"

"Corning. It was a woman."

"Oh, yes, Sheila. I'll get your records from her. Make a note of that, will you, Millicent?"

"Yes, Dr. Denardo," Mrs. Newell said. "I'll see to it immediately."

"Thank you. Now, then, shall we begin?"

He had me lie down on my bed. I knew that a midwife and *mi abuela* Anabela had delivered me in our *casa.* At school back in Mexico, we were given some inoculations, but there was never the kind of extensive physical I had here when I was enrolled in school. Of course, I had been examined at the hospital after the boating accident and at the clinic, but both cases were in a medical setting. To be asked to disrobe and do the things Dr. Denardo and Mrs. Newell asked me to do here in the bedroom made me quite nervous. He noticed that and remarked about my pulse and blood pressure. He tried to reassure me to keep me from worrying or being concerned. He repeated that everything he was doing was standard procedure. Even though I wasn't fond of her, I had to admit to myself that Mrs. Newell was efficient, anticipating things before he asked for them.

"Everything looks fine," he told me afterward, "and I think your estimate is very accurate. We'll get the results of our blood tests and all quickly."

"You know Señor Bovio will be calling every day," Mrs. Newell said.

"Yes," Dr. Denardo said. "That's all right." He smiled at me. "It's good to have a worrywart looking after you sometimes."

He then described some of the physical changes I should anticipate. He was very methodical when he spoke and repeated things often to be sure I understood. I had the sense that Señor Bovio might have described me to him the way he had described me to Mrs. Newell—a simple, rural Mexican girl, not very sophisticated about her own body, much less medical matters.

"I think it's very good that Señor Bovio has hired

Mrs. Newell to plan out your meals," Dr. Denardo continued, nodding at her. She gave him one of her blink smiles. "She happens to have an excellent reputation."

I glanced at her and saw how she was soaking up his endorsement.

"In fact, if you follow the diet she prescribes, you really won't need additional vitamins and supplements."

"I told her that myself," Mrs. Newell said.

He began to pack his bag, and I quickly dressed.

"I'll visit you regularly," he said, "but I want you to inform Mrs. Newell immediately if you experience any bleeding, abdominal pain, or swelling in your hands or feet. Mrs. Newell will check for these things, but if anything alarms you about yourself, don't hesitate to tell her to tell me. I find women are the best caretakers of their own bodies in the end," he added, smiling.

"Will you always come here? I'll never go to your office?"

"We'll have you at the office to do an ultrasound, perhaps in a month or so, and to do some testing for potential abnormalities, but from what you've told me, I don't anticipate anything."

He looked around the suite.

"You're in a beautiful place, and with Mrs. Newell on duty, you will get the best care. Señor Bovio will make sure of that."

"You have been friends with Señor Bovio long?"

"Quite a few years, yes," he said. "Of course, like everyone, I was quite upset about his son's unfortunate accident. You're doing a wonderful thing by giving him a chance to be a grandfather, Delia. I know what all of this means for a young woman your age."

"I am doing it for all of us, Dr. Denardo, especially my baby."

"I understand," he said. "You're going to be just fine."

"You didn't deliver Adan, did you, Dr. Denardo?"

He smiled, glanced at Mrs. Newell, who looked bored, and turned back to me. "Why do you ask that, Delia?"

"I have been told Señora Bovio gave birth in the *hacienda.*"

He nodded. "Yes, actually, right in this room."

"Why?"

He shrugged. "She was a beautiful young actress hounded by the paparazzi," he said. "She chose to do so for her own privacy, I suspect."

He and Mrs. Newell started out. I realized he hadn't really answered about whether he had performed the delivery. I started to call to him, but something stopped me. I couldn't say what it was. I only knew I didn't really want to learn much more.

Not long afterward, Señor Bovio came up to tell me how pleased he was with the doctor's report.

"He said you are an excellent patient and in remarkably good health. If we just do everything right, follow his and Mrs. Newell's instructions, we'll be fine. Are you pleased? You have everything you want and need here, right? It's all good, *sí*?"

"I'd like to get out more, *señor*. I need not take all of my meals up here, for example."

"No, but for the first week or so, I think it's best the servants don't pester you with their nosy looks and questions. I won't always be around to make sure of that. I'll always be sure there is proper security, however."

"You need not worry about uninvited visitors, *señor*," I told him, thinking he was mainly worried about Sophia and her friends barging in on me.

"I know, but it would please me to be certain. Indulge an old worrywart," he added, smiling. "I understand the doctor called me that."

"*Sí.*"

"I'm happy for you, Delia, for both you and the wonderful baby you're carrying."

"*Gracias.*"

He started to turn away.

"*Señor.*"

"Yes?"

"When you came to the clinic, you mentioned that I would have access to a car."

"Oh, yes. Where would you like to go?"

"I'd like to know I can go wherever I want whenever I want," I said.

"Certainly, of course . . . *sí*. My driver is at your disposal. It's easier. Just let me know when you want him available, and—"

"Tomorrow," I said sharply. "After my breakfast."

"Tomorrow?" He looked frightened for a moment and then smiled. "Fine. Sure. I'll have the car out front at ten A.M."

"*Gracias.*"

"Will you be going far, long?"

"Not far, *señor*."

He nodded when he clearly saw that I did not want to tell him much more.

"That's fine," he said. "I want you to be happy, comfortable. Do you need some money, perhaps for some shopping?"

"No, *señor. Gracias.*"

I did have his curiosity captured now, but he sensed he had questioned me enough.

He went to his wife's closet. "Have you found other things to wear?"

Before I could respond, he went in and came out with a blouse and a skirt.

"This would fit you, I'm sure, and you would look very nice in it wherever you go tomorrow."

I smiled at his interest in what I would wear. "*Sí, señor. Gracias.*"

"Don't forget, by tomorrow night, you'll have some new maternity clothing and perhaps new shoes. Well," he said, looking as if he didn't want ever to leave, "call down if you need anything more tonight."

"*Gracias, señor.*"

He looked around the suite again and nodded. "You will be very comfortable here. My wife used to call it her little piece of heaven on earth." He started out and stopped. "Oh, there is a wall safe in the closet. The combination is two-six-zero-eight. You will find beautiful jewelry, necklaces, watches, earrings. You might even be able to wear some of her rings. Use whatever you wish. It does no one any good to be shut up in there."

"*Gracias.*"

"*Sí.*" He stared at me and then nodded at the suite.

"It's good to have someone beautiful in here again," he said. "A woman becomes radiant during her pregnancy. My wife never believed it, but it was true for her as it will be for you, Delia."

With that, he left, closing the door softly.

I went to the safe to look and was shocked to see how much jewelry was in it. All of the pieces looked very expensive. I was happy he trusted me with it, but wearing some of it would make me very nervous, and where would I wear any of it, anyway? I didn't anticipate being invited to any parties or dinners, unless Señor Bovio had some planned. I wondered about that. Would he introduce me to his friends? If so, how would he refer to me? It was awkward for both of us. I couldn't imagine him doing so. This could be a very long pregnancy and a very lonely one, too.

It already had been a very long and, in many ways, tiring day. Except for the short time I had sat at the pool, I was continually on a bed of pins and needles. I was not used to being the center of so much attention. I couldn't make a move without someone watching me. Even now, I imagined eyes in the walls, as if the *hacienda* itself were alive and studying me. It was part of the reason I wanted to get away for a while, why I had asked about a car. I had been hoping to be on my own, but I could see now that Señor Bovio didn't trust me enough yet. He probably was afraid I would do what I had been tempted to do from the moment I had arrived, sneak away and return to Mexico. It was still something I toyed with in the back of my mind.

I began to go through the dresser drawers to look for a nightgown. I found two drawers full of them, primarily in red, some sheer, a few meant for cooler nights. There were matching slippers, as well, for almost every nightgown and robe. In one drawer, I found a box of old photographs and sat on the floor going through them. There were many people in the pictures whom I didn't know, but there were many of Adan at all ages. I noticed that in only a very few of them was he standing beside his mother. With her schedule as a movie actress, I imagined it must have been very lonely for him.

Finally tired enough to feel confident that I would sleep, I crawled into the oversized bed. The *hacienda* was very quiet and far enough from any street or road to be beyond the sounds of traffic. When I put out the lights, the glow of a half-moon came through the light curtains. I had not closed the drapes. Because even these curtains had a crimson tint, the moonlight that seeped in and over the bed and the room was the color of light-red rose petals.

I said my prayers.

I closed my eyes and thought about the baby forming inside me. Parts of Adan and parts of me were exploring and testing each other, finding ways to join with those that had already begun creating our child. Adan was still in me, still a part of me. Maybe it was his spirit that was in this bedroom suite and not his mother's, after all; maybe that was what Señor Bovio had felt.

Thinking about him and the accident on the boat, I wondered if, even for a split second, Adan had blamed me. Whether it was my own imagination at work or not, I sensed anger in this room with me. If I hadn't turned, slipped on the ladder, lost control of the boat at that moment, he wouldn't have been so badly injured.

If he didn't blame me, and Señor Bovio had decided it was more important for him to forgive me and care only about my giving him a healthy grandchild, then perhaps his mother's spirit was here and did blame me. Perhaps rather than keep me safe, she would be the vengeful one.

And then, I thought, if I considered Ignacio and his father, Tiá Isabela and Sophia as well, there was a great deal of rage swirling around me. Would all of the good spirits, those who had loved me, be able to come to my defense? What truly lay in store for me?

All of these thoughts troubled me and kept me tossing and turning, falling asleep and then waking with a start. By the time the morning light cleared away the shadows, I was mentally and physically exhausted. I slept later than I had intended, but I knew what I must set out to do. I rose, showered, and dressed.

Teresa was in with my "perfect" breakfast. Apparently, Mrs. Newell had arrived early because she had to oversee every slice of bread. She had created some nutritional drink that tasted like pure chalk to me. I drank what I could and then hurried downstairs. It was just about ten o'clock. According to what Señor Bovio had promised, the car and driver would be waiting.

I did not see Señor Bovio when I descended, nor was he waiting outside. The car was there, however, as was the driver he had simply referred to as Stevens. The moment I came out of the house, he got out of the car and hurried to open the rear door for me.

"*Gracias,*" I said.

He returned to his driver's seat and waited for instructions.

"Please, start for Indio," I told him. "I'll show you where to turn."

"Very good, Miss. If you want water or anything, there's a small refrigerator on the right."

He started away. I looked back at the *hacienda,* still surprised that Señor Bovio hadn't been there to greet me or watch me drive away. I did see that Stevens had an earpiece and was speaking softly to someone on a cell phone and imagined it might be Señor Bovio.

There wasn't much traffic, and less than thirty minutes later, I had Stevens turn on the street where Ignacio's family resided. I pointed out the house and driveway, and he turned into it.

"I won't be long," I said, and went to the front door.

Ignacio's brother answered the buzzer and stood there looking at me with such disgust on his face I thought he might attack me. He was as big as Ignacio now.

"*Quién es,* Santos?" I heard his father ask. The sound of his voice made me tighten up. I hadn't expected either of them to be home. I was hoping to speak only with Ignacio's mother.

"Her," Santos said, practically spitting at me. He left the door open and turned away.

I entered slowly.

Ignacio's father had his foot on a stool. It was bandaged. He looked up with surprise. Ignacio's sister wasn't there. I was sure she was in school. His mother came in from the kitchen and stopped when she saw me.

"Why did you come here? What do you want?" Ignacio's father asked.

"Just to talk, *señor*. What happened to your foot?"

"A broken ankle," he replied quickly. "Talk about what? Why have you come here?"

I looked at Ignacio's mother. She seemed ready to cry. Her lips trembled. Santos kept himself slightly turned away, his head down.

"I never had an opportunity to speak with you, to explain what had happened, to—"

"We know what happened. We don't need you to come here to give us any explanations. Please. Go. You bring only bad luck to my family."

Now I was the one near tears, but I wouldn't turn and run out.

"You don't know what happened, *señor.* I have tried to explain it to Ignacio as well. I wrote letters, but he does not respond."

"He's finally smarted up," his father said. "Too late to help himself, I'm afraid. You know what life is like where he is, what he will become?"

"I know, *señor.*"

"Then what is it you can say that would make any difference now?"

"I can say I'm sorry, but it wasn't my fault, *señor.* I did nothing to cause this to happen."

He smiled and looked at his wife. "Did you hear? She did nothing," he said. Ignacio's mother looked at me, the utter helplessness in her face so clear and tragic.

"Señor Davila, I have tried many times to explain. I had no idea that my cousin had found Ignacio's note to me and had told the police. She didn't even warn her own brother so he wouldn't get into trouble. She was always trying to hurt me. That was more important."

"So, if you knew that, why were you so foolish as to leave that note where she could find it? Didn't I tear up every letter Ignacio sent you after you had read it? Wasn't I afraid that something like that would happen?"

"It was—"

"What?" he nearly shouted.

"Important to me. I didn't want to tear it up."

"So, instead, you left it where she could find it and do this terrible thing to us?" He shook his head. "It doesn't matter what you intended or didn't intend, Delia. The result is my son is in a terrible place, and there is nothing I can do for him. *Nada.*"

"All I ask, Señor Davila, is that you please, please, tell him I didn't mean for this to happen. When you see him again, will you ask him to write to me?"

"Why?"

"Why? I'd like . . . to . . ."

"To do what? Haven't you done enough to this family? Go back to your wealthy friends. Leave us be."

He turned away from me. Santos had kept his head down the whole time and now lifted it and looked at me with the same anger that was in his father's unforgiving face. Only Ignacio's mother had any warmth for me, but she was too frightened to say or do anything. She simply shook her head.

"I'm sorry," I said. I put a slip of paper on the small table under the picture of Jesus. "This is my address now. I am at Señor Ray Bovio's *hacienda.*"

Ignacio's father looked up sharply. "The man whose son died on the boat?"

"*Sí.*" I imagined it wouldn't be long before they found out why. "I am pregnant with his son's child."

Ignacio's father stared coldly a moment. "Please, get out of my home," he said.

I stood a moment and then turned and hurried out, pursued for what I feared would be the rest of my life by the terrible pain and anger in Señor Davila's eyes.

"Where to now, Miss?" Stevens asked.

"Just back," I said, and turned to stare out the window. I said nothing more and barely moved until we had arrived at the Bovio *hacienda*. Stevens hurried around to open the door for me, and I charged up the steps and entered the house.

Señor Bovio was right there, waiting. He took one look at my face and shook his head.

"Look how you have upset yourself," he said. "Come into my office now," he added authoritatively.

I followed him down the corridor to his large, beautifully furnished office. He had a cherrywood desk with matching paneling on the walls and a slate floor. The room was bright because of the big windows and French doors that had a western exposure. There were two walls of bookshelves, an entertainment center, and an area with computers and printers. Two dark-red leather sofas were on the right and left of the desk, and there were matching chairs in front of the desk. I saw the pictures of Señora Bovio and various political figures and celebrities on the wall, where he had also hung pictures of Adan. There was an entire section of wall covered with movie photos from the films in which Señora Bovio had starred.

"Sit, Delia," he said, and then sat behind his desk. "Why did you go to see the Davila family?"

I was on the verge of crying, but the fact that he was aware of every move I made angered me. "Am I to be spied upon constantly, treated like a prisoner? I warned you about that when you came to see me at the clinic," I replied.

"I am not treating you like a prisoner or spying on you. I am only watching over you. I do not take my responsibilities lightly, and for now, your health and welfare are my responsibilities. Look," he said, taking a different, softer tone, "if you tell me what's bothering you, I can see about helping you. If I don't know, what can I do for you? It bothers me that you are obviously so upset."

I shook my head and looked away. "There is nothing you can do, *señor*."

"Are you so absolutely sure? I am a man of great means, Delia."

"You know what happened in Mexico, *señor*. I'm sure *mi tía* Isabela has cried about it on your shoulder many times, told you how I embarrassed the family and nearly ruined her good name and reputation."

"*Sí*, and . . ."

"And I do feel guilty and responsible, but not for her. I feel terrible for the Davilas, especially Ignacio's parents. They are suffering so much." Tears bubbled under my eyelids. "I will never get their faces out of my mind. Never."

"I understand."

"I don't think you can fully understand, Señor Bovio. You would have to have looked into Ignacio's father's and mother's faces as I just did and feel the knife in your heart."

He nodded. "It's not good for you to carry such a burden right now, Delia."

"Yes, well, it is nothing compared to the burden they carry," I replied.

He sat back and thought. "I may be able to help," he said after another long moment.

"Help? How?"

"I have some influence with some very important government officials. I can't say exactly when or how, but perhaps I can get Ignacio Davila released much earlier than his jail sentence demands."

"Can you?" I asked, now excited.

"I think so," he said.

"Oh, *señor,* that would be—"

"But I won't even try unless you promise me certain things," he said.

"What things, *señor?*"

"I don't like you doing these things to yourself. I don't want you returning to the Davila home. They are angry people in pain, and you never know how they will react."

"Oh, they would not hurt me, *señor.* That—"

"Will you promise me this?"

"*Sí, señor,*" I said, nodding. "I can do no good for them returning, anyway. I don't think they would even open the door for me."

"*Muy bien.* I will work on this, Delia, but you must promise to be a cooperative patient both for Dr. Denardo and for Mrs. Newell and, of course, for me. I don't want you to think of yourself as a prisoner, but for now, I want you to take extra good care of yourself and permit me to give you everything and anything you need. This is a very big property. There is much for you to do here to amuse yourself. I'll have any and all books and magazines for you. You have your own entertainment center upstairs. You ask for anything, and I will have it brought to you, anything."

"Are you saying you don't want me to leave the property?"

"Why would you need to leave? I just said I can have anything you want brought to you, including your schoolwork. Indulge me during this pregnancy. Afterward, you can do what you want, go where you want."

"What about our trip to my Mexican village to visit my family's graves?"

"I discussed it with Dr. Denardo, and he thinks we should wait until after you give birth. It's a very emotional journey for you. I promise you, the day after you can get up and leave, I'll have you delivered first class to your village. How's that?"

"I don't know," I said, all sorts of worry rising to the surface of my thoughts.

"It's not really all that much to ask of you, and everything I ask is for our baby's benefit, Delia. Look at how simple your sacrifice, if you want to call it that, is, compared to your friend's difficult and unpleasant situation in prison. Don't you want to do something about it?"

I looked up at him.

He smiled and turned his palms up. "What do you say?"

"How long will it take you to help the Davilas?"

"It's not something I can manage overnight, Delia. There are favors to call in, officials to convince, but it can be done." He smiled. "It's been done before, believe me. However, you must not speak of it. That could compromise my efforts, understand? Mr. Whitfield, the father of the boy killed, is also a man of some means, with influential friends. I don't want you to tell anyone anything, especially your aunt Isabela."

I had to laugh at that. "You have no worry there, *señor*. I doubt that she and I will be speaking again."

"*Bien.* So, we have a bargain?"

Again, I envisioned Ignacio's father's face and the pain in his eyes.

"*Sí,*" I said. "We have a bargain."

He smiled. "Good. Now, please go and rest. Take a warm bath, perhaps. All of the toiletries in the bathroom are fresh. I've restocked them for you, and they are all my wife's favorites. She was very concerned about her skin, her hair. You have it all up there. And," he said, rising, "just to put some icing on the cake, I'm going to have my wife's beautician and manicurist come to the *hacienda* tomorrow. I'll make sure you are pampered and more than comfortable. How's that?"

"I don't know what to say, Señor Bovio."

"Say nothing. Enjoy whatever I can do for you, and let me see about your friend's problem. I don't want anything weighing on your conscience and bringing you stress and unhappiness."

He came around the desk and offered his hand. I stood up and took it.

"We have a real bargain, then, Delia," he said, fixing his eyes on mine.

"*Sí.*"

"Good. You have made the right decisions for both yourself and little Adan or little Adriana."

I raised my eyebrows. Was he dictating the name I was to give to my own baby?

He smiled at my surprise. "Oh, of course, you will

choose whatever name you want. I'm sure you will make the right choice, as you have just made."

"*Sí, gracias,*" I said.

It felt good to know I finally was doing something real for the Davilas, but when I left Señor Bovio's office, I wasn't sure if I had made a bargain with a powerful man, concerned for his grandchild, or the devil, concerned with winning another soul.

I imagined it wouldn't be long before I knew.

4

Visitors

Early in the afternoon two days later, I was on my way to the pool to take my first swim, when I saw what I felt certain was my cousin Edward's car approach the main gate. When the driver rolled down his window and leaned out to speak to the security guard, I saw that it was indeed Edward.

A surge of excitement seized my heart. Finally, we would see each other again. I waved and shouted, but he wasn't looking my way, and the brisk breeze carried away the sound of my voice. The guard picked up the phone instead of opening the gate to let Edward onto the property. Seconds later, he hung up the phone and spoke to him again. Too impatient and too excited to wait for him to drive up and park, I had started down the driveway, when suddenly I saw him back up and drive off.

I stopped, stunned.

"Edward!" I shouted, even though his car was gone from sight.

Why hadn't he come in? I continued down the driveway, hoping he had merely, for some reason, parked outside the gate, perhaps just to the side, but when I got there, his car was nowhere in sight.

"Where is my cousin Edward?" I asked the guard. I did not know his name. He and another two men split the shifts, and I had never spoken to any of them.

"Who?"

"That was my cousin Edward who just drove up to the gate. What happened?"

"Oh. Yeah, Edward Dallas. He didn't call ahead, so I called up to the house and was told not to let him enter."

"Not to let him enter? Why not?"

"I don't know, Miss."

"Who told you that?"

"Mr. Bovio."

"I don't understand," I said. "Open the gate," I ordered. He hesitated. "Open it!"

"I have to call up to the house first, Miss. I don't open the gate unless I have permission or unless I'm told in advance that someone is coming or leaving. That's my job. Just a minute, please."

I stood there with my hands on my hips, steaming. I was in a robe and a pair of sandals. The new maternity outfits and shoes had been delivered as promised. Everything was stylish and fit well. There was already even a pair of specially designed walking shoes, but I favored the clothes in Señora Bovio's closet. As Señor Bovio had predicted, I found beautiful bathing suits that fit, and the sandals looked unused.

Impatient, I went to the gate and looked up and down through the bars, hoping that Edward would either come back or still be within close enough range to see or hear me. The distance between the bars was quite narrow, so I couldn't see too far down the street, but what I saw was quiet and empty. There was no sign of him. He had probably been very annoyed at being turned away and had rushed off.

I turned quickly when I heard the guard step out of the little guard house.

"I'm sorry, Miss, but I was told not to open the gate," he said.

"What?"

"I'm just following orders, Miss. Sorry. You'll have to speak to Mr. Bovio."

"This is ridiculous," I said, and charged back up the driveway, my heart pounding, the sandals clacking. I practically lunged at the front door and ran down the marble corridor to Señor Bovio's office. He was on the phone but waved me in when he saw me in the doorway.

"I know. I'm sorry, too," he told whomever he was speaking to on the phone. "I'll call you later. I did what you asked. Calm down," he added, and hung up. Then he shook his head. "What a mess. Sorry about all that," he said.

"What mess? Why was my cousin Edward not permitted to enter the property? Why wasn't I permitted out?" I demanded. "Why did you give such orders?"

He sat back. "Those weren't my orders, Delia."

"What do you mean, they weren't your orders? I just spoke with the gate guard. He said he called up here, and you said not to let Edward enter and not to open the gate for me."

"Yes, but those aren't my orders. They're his mother's standing orders. Apparently, and you probably know more about it than I do, Edward still has some agreement with her not to see you or speak with you. Nothing has changed in that regard. She said you were well aware of this, so it should not come as any surprise. I remember that she had informed me of the agreement between Edward and her a while back, when this whole Mexican mess started. When she was here the other day, she reminded me of it and made me promise that I would enforce the agreement should Edward come around. She asked that I inform her if her son tried to violate the agreement.

"That was Isabela on the phone just now," he continued, sitting forward. "I had to let her know he had come here. I don't want her troubling you."

"You don't want her troubling me? It's far too late for that, *señor.*"

"I understand. She's beside herself. She almost burned my ear through the phone," he said. Smiling, he added, "I wouldn't want to be in Edward's shoes right now when he gets home."

"This isn't right. I won't permit her to—"

"Relax, Delia. This is a very, very sensitive time for all of us. You asked me to look into the Mexican boy's situation and do something about it, didn't you?"

"Yes, but what does that—"

"Well, if Isabela starts rattling cages, it will complicate everything. Besides, this is between Isabela and her son now. You have enough on your mind without bringing in someone else's problems."

"It's not someone else's problems, Señor Bovio.

Edward is my cousin. He has always been a good friend to me."

"I understand, but nevertheless, you can't interfere between him and his mother," he said sternly. "Let it be for now. And I wouldn't go planning on some secret meeting with him somewhere, either," he warned. "That could be even worse. You've already seen what a secret meeting can do."

"This isn't what I expected when I agreed to come here," I said, flopping into one of the cushioned chairs. I was angry but not sure if I should be angry at him or at Tía Isabela.

"Look at you. All flushed. Did you run all the way up the driveway?"

I pouted and didn't answer.

"Listen to me, Delia. It wouldn't have been any easier if you had been sent back to Mexico, would it? Edward couldn't go there to find you."

"Why not?"

"It was part of my deal with the Mexican authorities when I got them to release both of you," he said. "Actually, Isabela insisted on that."

"Of course, she would insist on that. She always expected I would go back, and she didn't want him following me."

"Whatever. You know you and he and his friend were actually arrested, and you were being charged. I don't think you would have liked being in a Mexican jail. It was very serious. Your aunt saved all three of you from a terrible time when she called me. I repeat, let it alone for now, Delia. What you do afterward with yourself is your own business."

"Afterward?"

"After you give birth. You don't want to do anything to jeopardize that, now, do you?"

The frustration washed over me. Would this be the way every argument or discussion we had would end? Would I always have to give in for the sake of my baby? And I didn't like the way he said "afterward with yourself." We had had a discussion about "afterward" when he came to the clinic. I had told him I would never desert my baby. I could see he still thought I might, that I might think more about myself and my future.

"It's all ridiculous," I said, not hiding my anger at him now. "I do feel as if I'm locked away here. I was standing there looking out that gate like some prisoner looking through bars. I won't be locked in like this!"

I stood up and stamped my foot, well aware that I was behaving just the way my cousin Sophia behaved when she was frustrated or told she couldn't do something.

"Take it easy. You're getting overwrought for nothing. It was an incident. It's over. No one is keeping you locked in. I had my driver take you to the Davilas', didn't I?"

"It's not over! Don't say this is over just because *mi tía* Isabela got what she wanted."

He saw the rage building in me, and his expression quickly softened. "All right, all right. Look, I tell you what. I'll speak with Isabela about it again. Give me some time to calm her. I'll explain why it would make you happy to be able to have your cousin visit from time to time. She's very upset right now, but I'll get back to her. That's a promise," he said. "She usually listens to me after a while. Just don't expect any miracles overnight. She's not the easiest mountain to move." He smiled.

"No, she's not. But move she will," I told him. "Or else."

"Threatening Isabela is the wrong approach to take," Señor Bovio said, shaking his head. "I know something about politics, diplomacy. She would only dig her heels in deeper and make even more trouble for you both, Delia. Don't forget that you and your cousin and his friend were involved in what amounted to an international incident. This isn't some parlor game we're playing. If somehow she got wind of what we're trying to do for that Mexican boy who was at the center of it all, she would really explode."

He was right. I felt myself calm down. "I know," I said in a voice of defeat.

"Besides, this is exactly the sort of thing I am trying to keep away from you while you are pregnant," he continued softly. "Let me use all that I have at my disposal to make your life easier, comfortable, and healthy, especially healthy, during these months. If Adan were here with us, he'd be asking you the same thing."

I raised my gaze quickly. He was looking to the side and smiling, as if he could see Adan standing there, agreeing. Then he turned back to me.

"I'm a grandfather who has to think like a father, too. I didn't ask for this," he said, sounding a little cold. "Fate imposed this on me, but I am not the sort of man who shirks his responsibilities. I am determined that this baby will be born healthy and strong."

"I am not arguing about that. I, too, want nothing else, Señor Bovio."

"Good. Good," he said, relaxing. "Now, let me change the subject. I have some good news for you. This afternoon, a teacher, James McCarthy, will be bringing you books, manuals, whatever you need to finish your high school diploma requirements. He will supervise your work, leave you the assignments to complete, and then, when the time comes, administer your exams. If you get busy with it, you should be able to graduate about the same time as the students attending the school.

"In the meantime, I have spoken to my friends at the education offices, and we will receive a list of the best schools of nursing to which you can apply. I'll get you all of the information on all of the schools, and you can spend time thinking about each one and deciding. When you are able to attend such a school, the tuition and living expenses at whatever school you choose will be taken care of, so you will have absolutely no worries in that regard.

"After you give birth, I'll see to it that you have an automobile of your own, clothes, whatever you need or want, for as long as you want."

"How long do you expect my baby and me to live here, Señor Bovio?"

"You can live here as long as you wish, Delia. I am willing to do anything to make you happy. There's no reason to worry about all that now, anyway." He waved the air as if he could wave away the words and thoughts.

"I'll try not to worry about it, but I'm sure I'll think about it, *señor*."

"Of course, of course. So," he said, pressing his hands together, "as you see, in the meantime, your days will soon be filled. Mrs. Newell is, in fact, at this very moment working out a schedule for you that will include exercise as well. All of your physical examinations, evaluations, whatever tests are needed, will be scheduled.

"Now, please, do me a favor. Go up to your room and rest, and get yourself in a calmer mood. I'll have you called the moment Mr. McCarthy arrives with your school materials."

He smiled. It was difficult for me to hold on to any indignation in light of all that he was doing and promising. And when I thought about it, it was true that Tía Isabela was really responsible for this. She was just trying to get back at me. I could just imagine how Sophia was teasing and tormenting her about Señor Bovio stopping her from getting her satisfaction.

"I'm all right," I told him. "I was in the middle of going to the pool to get some exercise and air. I'll go back to that. It relaxes me."

"Good. If it relaxes you, please continue," he said. "Swimming is an approved exercise, but don't overdo it."

His phone rang, so I nodded and left when I could hear that it was business and not Tía Isabela again.

I could see his logic. Everything he was saying sounded reasonable, but nevertheless, I was terribly disappointed. It had been quite a long time since Edward and I had had an opportunity to talk. There was so much more I wanted to say to him, to explain more about what had happened in Mexico. I was sure he was curious about all that was happening to me now, and I needed him. I desperately needed someone to talk to, someone I could trust. For as long as I had been in America, he had been that someone. He and his companion, Jesse, had been my knights in shining armor.

Everything was set up at the pool as usual, so I chose a lounge, slipped off the robe, and went into the water. I began to do some laps, enjoying the water and losing myself in the exercise. When I reached the side of the pool after my fifth lap, I looked up at the polished toenails and shapely legs of Fani Cordova. She was standing in a pretty yellow skirt and blouse and smiling down at me. She wore a pair of designer sunglasses that were studded with jewels. Her hair was pinned up. I thought she looked more beautiful than ever.

"I see you've adjusted to your new life pretty quickly," she said.

I pulled myself up and out of the pool. "Hi, Fani."

"My cousin called me to come see you, but I already knew you were here. Sophia didn't waste a second getting out the news about you all over the community."

"I expected that."

"Yes, well, you don't look pregnant to me. Is this another scam you're pulling?"

"What?"

She sat on a lounge and watched me take my towel. "Another scam, like that whole charade you created with what's his name, the Mexican boyfriend."

"It wasn't a charade, Fani, and it wasn't a scam. I couldn't talk about it at the time. There was too much danger for him and his family."

"You sure had me believing you about all that terror crossing the desert and his dying. I thought I was the

best when it came to pulling wool over other people's
eyes."

"Pulling wool?"

"You can stop that ignorant Mexican girl act, Delia,
especially when you're talking to me," she snapped. "I
know you're smarter than almost any of the other students who were in our classes."

I put on my robe.

She was glaring at me with daggers in her eyes.

"I'm sorry you are so angry at me."

I sat across from her and started to dry my hair.

"Sorry? What did you expect? I loved Adan, and I
don't mean just as a cousin."

I stopped drying my hair. "What do you mean?"

"There was a time when I thought he and I might tie
the knot. Know what that means?"

"You never said anything like that, and you were
happy that he was seeing me."

"Well, that was because he didn't see me as I saw
him, so I gave up on it and settled for a closer friendship. We got so he would confide in me as much as he
would in any of his male friends. That's how I knew he
was so bonkers over you and that it was hopeless. I
tried to talk him out of going back to you, telling him
not to feel so sorry for you, that you were much
smarter than he could imagine. I did keep him away
for a while and got him fixed up with Dolores Del Ray.
I had his father convinced it would be a good match,
but he threw that out the window to go back with you.
He'd be alive today if he had listened to me."

Tears froze over my eyes.

She opened her purse and took out a cigarette.

"You are smoking?"

"Since Adan's death," she said. "Maybe I'm suicidal. Didn't you once tell me everyone who gets close to you suffers some way, somehow? One of your other big secrets, I imagine."

"I was being honest with you, Fani, and trusting. I thought you were my friend then."

"I was your friend, probably your best friend." She puffed again and looked at me, moving her closed lips from side to side as if she were washing the inside of her mouth with a new thought. "Maybe I still am or could be. It will depend on what you do now."

"What do you mean? What will I do?"

"I hope nothing more to hurt my cousin. Señor Bovio lost the election because his son died, you know. He lost his whole great future. And let me tell you something, Delia," she said poking the air between us with her long cigarette. "He would have been a great U.S. senator for our people. A great many people lost when he lost."

"Why did he lose?"

"Why did he lose?" She laughed coldly. "His heart fell out of his body, and he had no energy or interest in the campaign after Adan died."

She blew her smoke straight up and then studied me again. Her critical gazes made me very uncomfortable. I tightened the robe.

"How many months are you supposed to be?"

"It's not what I'm supposed to be, Fani. I am about three months," I said.

"Right."

"I am, Fani." She was infuriating me now. "Some women don't show for many months."

"Some never show," she said.

"Why would I lie about this?"

"Why?" She laughed and waved her hand. "To be here for a while, that's why. I'm sure it's a little better than the Mexican village you were returning to, isn't it?" She smiled. "From what I was told, you certainly didn't behave like a pregnant woman the day you came."

"What? What does that mean?"

"You and that José or whatever his name is, the pool man. My cousin had to fire him."

"He fired him?"

"Ray said you were flirting with him. Not that I blame you. I've seen him. He's got quite the body. If I ever felt like slumming, he'd be my choice."

"I did not flirt. I am sorry Señor Bovio thought that and did this. I don't like that someone lost his job over me."

"Right. You'll lose sleep over it. So, you're sure you're really pregnant? Lots of times it's a false alarm, or it's something a woman wishes."

"Doctors examined me, took tests, Fani. I couldn't make this up just to live here, and I wasn't exactly feeling that I should live here."

She laughed. "I bet not."

"You're being very cruel, Fani."

"Yeah, well, I haven't been exactly Miss Congeniality these days with anyone, so don't feel bad." She smoked some more and then said, "Things aren't so good at my house."

"What do you mean?"

"My parents."

"What about them?" I expected she would tell me they had become stricter after Adan's death, imposing curfews and restrictions on her. I was sure she would blame that on me as well.

"I think they're heading for a nasty breakup."

"A breakup? Why?"

"My mother found out something about my father that has turned her against him. It's like living in the land of the dead these days."

"Oh, I'm sorry. What did he do? Is he seeing another woman?"

She blew more smoke straight up again and looked away. There was a long silence, and then her shoulders rose and fell. "I don't know why I'm telling you anything," she said. "Except," she added, looking back at me and smiling, "you've proven you're real good when it comes to keeping secrets. My cousin, Ray Bovio, doesn't even know what's happening with my parents yet. And I don't want you telling him! He has enough to worry about, and he's had enough unhappiness, thanks to you."

I just stared at her a moment. "Maybe," I said, "it's better you don't confide in me, Fani. Yes, I keep secrets well, but secrets burn you from the inside out."

"Thanks. I just knew I could depend on you when it came to being a friend."

"I don't know what to say to you, Fani," I said, exasperated. "Do you want me to be your friend or not? Sometimes you sound as if you don't, and sometimes you sound as if you do."

"I'm here, aren't I? I didn't have to come."

"*Sí*. Okay. You can tell me your secret, and I won't tell anyone. Why is your mother angry at your father, so angry that she would leave him?"

"He has a boyfriend," she said.

"What? What does this mean, a boyfriend?"

"He goes both ways, Delia, but mainly with his boyfriend these days, it seems. You know what going both ways means, don't you?"

"*Sí.*"

She looked angry, but I could see tears glistening in her eyes. She looked out toward the stables. "Anyway, who cares what they do, right? I'm going off to college in late August, and I won't be back much."

"I'm sorry, Fani."

She turned her now fiery eyes at me. "Stop saying that. One thing I won't stand for is you feeling sorry for me. You're the one who should be pitied. What do you think your future is going to be once you have your baby? A few years from now, you'll probably be working as someone's maid. Maybe I'll hire you myself."

I felt my blood boil. "No, Fani. Whenever I am ready to go, Señor Bovio is paying for my college. I'm going to become a nurse."

"How would you go to college when you have a baby?"

"I won't go right away, but he's buying me a car and paying all of my expenses." I smiled. "I'm thinking I'll get my own apartment, and maybe," I said, still smiling, "I'll have a Mexican lady babysitter. He would pay for it if I asked."

She looked skeptical. "Why would he do all that?"

"It's a bargain he has made."

"What bargain?"

"I agreed to live here during my pregnancy and let him take care of me so that my baby, his grandchild, would be born healthy rather than go back to Mexico.

In return, he has hired a private-duty nurse and nutritionist, bought me personally made maternity clothing, even maternity shoes, and has the doctor coming here and giving me very personal attention. He's arranged for me to finish my high school work here. A teacher is bringing everything to me today."

"Buying you a car, paying your expenses after you give birth? You fell into a gold mine, didn't you? I hope you planned all this. I hope it wasn't all accidental."

"What? Why?"

"Why? I'd like you more if I knew you were as good a schemer as I am, if not better."

"You're not going to like me very much, then," I told her.

She paused for a moment, and then she laughed. "I do miss you, Delia. It's been rather boring at school, as a matter of fact. I'm not even interested in picking on your stupid cousin Sophia. It was always like shooting fish in a barrel, anyway," she said, and blew some smoke.

"What are you doing?" we heard Señor Bovio cry out.

Both of us turned to see him walking quickly in our direction.

"Fani!" he screamed louder.

"What?"

"I asked you to come by and be a companion for Delia but not to blow smoke in her face," he said, drawing closer.

"I'm not blowing smoke in her face, Ray. Calm down. Jesus."

"Put that cigarette out," he ordered. "Don't you

know it's bad for pregnant women to be around smoke?"

She stared at him and then stamped it out. "Sorry, *mi dios.*"

"I don't want smoking anywhere on my property."

"What about your Cuban cigars, Ray?"

"I've locked them away for now," he said. He turned to me. "Mr. McCarthy is here to see you. He has all of your books and materials. Go change and meet him in the library. He's waiting there. You don't want to catch cold walking around the air-conditioned house in a wet bathing suit."

"Why are you getting so hyper, Ray? She's not that fragile," Fani told him.

He turned to her with a look of pain in his eyes. "I would have expected you to think like I do, Fani. She's carrying Adan's baby."

Fani glanced at me and then looked away. "I've got to go," she said. "I have a few silly errands to do for my mother. I'll call you sometime, Delia."

"I'll walk back with you," I said quickly, and joined her.

Señor Bovio remained standing there as we walked off toward the house.

"Maybe I was wrong," Fani told me as we drew farther away.

"Wrong? About what?"

"About your falling into a gold mine. Maybe you just fell into a dark hole. I'll call you," she promised, and walked to her car.

I watched her get in, looked back at Señor Bovio, who was still standing at the pool looking our way, and then I hurried into the house to dress and meet my teacher.

Mrs. Newell was waiting for me at the top of the stairway. She seemed to pop out of nowhere.

"I'm happy you've come back inside. I see you went out without putting any sunblock on. We don't want you getting a heat rash or sunburn."

"I have lived in the sunlight all my life, Mrs. Newell. I know when I'm getting too much."

"You haven't been pregnant all your life, have you?" she shot back at me. Then she paused with a new thought. "Were you ever pregnant?"

"No, of course not."

"It's not a foolish question to ask. Girls even younger than you are often married and mothers back where you're from, aren't they?"

"I was not," I said.

"Um. Next time, put on the sunblock. I left it on the dresser in your room. People don't understand," she said in a more thoughtful, calmer voice. "Young girls can be physically mature enough to conceive, but that doesn't mean they have the basic intelligence necessary yet to take care of themselves and their children. Sex is easy; motherhood is not." She smiled. "It's why we have so many problems with young people today."

"Do you have children, Mrs. Newell?"

"No, but . . ."

"Why don't you have children?" I was going to add, *if you're so smart about it.*

"That's not your business. We're here to deal with you, not me."

"Deal? I don't want anyone dealing with me, Mrs.

Newell. I'm not a deck of cards," I told her, and went to my room.

Fani would have liked that, I thought, smiling to myself. I made a mental note to tell her. We'd have some good times laughing about it. Despite all she had said, I was happy she had come to see me and looked forward to the next time. I hoped she wouldn't wait too long.

When I stepped into my room, I saw the schedule Mrs. Newell had prepared for me. She had left it on my pillow so I couldn't miss it. It was quite detailed, with almost every moment of my day accounted for, right from when I awoke, had my breakfast, and then, according to her wishes, took my morning exercise, which she specified as only a ten-to-fifteen-minute walk. She had even outlined where I should walk.

After that, I was to go to the library to do my schoolwork until lunch. I would then return to the library, where, on Wednesdays, Mr. McCarthy would meet me at two P.M. to review what I had done and to see if I had any questions or problems. He would leave me the next week's assignments.

Following that, Mrs. Newell would take my blood pressure and check to be sure my feet or hands weren't swelling. I was always to tell her if I had any problems, but she would consider this to be her examination. Since the sun was lower, I could, if I wanted, go for a fifteen-minute swim. She dictated that I would then take a nap, to relax before dinner.

My time after dinner was my own, but I was to be in bed by ten P.M.

Every other day, I would be weighed in the morning before breakfast.

The doctor's visits were clearly indicated on the calendar she had created. I did see that I was scheduled to be taken to his office for the ultrasound test and something called chorionic villus sampling. She didn't explain it but told me to see the pamphlet she had left on my desk. Three weeks after these tests, I was to have an amniocentesis. I read in the pamphlet about each exam. She had underlined that chorionic villus sampling was generally done when the mother or father had a genetic disorder that ran in the family.

"Since medical records for poor rural Mexicans are nonexistent, this is important," she had written in the margins.

My first reaction was pure anger, but then I thought it was not untrue, although I could not recall *mi abuela* Anabela or my mother ever mentioning such problems in either my father's or her family. Since Señor Bovio was paying for all of this, how could I object?

My phone rang. My first reaction was hope and excitement. Perhaps it was Edward, but it turned out to be only the intercom.

"You are keeping your tutor waiting unnecessarily," Mrs. Newell complained.

"I'll be right there."

I hung up, quickly took off my bathing suit, and dressed in a skirt and blouse. Still in sandals, however, I rushed out and down the stairway to go to the library.

Mr. McCarthy sat at the long, light-walnut desk with my books, workbooks, and other school materials spread before him. He was a stout man with thin, balding gray hair and a round face that looked swollen because his small dark-brown eyes were so sunken. His complexion was smooth, however, so smooth that he looked as if he never had to shave. He stretched his thin, pale lips into a smile that seemed to sink into his cheeks and disappear. He wore a brown-and-white-striped sport jacket with a coffee-colored bow tie that was so tightly tied it moved with his Adam's apple when he spoke.

"Hello there," he said.

I hurried to the desk.

"Hi."

"So," he said, getting right down to business, "I met with your teachers before I came here today to learn where you were in your studies before you stopped attending school. If you'll sit down," he said, pausing. "I don't like having to look up at students when I speak to them."

"Oh. Sorry."

"You'll notice that I have marked each textbook where you should have been at that time. Under each book are the assignments to follow once you read the text assigned. I have also created a time line for it all. I understand you hope to take your exams at the same time as the students in your old school?"

"Yes, I would."

"We'll see," he said. "You have to be ready."

"I'll be ready," I said. "I have not much else to do but my schoolwork."

"I don't imagine so. You're not the first prospective teenage mother I've had to tutor. In fact, these days, it seems like an epidemic." He dropped the corners of his mouth even deeper into his cheeks.

I felt my whole body tighten and close like a fist, but I said nothing. I dropped my gaze to the books.

"Well, then, I'll leave it all with you and see you next Wednesday. We'll go over what you did and see what you didn't understand."

He rose. His waist was as wide as his shoulders, and he wasn't much taller than I was. Didn't he want to tell me anything else or ask me anything?

"I was always a little ahead in all of my classes," I said, "even though my grades weren't perfect."

"That should make things easier, assuming, of course, that you knew what you were doing. You're right about your grades. They weren't all that impressive," he added, bending over to whisper. His breath smelled like sour milk. "This is not going to be a walk in the park. I'm a private tutor since retirement, but I'm not for sale. I have my standards, and I don't compromise them to please my employer."

"I don't think you should, either."

"Good. Then we have an understanding. I left my telephone number if you have any problems that can't wait until next Wednesday." He nodded and walked out.

I looked at the books and the assignment sheets. He was right. I hadn't done as well as I could have in the public school, but that was because I was very depressed and unhappy after we had returned from Mexico. I would do well now, I thought. I wanted a future.

I sat and looked at the doorway through which Mr. McCarthy had just walked. He was very different from the pleasant teachers I had at the private school and the public school and not very encouraging. But beggars couldn't be choosers. Perhaps all of these challenges, the lonely world I was living in, were of my own making and not just the work of some evil eye that had chosen me for torture and unhappiness.

I always had trouble blaming God for our misfortunes, always had difficulty believing that he kept track of every little thing that happened to us or whatever we did. We wrote our own stories. I wasn't pregnant because of some unexplainable accident. I had wanted to make love with Adan. Deep in my heart, I wanted his child, a child who would be our child.

And so I was here and would have to do whatever was necessary, walk over whatever hot coals I had to walk over. If I kept feeling sorrier and sorrier for myself, I wouldn't have the strength or the will to get to a brighter future for myself and for my child.

As *mi abuela* Anabela would say whenever she heard or saw someone full of self-pity, "*Gato llorón no caza ratón.*" A crying cat catches no mice.

I will not be a crying cat, I thought.

Almost out of anger as much as out of ambition, I set forth to attack the work Mr. McCarthy had detailed for me. I vowed to myself that I would do it so well that I would wipe the smirk off his marshmallow face.

5

Clear Sailing

Marking off the days designed for me on Mrs. Newell's schedule was like counting drips of molasses falling into a bucket. Even though I followed her orders and kept myself busy with my schoolwork, the monotony began to wear on me.

In fact, the days became so dreary that I actually looked forward to being taken to Dr. Denardo's office for my tests. As promised, he stopped by every other week to check on how I was doing and get a report from Mrs. Newell, but he did very little and was very happy with what he saw. He never failed to compliment Mrs. Newell on how well she was managing my pregnancy. They discussed me in front of me as if I were invisible.

"How is her appetite? How is she sleeping? Does she have any unusual pains?"

It made me feel like some controlled laboratory animal.

Finally, the day for my ultrasound arrived. Señor Bovio surprised me by insisting that he would drive me to Dr. Denardo's office himself.

"This is too important to send you off with surrogates," he told me. "If fate had permitted Adan to live, he would surely be going with you today."

Even though he had said it was for family, he told Mrs. Newell to come along.

"She needs to hear everything, just in case there is a problem," he told me.

It was then that I became nervous. I wanted to ask Mrs. Newell what sort of problems could be determined, if any, but I didn't want to hear her doom and gloom. Whenever she warned me about anything happening to my baby, she always made it sound as if it would be the direct result of something I had done, some way I had lived, or simply something genetic in my family. Nothing could ever be the fault of Adan's family line.

Dr. Denardo had a very modern office with a plush waiting room. There was a small area off to the side for the children of the mothers and prospective mothers. In it was a television, toys, and even a sandbox. The lobby itself had three soft-cushion sofas and a half-dozen comfortable chairs, shelves of magazines, mostly about raising children but a good variety of others, a machine for hot water to make tea, all decaffeinated, and a refrigerator with juices and soft drinks. Light, soft music was piped through two speakers.

He had two nurses and a receptionist. There were four examination rooms just past the reception desk.

Almost the moment we arrived, we were brought into the room that contained the ultrasound equipment. One of the nurses, Betty Rosen, apparently knew Mrs. Newell, but I sensed she was not very fond of her. They eyed each other like two gunslingers, with Mrs. Newell looking as if she was evaluating everything Betty Rosen did. I could feel the tension and was happier when Dr. Denardo entered.

"Okay," he said, "let's get right to it. This is going to give us an even more accurate idea of gestational age," he explained.

Everyone's attention went to the screen as Dr. Denardo pointed out my developing baby's head and spine, chest and heart, abdomen, liver, stomach, and kidneys, as well as the arms and legs and hands and feet. He announced that everything looked perfect.

"And," he said, turning to Señor Bovio, "she is carrying a boy."

Señor Bovio's eyes lit up with such joy it nearly made me cry. He surprised me by putting his hand on my stomach and closing his eyes as if he could communicate with my developing child. No one spoke. Even Dr. Denardo looked moved.

"It is truly a resurrection," Señor Bovio whispered.

"Well, Millicent," Dr. Denardo said after completing his evaluation of my health, "continue to do what you're doing. She's in perfect shape."

Mrs. Newell gloated and eyed Betty Rosen, who busied herself with other preparations.

Afterward, Señor Bovio was so pleased he decided to take us to lunch. The prospect of eating something other than the bland, so-called perfect foods Mrs. Newell had prepared for me daily cheered me, but when we sat in the booth at the restaurant, she was highly critical of almost everything on the menu. Señor Bovio could see my displeasure growing.

"Oh, I think we can loosen the reins a bit today, Millicent. Go on, Delia, order whatever you like."

Even with this permission, Mrs. Newell's disapproving and critical eyes intimidated me. I ordered and ate less than half of what I wanted.

But Señor Bovio's joy at discovering I was carrying his grandson and not a granddaughter spilled over in many different ways once we returned to the *hacienda*. He showered me with more gifts. Every day following, either Mr. Blumgarten or Mark Corbet appeared with something new. My protests were useless, even when I pointed out that I couldn't possibly wear everything enough times before I gave birth, after which I would have no use for it.

"Unless, of course, you have another child relatively soon after," Mrs. Newell couldn't help but point out. She always managed to hear our conversations. "But perhaps you've learned something about birth control now."

"If it would mean having to go through every day like this, I think I'd become celibate," I responded. Instead of being upset by my remark, she smiled that self-confident, know-it-all smile that was longer than her usual blink.

"I doubt you would have that concern, Delia. You wouldn't have another Bovio."

It was as if her words went directly to my heart and not through my ears and brain. I felt the pain under my breast, a pain that was so sharp it pierced on through to my spine. For a moment, I lost my breath.

"That comment was unnecessary, Mrs. Newell," I said.

She shrugged, unremorseful. "It's always better to face reality, Delia. If young women did that, for example, there would be fewer unwed mothers."

She gave me one of her blink smiles before walking off full of self-satisfaction.

After that, I finally expressed my dissatisfaction with her to Señor Bovio.

"She's making everything very unpleasant for me," I told him.

"What? You saw how pleased Dr. Denardo is with her. You mustn't take her too personally," he said. "She's here in one capacity only and is the best at what she does. Pay no attention to anything else she says or does."

"That is not easy to do most of the time, *señor.* She hovers over me so much, I feel as if she's attached herself to my shadow."

"Please, please, do it for me. I promise you, she'll be gone as soon as she is no longer necessary."

I said nothing more. I had no one else to talk to, really, no one else to confide in. To my disappointment, Fani had not called or returned since the day she had met me at the pool. I waited each day for some word from her or about her but heard nothing. Señor Bovio did not mention her parents breaking up, either, nor did he mention her. Finally, I asked him about her, and he told me he hadn't heard from her or her parents.

"Everyone's busy. I'm sure Fani has many friends. You know she is a very popular girl at school. Maybe she no longer feels she has anything in common with you because you are pregnant."

He might very well be right, I thought. I was disappointed but said nothing. Of course, there was no word from or about Edward, either, since the day he had been turned away at the gate. I attributed that to *mi tía* Isabela, who had yet to stop by even to threaten something new since the first day I had come to the Bovio *hacienda*. Still, I hoped that Edward might at least call me, but the phone never rang.

I always asked Teresa if any messages had been left for me when I was out of the house, but she never said there had been any. I became suspicious about it and for the first time used the phone in my room to call out. I was just testing, so I called the telephone number of a nursing school I was considering. I couldn't get an outside line. The phone kept going back to the dial tone.

I went down to ask Señor Bovio about it, but he wasn't in his office, and no one else knew anything about it. I waited for him in the living room, and the moment he entered, I asked him about my phone.

"Oh, that was shut off shortly after my wife died," he said. "Only the intercom works."

"Well, can you get it back on for me, please, *señor*?"

"I'll see about it," he said, but he didn't, and when I reminded him, he apologized. Finally, he told me the technician was having some difficulties and would have to do some rewiring. I asked him to get me a cell phone in the meantime. He was surprised, but he always said I could ask for anything I wanted.

"If I should go somewhere, I might have to call you or Mrs. Newell," I suggested when he looked hesitant.

"*Sí.* You're right. I'll see to it immediately," he told

me, and to my surprise, the following day, a cell phone was delivered for me.

The first thing I did was call Fani. I hadn't forgotten her private number, but I was surprised to learn that it had been changed, so I called her house, and the housekeeper told me she wasn't home. I left my name and my new phone number, but Fani did not return my call.

During the weeks that went by, I often asked Señor Bovio about his efforts to reduce Ignacio's prison sentence. He told me it was in the works, but it had to go through a chain of command that would take more time. Finally, a little annoyed about my frequent inquiries, he said, "You don't have to keep asking me about it, Delia. You don't push people who are doing you favors. I don't mean me. We are working with bureaucrats who are quite self-important. There are egos to stroke and palms to fill, if you know what I mean. Be patient."

I could do nothing but nod and hope. To keep myself from thinking about it too much, I put most of my energy into my schoolwork, usually doing more than was required. Mr. McCarthy's smirk of pessimism didn't fly off his face, but it began to dwindle as he reviewed my work every Wednesday. Just before he prepared me for my final exams, however, he did admit that he expected me to do well. He administered the finals over two days and then called Señor Bovio to tell him that I had passed everything and would be getting my high school diploma.

Although it was unusual for him to do so, Señor Bovio came up to my suite to invite me to have dinner with him the night after I had passed my exams.

"It is a very special occasion, after all," he said. "I am proud of your accomplishment, Delia. To be honest, I didn't think you would be able to do it so quickly."

"*Gracias, señor.*"

"I know it was a real accomplishment. Your tutor has a reputation for being very strict."

"He was."

Señor Bovio nodded. "You should look special tonight," he said. He went to the closet and sifted through my maternity dresses. "I like this one very much. It reminds me of one my wife wore."

Dozens had been made for me and delivered, especially after the ultrasound results. Señor Bovio had Mr. Blumgarten come to do his new measurements every ten days now, instead of every three weeks. At the last session, he admitted being surprised at how quickly I was showing. He wondered if I were having twins. Mrs. Newell, who overheard, immediately assured him that I wasn't and that I was not gaining any more weight than expected. Obviously taking it as a criticism of her, she dressed him down so sharply with her remarks that he seemed to shrink and couldn't get his work over and leave fast enough. However, he did create beautiful clothes.

"It is very pretty, *señor*. I'll wear it."

"Good."

Señor Bovio continued to look in the closet and surprised me by bringing out one of his wife's wigs.

"Try this on tonight," he said. "I think the color suits you."

I stared, amazed.

He smiled. "I know you young women like to dabble in all this. Go on," he said, holding it out.

I took it because I could see that it was important to him.

Later, dressed in the wig and the maternity dress he had chosen for me, I entered the dining room. He was already there and immediately registered delight. He stood and pulled out the chair for me.

"You look absolutely beautiful, Delia. I was right about that wig. It suits you. I knew you would soon bloom. I told you that you would be even prettier during your pregnancy. My wife never believed me. I hope you do now."

The wig did change my look, but I didn't think it was flattering. It wasn't me, and I wore it only to please him.

"We don't see ourselves the way others see us sometimes, *señor*," I said, coming as close as I could to telling him the truth.

"Very true, very true. You are a wise young lady. More and more, I understand why Adan was so attracted to you, Delia."

I thanked him, but he looked very thoughtful for a moment, and then, after a moment, he asked, "How would you like to attend a nursing school in California?"

"I have been considering a few, *sí*, but as I have told you, *señor*, I would first like—"

"I have an idea for you." He put his fork down and sat back. "Why not attend the nursing school in San Bernardino, which is only about an hour away? As I told you, I am buying you a car. You could attend that school and remain living here. To help you go to school and still care for our baby, I will hire a nanny to take care of the *muchacho* while you are at class and whenever you need to be away or work in quiet. How does that sound?"

When I was silent, he continued.

"There is no reason for someone as intelligent as you to delay her education. You're comfortable here. Imagine a child growing up here," he added. "Adan had a wonderful childhood."

"With his mother being away so much?" I asked. It came through my lips so fast I didn't have time to intercept the thought. I saw that my remark stung him and brought small white blotches of anger into his cheeks.

"We managed," he said. "I did the best I could running a major business simultaneously. He grew up to be a fine young man, didn't he? A father couldn't be any prouder of a son, could he?"

"No, *señor*, of course not."

"So? Why do you resist my offers?"

"I don't know, Señor Bovio. Let me think about it all."

"Think, sure, but you could start this schooling much sooner than you would if you went off on your own. Besides, it would be wonderful for a child to have a nurse, and peace of mind for a mother who was otherwise occupied with important things."

I couldn't deny any of that, but in my vision of the future, I saw myself being far more independent. And what if I found someone new to love and to love me? How difficult that would be if I still lived in Señor Bovio's house. I wouldn't bring up such a possibility now, of course, but it hung in the air like something inevitable.

We ate the remainder of our dinner in relative silence, but he did not retreat from his suggestion afterward. The following day, I found a pamphlet in my room for the school he had suggested in San Bernardino, and then he began to parade a variety of automobiles for me to consider.

"I'd turn over one of Adan's many cars to you, but it would be too painful for me to see them without him driving them," he said.

"I understand, of course."

"I'm in the process of getting rid of them, actually. It's one of the more painful things for me. It was hard enough donating most of his clothing to Angel View, the charity in Palm Springs. I am saving all of his precious personal jewelry and other mementos for little Adan."

On a number of occasions since I had been given the ultrasound, he referred to my baby as little Adan. I knew he was hoping I would not object to naming him Adan. A part of me wanted simply to say I would, but another part of me wondered if my baby shouldn't have his own identity and not be made to live in his dead father's shadow. I was afraid even to bring up this conflict in my mind. How I longed for a companion, a trusted ear to listen to my most troubled and intimate thoughts.

Again, I tried reaching Fani and even considered calling Edward. I almost did, but I stopped myself when I thought I would just be getting him into deeper trouble. I had done enough to him as it was. He didn't need me bringing him down any more.

However, whenever I saw the pile of mail being brought to Señor Bovio's office, I wondered if there could be a letter from Edward or possibly, finally, a letter from Ignacio. Perhaps his mother had mentioned my visit when she had visited him in prison, and perhaps she had suggested that he write to me. It was truly a dream, I knew, but I couldn't help fantasizing about it.

In my fantasy, Teresa would bring Ignacio's letter to me, and I would hold it for hours without daring to open the envelope and read the letter. I would be too nervous. What if it was a letter filled with anger and curses? What if there were no forgiveness and understanding? It would be too painful.

But what if it was a letter filled with hope and love? Would I dare write back and tell him that Señor Bovio was working on getting him out earlier? What if I told him and Señor Bovio was unable to do much at all? It was much crueler to make a promise and have someone expect it than not to make any promise at all. He could hate me again. I spent hours thinking about all of this, even though it was something that hadn't happened. I lived with the hope that someday it would.

Another three weeks went by, and my scheduled second visit to Dr. Denardo's office occurred. This time, Señor Bovio was more nervous. I had the feeling that Mrs. Newell had unloaded her litany of terrible scenarios on him as well. I was having an amniocentesis, which was a test to see if there were any genetic abnormalities. I was sure she had told him, as she had made sure to tell me, that the test could detect chromosomal disorders such as Down syndrome or the structural defect she had described earlier, spina bifida.

Señor Bovio tried to be nonchalant when he asked me questions about my family, my relatives, but I knew why he was asking.

"We have always been healthy people, *señor.* Anyone who died young in my family died because of an accident," I said, making sure that Mrs. Newell clearly heard my answers. "Perhaps I don't need this test," I suggested. "I understand it is expensive."

Mrs. Newell made a sound under her breath.

"No, no, it's good we do it," Señor Bovio said. "The cost is not important, and Dr. Denardo is a talented doctor."

I said nothing more about it. The test was completed, and the results were good. Dr. Denardo concluded by telling Señor Bovio and me that the rest of my pregnancy should be "clear sailing."

After that, I had good days and bad days. Sometimes I was simply depressed and glad that everything was being brought to me. Just like Señora Bovio, I found it easier to remain all day in my suite. However, despite Señor Bovio's having a beautician and a manicurist visit frequently and despite the many new gifts, I seemed to sink into a deeper depression. Dr. Denardo had warned me about experiencing emotional highs and lows, but when I began the sixth month, I found myself stuck in the lows more often.

I began to suffer some of what Dr. Denardo had described would be the minor disorders of pregnancy. Everything that happened seemed to please Mrs. Newell. At first, I thought it was because it verified all of the things she had predicted, but I began to wonder if she wanted me to have the discomforts because I was an unwed mother. She never failed to add a comment such as "If you want to dance, you have to pay the piper," "A night of joy can lead to a morning of regret," or simply "You should have thought about this."

When I complained about heartburn, she made my meals smaller and more frequent. She advised me to drink milk, and that did appear to help, which was what made it more difficult for me to complain about her. Her little quips were biting, but her treatments were soothing. It was the same with my constipation, backaches, and muscle cramps. Although I cringed at her touch, I couldn't help but enjoy the massages, and she was right there with an antidote or a suggestion as soon as I uttered a complaint. Whether she was doing it to make things better for me or to impress and satisfy Señor Bovio didn't matter. The result was the same.

One Saturday afternoon, while I was lying on the love seat, bored with what I had been reading, aching, and feeling sorry for myself, I heard a knock on my door.

"Yes?" I called, sitting up, and was happily surprised to see Fani.

She looked as beautiful as ever in a light blue, tightly fitted cotton sweater and designer jeans with sequins running up the sides. She had her hair flowing down under a USC cap. The air around her seemed charged with electricity as she burst into the suite wearing her best glittering smile.

"Where's our teenage mother?" she cried, laughing. "*Mi dios,* you do look pregnant now."

"I was always pregnant, Fani. I couldn't help your not believing me."

"Whatever," she said, practically floating down to me. "How are you?"

"Miserable," I said, which made her laugh again. "I feel like I'm becoming a blimp. Look at my legs," I said, showing them to her.

"Ugh," she said, sitting at the foot of the love seat. "I may never get pregnant. I might just hire someone like you to carry my egg and my husband's sperm."

"I don't doubt it," I said. "Where have you been, Fani? Why didn't you ever come back or return my calls?"

"I didn't think Ray wanted me to," she said.

"Why not? He never told me such a thing."

"He didn't tell you, but he called my mother and complained about me blowing smoke in your face and not being the right sort of companion at this particular time."

"I don't like that," I said.

"Forget it. He was just being overly protective. Anyway, as soon as school ended, I went on holiday with some friends to France. As you can see," she said, tapping her cap, "I decided to attend USC." She smiled, raising her eyebrows. "And guess whom I see quite often on campus."

I sat up, excited. "Edward?"

"*Sí, su primo* Edward. He always seems uncomfortable when he meets me, but I deliberately go out of my way to force him to run into me. I enjoy teasing him. Jesse left him, you know."

"No, I didn't know."

"Seems that even gay lovers can be fickle." She paused. "Don't you want to know if he asked about you?"

"You know I do, Fani. He tried coming here, but *mi tía* Isabela—"

"I know, I know. I heard all about the deal she made or the threat, whichever way you see it. At the time, I told him you were doing rather well and being treated like Señor Bovio's daughter-in-law would, if he had one. He was happy about it. I also told him I hadn't seen you and why."

"How come you're able to visit me now, then?"

"For just this reason, I guess," she said, holding her hands out to me. "Ray's worried about you. Your nurse has told him you've been more depressed than expected, whatever that means, and he thought if I visited you, it might cheer you up and bring you out of your funk. Why are you depressed? You have everything you could want here, don't you?"

"*Sí.*"

"So? You're not getting as spoiled as I am, are you? Then nothing's enough."

"No, Fani," I said, smiling at her honesty. "The truth is, I miss my family. I am still quite unhappy about what has happened to Ignacio and his family. Señor Bovio has not yet worked out a way to get him out of prison sooner. I can't see my cousin Edward. And I have a nurse who might once have worked for *el diablo.*"

She roared with laughter. "Well," she said, "I'm occasionally home on weekends, as I am this weekend. Maybe we could hang out, go to the Fountain."

The Fountain was a dance club.

"I don't think I'd be much fun there."

"You never know. I heard pregnant women turn on some boys. One thing's for sure, they can't get into trouble. You're already there."

"Very funny. You're not saying anything about your

parents. Señor Bovio has never said anything to me. What is happening with them?"

"They have reached an understanding. There's a truce under way. They don't talk about anything but necessities, and they live separate lives. They hardly ever eat dinner together. Oh, they do when I'm home, just to put on an act, but it's like sitting with two people who speak different languages or are deaf. Practically everything's said with a gesture. I don't care, as long as they don't get in my way."

She looked around.

"It's quite a suite, but it's still a prison," she said. "I have an idea. You need some excitement, some fun in your life, don't you?"

"I don't know."

"Of course you do. Especially now. How would you like to see Edward?"

I shook my head.

"Is that a no?"

"I don't want to cause any more trouble for him, Fani."

"You won't. It's not your fault if you accidentally meet him, is it? That could happen."

I still shook my head.

"C'mon. It will be fun for you. I won't tell him anything. I'll invite him to my house next weekend. He'll come. He's been pretty depressed about Jesse and needs a change of scenery. I'll invite him to play golf on our course. I won't tell him you're coming, too. You'll just drop by. That way, neither of you will look guilty."

I remembered Señor Bovio's warning about arranging another secret meeting.

"It frightens me, Fani. He could get into serious trouble with his mother again."

"Good. That makes it exciting," she said, jumping up. "Then it's settled. Next Saturday. It's actually a perfect Saturday for it. Both of my parents are going somewhere. I'll get Ray to have his driver take you to my house. I'll tell him I'm having you to lunch. I'll promise no smoking. Actually, I've given up smoking. I realized it was making my teeth yellow and affecting my complexion. I know," she added. "I'll get the suggested menu from your nurse from hell and promise to serve it. That should nail it down. Okay?"

"What if Edward doesn't come?"

"It won't be a total loss. We'll simply have a nice time ourselves. I'll serve you something you're craving. Don't worry. Settled?"

I took a deep breath. She was right. The prospect of seeing Edward made it enticing.

"Okay," I said.

"Good. Now I'll tell you about my little romances at college," she said. "Let me open one of those bottles of wine." She nodded at the wine cooler.

"I don't dare have any. Mrs. Newell—"

"I'll give you a sip." She went for a bottle. "Oh," she said, turning back. "Ray did make me promise to do something if I paid you a visit."

"What?"

"To talk you into going to nursing school sooner rather than later and remaining here. I have a feeling he wanted me to visit more to do that than simply to cheer you up, but think about it. You'd have to be an idiot not to take him up on it."

"I see."

"Why, just imagine, Delia. You could even pretend you didn't have a child! The boys you meet at school won't be immediately turned off, and you could reveal it casually later. That's exactly what I would do if, God forbid, I was ever in your situation."

She laughed and returned to the wine.

Who worked for *el diablo*? I wondered. Mrs. Newell or Fani?

6

Reunion

"I understand," Señor Bovio began at dinner that night, "that you would like to spend a day with Fani? Go to her home?"

"Yes," I said. I searched his face, looking for some sign of suspicion.

"Fani came to me to ask, and I sent her to see Mrs. Newell."

"Mrs. Newell? Why, *señor*?"

"I trust her judgment with these things totally," he said. "She would know if Fani would be good for you now or not. They spent quite a bit of time together," he added. "Mrs. Newell made everything very clear to her, I'm sure."

"Everything?"

"What you should and should not eat, do, that sort of thing," he said, waving his hand. "She is sufficiently comfortable with Fani and agrees that a change of scenery will probably do you good. However, she would like to speak with you, too, about it."

Later that evening, she came to see me.

"I'm approving this trip," she began.

I wanted to say that I was not in prison here, but I held my tongue. After all, I would see Edward.

"However, despite my talk with Estefani Cordova, I still have concerns. Most young women who aren't pregnant and who've never been pregnant don't appreciate your condition. I'm sure she'll offer you things that will not be good for you."

"I know what's good for me and not by now, Mrs. Newell." *Thanks to you,* I wanted to add, but I didn't.

She just shook her head skeptically, but she didn't stop her admonitions.

"If you drink alcohol, it will go directly to your baby. If you smoke or take anything in the way of drugs, you can damage your baby's brain and nervous system."

"I would never do any of that."

"I bet you told yourself you would never be pregnant before you were married, too," she replied, and left.

I swallowed back my rage, believing that was it. However, the day before I was to visit Fani, Mrs. Newell embarrassed me in front of Señor Bovio with what was surely the bottom of the barrel of warnings but was just as cutting.

"I'm sure there will be boys there. I know what happens when young women your age have such freedom. Don't be surprised if you are in some bizarre way attractive to one of them. Look at your bosom. They'll all want to put their hands on your abdomen to see if they can feel the baby's movements, and that can lead to other things. You're even more vulnerable now than you were. I know how much pregnant women want to be attractive to men," she said, nodding to confirm her own statements. She always spoke as if what she said was gospel.

I glanced quickly at Señor Bovio, who wore an expression of fear. It was as if the scene she drew up were actually taking place right before his eyes. With all of these warnings and predictions of dire consequences, I couldn't help but wonder why she had approved the trip at all. Perhaps Fani was better at convincing people, even people like Mrs. Newell.

"You don't know me," I said. "I'm not at all the kind of girl you are describing, Mrs. Newell."

She blinked her smile and nodded at Señor Bovio before turning back to me.

"I know you. I know all of you."

What a strange thing to say, I thought. Instead of driving me away from even the sight of her, however, my interest in her suddenly grew stronger. I couldn't help wondering what had made this woman see the world only as a place for diseases and unhappiness. That afternoon, I cornered Teresa, who was vacuuming and dusting a guest room. My curiosity was at first about that.

"Is Señor Bovio expecting a guest?"

"I do not know, Delia. I was only told to get the room prepared, clean and polish and put fresh linen on the bed, restock the bathroom, and vacuum the carpet."

I lingered. Finally, she realized I wanted more and stopped working when she saw I was waiting there.

"Do you need something?"

"Yes. Information."

"What information?"

"What do you know about Mrs. Newell?" I asked.

My question obviously surprised her. "Mrs. Newell? What do you mean?"

"She never talks about herself. She never mentions her husband or where they live, anything. If I ask a question, she always tells me she's here for me and I'm not here for her, something like that."

"I don't know anything," Teresa said quickly. "I don't see her except for here."

"You know more than I do about her, Teresa. Don't worry. Whatever you tell me will stay right here in this room."

She started to shake her head.

"I know you don't like her. I don't, either, but I put up with her just like you do to please Señor Bovio. I can't wait to be rid of her. I know she really doesn't like me, either, and she certainly has little respect for you."

"I can't lose my job here," Teresa said. "I haven't saved all that much. I send money to my brother back in London."

"You won't lose your job. If she in any way caused Señor Bovio to fire you, I'd leave the same day, and you know he doesn't want that," I said firmly enough to impress her.

She considered. I saw that the open doorway made her hesitate, so I backed up and closed it softly.

"Well?"

"I don't know anything firsthand, Miss, but in a

house as big as this, employees gossip about other employees."

"*Sí,* I understand. And?"

"Mrs. Newell was pregnant once herself but suffered a miscarriage."

"I knew it. In my heart of hearts, I felt it," I said, excited.

"She wasn't a nurse then."

"Really?"

"It wasn't until after that tragedy that she became a nurse. She's still married, but she and her husband don't have much of a life together. He sculpts and makes clay pots and such. He's not famous or anything and just scratches out a living. She brings home the bacon, as we say. She worked in a hospital first, and then she started doing private duty. Now she's highly regarded and highly paid."

"There's something else, isn't there?"

"It's silly, Miss. I don't want to upset you."

"It's too late for that," I said dryly. "If I were any more upset than I am, I'd be walking on my hands."

She laughed and then grew serious again, but she was still hesitant.

"Well? You might as well tell me the rest of it, Teresa. You've told me this much."

"I've heard it said that she gets so close to the pregnant woman she's caring for, especially in the last month or so, that it's . . ."

"Yes? It's what?"

"It's as if she's having the baby, the baby she lost."

"How does she do that?" I asked, now confused.

"Oh, people just talk, Miss."

"How? Tell me what they say, Teresa. I should know."

"It's just talk."

"Tell me," I insisted, stepping toward her.

"It's rumored that sometimes she behaves as if she's the one in labor. I'm sure it's all an exaggeration," she added quickly. "What people, other pregnant women, mean to say is that she takes it all so personally and seriously, she acts as if she is the one having the baby. She does follow the same diet, avoiding the foods she tells her patients to avoid."

"And she's doing that here?"

"Yes, but it's not a bad diet to follow, so that doesn't necessarily mean anything sinister, Miss."

I could see she was still holding back.

"What else, Teresa?"

"I did hear that she was let go once. The pregnant woman insisted that she was pandering to her husband."

"What did that mean?"

"Oh, you know, coming on to him, but pregnant women can get paranoid about that sort of thing, being in that condition, you know. Mrs. Newell threatened to sue her and her husband if they spread any stories, so no one knows exactly why she was let go."

She paused and shook her head.

"Now, look at you, look at what you've made me go and do. I'm just behaving like some pantry gossip. Nothing I've said has a tinkle of truth to it, I'm sure."

"No, no, it's okay. Nothing you've told me changes anything. I've never been comfortable with her from day one. I'm glad to hear others have felt that way about her."

"If you go to Mr. Bovio with any of this, I'm a goner, Miss. I'm out in the street. That I am."

"I promised you it wouldn't leave this room, and it won't. I wouldn't tell anyone anything I didn't know firsthand, Teresa. I've been the victim of gossip so much here. I can appreciate how it poisons your life."

"Yes, it does, Miss. That it does. As I said, everything told to me about her could very well be just that, nasty exaggerations. She might just be what you see, a stern, professional nurse who takes her work too personally. You don't have to be her best friend or anything, and, as you say, once you give birth, she's gone on to another job, and you would probably never see her again."

"Okay, Teresa, thank you. Thank you for trusting me."

She smiled. "You'll be fine, Miss. Everything will be just fine, I'm sure."

I nodded and left her working, but despite what I had told her, I was upset. I just had to control it. Going to Fani Cordova's *hacienda* and finally seeing Edward again was just the medicine I needed at this point. Now I was happy I had let her talk me into it.

In fact, I was impatient with the remaining time. It couldn't go fast enough for me. I distracted myself with reading and television and my walks. I no longer swam, even though the pool was heated for me. My pregnancy seemed to be maturing at a geometric rate every passing day. Every day, I studied myself, measured my waist and my breasts, and saw how quickly I was growing. I did begin to have some small milk leakage, too. It put me into a little panic. To her credit, Mrs. Newell saw that and reassured me that I was textbook perfect and nothing that was happening was un-

124   VIRGINIA ANDREWS

usual. Of course, she never failed to imply or even come right out and say that it was a result in a large part of her care and supervision.

On Saturday morning, I was almost too nervous and excited to eat any breakfast. I did the best I could to appear nonchalant about my day with Fani. Just before Fani arrived, Mrs. Newell repeated her list of warnings.

"Spicy food and alcoholic beverages are out. Don't be too active. Don't let them talk you into riding in some all-terrain vehicle or going on a motorcycle."

"I would never do such a thing, Mrs. Newell."

"I've seen young, pregnant girls do things as stupid, believe me. If people are smoking around you, ask them to stop or move far away. As you know, you'll be urinating more frequently, so don't go far from a bathroom. Now, what are you wearing?" she asked, and reviewed my choices. She made sure I put some pads in my bra.

"Just in case," she said.

I expected Señor Bovio to behave like the worrywart Dr. Denardo had playfully called him, too, but to my surprise, he had already left the estate for a meeting. There would be no last-minute admonitions from him. Mrs. Newell was right beside me, however, when Fani appeared, bursting in with her characteristically explosive energy.

She wore a red tank top and dark yellow shortshorts with a tie-dyed bandanna around her forehead and a pair of ridiculously long red shell earrings. The fingers of both hands were filled with a variety of colored stone rings, and both wrists were wrapped in turquoise Indian bracelets. She looked like a rainbow gone wild.

"We have a perfect day, almost no humidity. My father calls these days 'dry heaven,'" she told Mrs. Newell, who just stared at her as if she were from another planet.

She then pulled herself together and proceeded to dictate what foods were restricted and what were not. She emphasized the danger of smoke and alcoholic beverages and left Fani with the warning that I was now her responsibility.

"I think Delia is old enough to take care of herself, Mrs. Newell," Fani told her.

"I doubt she would be in the condition she is in if that were so. You should take a lesson yourself," Mrs. Newell countered, smirked, and turned to walk away.

Fani rolled her eyes. "Where did Ray find her? Death row in some women's penitentiary?"

I laughed and followed her out. She had a brand-new ruby Mercedes convertible with the top down. It brought back memories of the car Edward had bought me before all hell broke loose after our trip to Mexico. It was one of the first things Tía Isabela had gotten rid of following our return. Once, I thought, I was on top of the world. I had a beautiful car, beautiful clothes, and a palace in which to live. *Mi tía* Isabela was actually getting to like me, or at least I thought she was.

"Isn't it a beautiful car?" Fani asked, pausing for both of us to look at it. "Daddy bought it for me last month. I call it a 'guilt gift'—his guilt, of course. But you know me, Delia. I'll take whatever I can get any way I can get it. *La caridad empieza en casa y luego se traslada a los vecinos, no?*"

She was telling me that the best charity begins at home and then moves on to the neighbors. I had heard the saying before, but *mi abuela* Anabela had told me it was just an excuse for selfishness.

Fani saw the disapproval in my face. "Oh, stop being such a goody-goody, Delia. Have some fun, damn it. You've been locked away with Nurse Diablo too long."

I did laugh at that and got into her new car. It was so plush inside I thought I was wrapped in soft leather.

"It's so hard being me," Fani kidded, "but someone has to do it."

We took off, driving too quickly down to the gate, I'm sure. I was also sure she was doing it just for Mrs. Newell's benefit. We both knew she was watching from some front window. The guard gave Fani a disapproving look and took his time opening the gate, but she threw him a kiss and shot out the moment he had done so. I screamed, and she laughed.

"Edward is already there waiting eagerly for you," she told me when we calmed down.

"I thought you weren't going to tell him."

"I wasn't, but I was afraid he wouldn't come. He was hemming and hawing and searching for one excuse after another until I mentioned your name."

My heart started to race faster than the car.

"He came directly from college, so his mother doesn't even know he's in the desert," she continued. "Don't look so worried," she said, glancing at me. "My house isn't exactly visible or accessible to anyone we don't want it to be visible or accessible to, Delia. You couldn't ask for a more private location."

"I know. It still makes me very nervous. I can't help

it. You don't know *mi tía* Isabela. Nothing enrages her more than not being obeyed or not getting what she wants. She can make trouble for you, too."

"Me?" Fani laughed. "If she starts with me, she'll be sorry."

"I don't want anyone to start with anyone," I said.

Edward's car was parked in front of Fani's family home. It wasn't immediately visible when we entered the property. She was right about that, because the driveway was so long.

"You haven't seen each other for quite a while, have you?" Fani asked. She looked almost as excited about Edward and me meeting as I did.

"It has been a long time, yes," I said.

She pulled up behind his car.

"Okay. He's cloistered in my bedroom, away from the servants and any other inquisitive eyes."

I followed her into the house. One of the maids glanced our way but hurried off quickly.

Fani smiled. "They don't like me. I'm always asking them to do something else," she said. "It keeps them out of my hair."

We went up the stairway to the wing of the *hacienda* that was practically all hers. Her bedroom, like mine at the Bovio *hacienda,* had a sitting room with an entertainment center. When we stepped into the suite, I saw Edward sitting and watching television. The moment he saw us, he stood up and smiled at me.

"Hi, Delia. How are you?"

I said nothing. He looked as handsome as ever, even with his eye patch. My eyes were filling so quickly with tears I was afraid I would just stand there and bawl like a baby. He laughed and came quickly to hug me. I held on to him a moment longer than he held on to me. Fani was standing to the side with a wide grin smeared over her lips.

"Are you sure you're gay, Edward?" she teased.

"If I weren't, you'd be the first to tell everyone," he replied, and she laughed.

"I'll leave you two to renew old bonds. I have a maid to terrorize below working on our lunch. Enjoy yourselves," she said. "I'll be back in a half hour, unless you need more time."

"No, that's fine," Edward said.

She nodded and left, closing the door behind her.

"You look well, Delia. Pregnancy makes you blossom."

"That's what Señor Bovio has been telling me. I don't feel like a blossom. I feel like a stuffed tamale."

He laughed and led me to the sitting room, where we sat on one of the sofas.

"You know, I tried to see you a while ago, and that caused a small hurricane at my house."

"Yes. I saw you and tried to get to you before you drove away."

"We would have been talking to each other through bars, I'm afraid. When I got home, my mother had called a friend of hers at the district attorney's office. They sent over an assistant district attorney to reveal to me that our international incident, such as they call it, has not been officially closed."

"*Mi dios.*"

"Yes, I was surprised but not sure if my mother was just calling in some favor and getting him to tell me that. I wasn't about to challenge her, however. I let her whip me with her threats and then returned to college."

"I'm sorry, Edward."

"It's not your fault." He paused. "I've been feeling guilty about deserting you ever since we returned from Mexico and I overheard Sophia confess to getting us in trouble. I haven't spoken to her since, not that it bothers her too much."

"It was never my intention to cause such turmoil in your family. I am sorry I didn't tell you my secret about Ignacio, but I was afraid to burden you with it."

"I know. I never imagined that you didn't trust Jesse and me."

"Fani has told me about you and Jesse no longer being together."

"I don't blame him. I've been impossible to live with these past months. No fun."

"Something else that's my fault," I said.

"You can't blame yourself for how other people behave. We all make our own choices and bear responsibility for ourselves. Now, tell me about life at the Bovio estate," he said, sitting back.

I began slowly, describing my reasons for moving in and telling him about all of the attention and all of the gifts Señor Bovio had lavished on me.

"I'm glad of that," he said. "I do feel sorry for him. It's a nice thing you're doing."

"Sí," I said.

Edward was always able to read me well. He stopped smiling. "What's wrong?"

I began to describe Mrs. Newell, but as I did, I realized that anyone who didn't live under her supervision might easily interpret it all as simply good and prudent care.

"Well," he said when I was finished, "at least you don't have much longer to go."

"A little less than eight weeks," I said.

"And then what?"

"I'm not sure, Edward." I told him about Señor Bovio's offer, including the car, the money, the nanny.

"That would be hard to turn down," he said. "I think nursing is a good career, and I know you'd be very good at it, Delia. After having been to your little Mexican village and seeing what you'd return to, I would hesitate before advising you to return. It's charming in its way, but it doesn't offer you a tenth of the opportunities you have here, and I don't just mean educationally. You're very young. There'll be someone else in your life, I'm sure."

I told him about Señor Bovio's offer and efforts to help Ignacio.

"I see. It sounds like he's doing everything he can to make you happy and keep his grandson in his life. But you have to start being a little selfish, Delia. Choose what you want for yourself and your baby first."

"I will," I said.

He smiled. "I won't hold my breath waiting for you to do that."

"No. I mean it. I'll try," I said. "Now, let's stop talking about me. Tell me about yourself and your college and if you have made some new friends."

He described his classes, his teachers, and his plans

to go to law school. He said everything that had happened with me had caused him to take more interest in international law, and that was where he wanted to be eventually. He didn't sound as if he had much of a social life, but he talked about college functions and living in Los Angeles.

Fani came back, knocking softly on her door before entering.

"How are we doing?" she asked.

"Good," I said quickly.

"Let's go out on the rear patio. It's beautiful, and I have a great lunch organized for us. Unless you need more time to be alone, that is."

"No, that's fine," Edward said.

We rose and followed her down the stairway to the French doors that opened onto the rear patio. It was a beautiful day, and the table she had set up for us was decorated with fresh flowers. There was an opened bottle of white wine and an opened bottle of red wine.

"Little Mama isn't supposed to drink. Did she tell you about Nurse Diablo?"

Edward laughed. "She's not wrong, Fani."

"Oh, a little bit can't hurt. Let her enjoy her freedom for a while," she said.

"You were always the little instigator," Edward told her. "Maybe you're Miss Diablo."

I knew he meant it as a criticism, but she loved that. I sat and did sip a little wine before we were served our fruit cups to start. Edward and she talked about the college, discussing the campus, the events, and some of the teachers they both knew. I felt as if I had disappeared.

"Oh, but we're boring Delia to death," Fani said.

I protested, but she said they would talk only about me and my future.

She had designed a wonderful lunch for us. There was a variety of choices, almost all of which Mrs. Newell would have me reject, but I did feel defiant for the moment and deliberately ate what I shouldn't. Later, I realized that I would probably pay in the form of heartburn. I had to go to the bathroom twice, which Fani thought was amusing, and then, after a rather rich, decadent chocolate cake dessert, we tried to take a walk, but I found my bladder complaining again and had to rush off to the nearest bathroom.

Edward decided it was time for him to start back to Los Angeles. He claimed he had promised some friends that he would go out with them that evening, but just as he could easily read me, I could easily read him and knew he wasn't telling the truth. He would probably return to a lonely room.

When I got back from the bathroom, Fani stayed in the house while I walked him out to his car to say good-bye.

"This is my cell-phone number," I said, handing him a slip of paper with the number on it.

"Good. I'll call you before I come back to the desert. Give me your phone," he said. I handed it to him. "I'll punch in my cell number for you. Call me whenever you want." He handed my phone back to me. "Don't look so worried, Delia. It's all right. We'll both be fine."

He hugged me and got into his car.

"I'll tell Jesse you said hello. We still talk occasionally, and he has asked me about you," he added.

"Good. Drive carefully, Edward."

"Don't worry. I'm a better driver with one eye than most drivers are with two."

He waved, started his car, and drove down the drive. I watched until he disappeared below the knoll.

Fani was sipping wine at the table when I returned.

"Well? Was it a good visit?"

"Yes, Fani. Thank you so much for arranging it."

"You want to hang out longer or . . ."

"No, I get tired."

She nodded at my stomach. "So, it's a boy in there?"

"That's what the doctor said."

"Considering all that Ray's done for you and is doing, you should definitely name him Adan Jr."

"That's pretty definite."

"Good. He deserves some happiness." She stood up.

"I do my best," I said, rising.

"Well, let me take you back," she said, and we went out to her car.

She was quieter on the way back. I wondered if she was thinking about Adan, as I was.

"I think I'll head back to college tonight, too," she told me as we approached the Bovio gate.

"Haven't you met anyone you like at college?" I asked. She didn't talk much about the boys there, and she obviously didn't have a date this weekend.

"Not yet. There's this young English associate professor I'm eyeing."

"Isn't that forbidden?"

She smiled. "Only for him."

The guard opened the gate for us. He glared at Fani, remembering the way she had jetted out earlier. She

smiled at him, and we started up the driveway. Half-
way up, I saw *mi tía* Isabela's car. Señor Bovio's car
was there as well.

"*Mi tía* is here."

"Lucky you," Fani said. "Say hello to Nurse Diablo
for me," she added when we stopped. "Here," she said,
offering me a stick of gum. "Just in case she smells
your breath and picks up on the inch of wine you
drank."

I took it and folded it into my mouth, still staring at
mi tía Isabela's car.

"*Mi tía* Isabela hasn't been here since the day I arrived," I muttered.

"Maybe she's come to her senses and has decided
to be your aunt again. My cousin Ray isn't someone a
woman her age should ignore, no matter how much
money she has. He can pull lots of strings."

"He hasn't yet pulled the one that would release Ignacio."

"I'm sure he will when he can. Take it easy, Mama
Delia. I'll call you next time I'm home," she promised.

"*Sí. Gracias,* Fani."

She leaned over to kiss me on the cheek. I opened
the door and got out. The moment I closed it, she shot
off. I smiled to myself, imagining her whipping past
the guard at the gate again. Then I went into the *hacienda.*

It was so quiet that my footsteps echoed over the
tile as I walked through the entryway. I paused, because Tía Isabela was sitting on the chair that faced the
front, just the way she often sat in her own *hacienda.*

Señor Bovio, sipping a glass of red wine, sat on her right. He turned to look my way.

"*Hola*, Tía Isabela," I said, deciding to be civil. "*Como es—*"

"Don't even begin your performance," she said.

"What?"

"I know you just had a secret meeting with Edward, and you'll both be sorry."

7

Lockdown

Señor Bovio, although obviously quite angry himself, leaped to his feet immediately and became a wall between Tía Isabela and me.

"Wait!" he cried at her, holding up his hand. "Mrs. Newell," he called.

She came quickly down the corridor.

"Take Delia up to her room, please, and see that she is comfortable."

"Comfortable," Tía Isabela practically spat at me. "You're worried about her comfort?" She pointed at me when I started to step away. "Don't think you two pulled anything over on me. Edward will pay for this deception. He's not as independent as he thinks. He's in for some big surprises."

"Isabela, you promised to let me handle this," Señor Bovio said.

She swallowed back her torrent of threats and

curses and looked away. "Then handle it," she told him with a backhand gesture in my direction.

"Mrs. Newell, please," he told my nurse.

She actually took my arm to turn me toward the stairway. Stunned, I began to walk and then stopped when I fully realized what had happened. I turned back to them.

"What did you do, have me followed?"

"No," Señor Bovio said. "No one follows you."

"Then . . . what did you do, Tía Isabela, hire a private detective to follow your own son? Or was Sophia responsible for this as well? What has she been doing, hiding in the bushes, waiting to pounce?"

"Sophia had nothing to do with it," *mi tía* Isabela said, still not looking directly at me. "She hasn't had anything to do with her brother since you deceived this family and he was sent back to school. You're poison to this family."

"I'm poison? You broke your parents' hearts. How low can you sink before you stink, Tía Isabela?" I said.

"Delia!" Señor Bovio shouted. Then he calmed. "Please, go upstairs," he said before I could continue. "We must talk when everyone is calmer. It's not good for you now. Go on, *por favor*."

I pulled my arm from Mrs. Newell's hand. "I'll walk myself, thank you."

I went up the stairway, feeling as if my baby had been cringing inside me. Mrs. Newell followed a few feet behind me and saw to it that I changed and went to bed.

"You need a nap," she said. "I can see it in your face. I can just imagine what your blood pressure is. If you don't do what I say, you could bring on a miscarriage."

The word spun me around to face her. Anger smothered any fear.

"Is that what happened to you? You miscarried because you were emotionally upset?"

Her face became so bloodred that she nearly glowed.

"We do not have now and never have had anything in common," she replied in sharply pronounced consonants and vowels. "Concern yourself only with yourself."

I didn't respond. I turned away and closed my eyes. Mrs. Newell wasn't really what concerned me at the moment, anyway. Instead, I wondered what sort of new trouble Tía Isabela would make for Edward. If it truly wasn't Sophia who had told her about us, how did she find out? Why couldn't she just leave us alone? Why was this so important to her?

Mrs. Newell left, closing the door. Suddenly, the stillness was overwhelming. It was like the quiet that often followed a devastating storm, as if nature were holding her breath. I listened hard for a moment, expecting Tía Isabela's footsteps in the hallway, perhaps, or Señor Bovio's, but I heard nothing. The tension had worn me out, and I finally did fall asleep. I slept for hours. When I awoke, it was dark outside. There was just a table lamp lit in my suite, but the bedroom door was now open. At first, I didn't realize she was sitting there, but when I turned slightly to my left, her silhouette so surprised me it made me gasp.

"Good, you're awake," Mrs. Newell said. "I'll get you some dinner."

I simply stared at her. How long had she been sitting there waiting for me to awaken? What had she been doing, counting every breath I took? Had Señor Bovio insisted that she hover over me like this? Was he really worried that I might miscarry? It made me think about all she had said. Perhaps I really had been brought to some brink and had been in some danger.

She rose, turned on more lights, and left. I sat up and ran my fingers through my hair. I still felt groggy and dazed, so I rose and went to the bathroom to wash my face. Ten minutes later, Teresa arrived with my dinner.

"Do you want it on the bed table?" she asked.

"No, I'll sit where I usually sit, thank you," I told her.

I was happy I hadn't suffered any heartburn from my elaborate lunch. Actually, I was surprised at my appetite after all that had happened, but I was so hungry, in fact, that I was very unsatisfied. The moment Mrs. Newell appeared, I let her know it.

"The portions are too small."

"I explained about the pressure on your abdomen and why the portions have to be smaller."

"Yes, but I should have them more frequently, don't you think?"

"No, I don't think." She blinked a smile. "This is a common complaint of pregnant women, and this is about when most pregnant women go bad. Later, after they give birth, they have a harder time losing the weight, and many, if not most, don't. It ruins their lives. They start hating themselves for being so fat, and they believe their husbands aren't attracted to them anymore. They get themselves depressed, and they eat more, not less, and get even fatter. It feeds on itself, and all of it could have been prevented with some self-control. Consider me your self-control."

"I've gained only fifteen pounds. You said that I was doing well."

"And we're keeping it that way. However, I want you to start drinking this at night after your dinner." She handed me a covered cup. She took off the cover when I didn't move fast enough to do it.

"What is it?"

"Supplements I have designed for this stage of a pregnancy."

"But I thought you said I wouldn't need any if I followed your nutritional design."

"Exactly. This is not something you buy in a drugstore. It's part of my program."

"Does Dr. Denardo know about it?"

"Of course he does. We've worked together with many patients."

I shrugged and drank the tasteless liquid and put the empty cup on the tray just as Señor Bovio appeared in the doorway. He looked at Mrs. Newell, sending her silent commands. She took my tray and marched out, giving him a slight nod, which, to me, looked like permission for him to come into the bedroom. He did so and sat as if he had aged twenty years in a few hours.

"You don't have to worry. Your aunt's gone," he said. "She left shortly after you went up."

"I don't want to see her anymore, Señor Bovio."

"No, she won't be back until after you've given birth. We've agreed about that."

"I don't want to see her after I give birth, either. In

fact, I don't think it's a good idea for me to remain in the area."

"What?"

"Things will never improve. I wouldn't even want to see her from a distance, and I certainly don't ever want to see my cousin Sophia."

"I wouldn't make such decisions in your present state of mind, Delia. We can talk about all that later. However, there are other problems now."

"What other problems?"

"Why did you betray me?" he asked softly. "I warned you not to do another secret meeting, and I assumed you were listening and would obey."

"Señor Bovio, Edward is a grown man, and I am a woman, not a little girl. We have a right to remain close and friendly. Tía Isabela is simply a spoiled, mean-hearted woman. I won't let her do this to us. She doesn't have that right."

"Delia, Delia, Delia," he said, shaking his head. "You are a young woman, yes, but you are not yet strong enough or mature enough to battle in this world. Your aunt, as you must know, mixes with the same powerful people I do. She knows many of the same politicians, government officials. She learned about my attempts to help your friend Ignacio Davila, and now she is threatening to interfere. I fear she has the power to do that, Delia. If she should call the father of the boy who was killed and tell him of my efforts, for example . . . well, you can just imagine what he would do and what would happen. They would stop any parole hearing, and Ignacio would remain in prison to the very last minute."

I looked away, biting down on my lower lip. He was

right. In this world of the rich and the powerful, I was helpless. I might as well be a child.

"What should I do, Señor Bovio?"

"For now, you must not leave the estate, especially to be with Fani. I have called her and told her it would be better if she stays away until you give birth."

"That's not fair, *señor*. She was only trying to make me happy."

"I know, but there would be less chance for another mistake. All of this tension and nastiness when you are so vulnerable and our baby is in such a dependant state is very, very dangerous. Dr. Denardo agrees that you should be kept from any more turmoil. Mrs. Newell told me she served a pregnant young woman not much older than you are who had a nervous breakdown and miscarried. What a horror it must be to come this far and lose a child."

I was quiet. In the back of my mind, I wondered if Mrs. Newell had been talking about herself and not some patient. Was Señor Bovio aware of her past? Should I mention it now, or would that only cause more trouble?

"Will you still be able to help Ignacio?" I asked.

"I was making some headway. I think I can keep Isabela from doing any damage, but you absolutely must listen to me this time."

"Okay, *señor*."

"Good. Now, please, rest and take care of yourself," he said, rising. "We'll take better care of you. I promise you that."

I thought that was a strange thing for him to say. How much better care of me could they take? He left, closing the door softly behind him. Despite what I had promised, I couldn't help but be worried about Edward. Did he even know yet that his mother had found out about us?

I went to my purse to get my cell phone to call him. I could warn him if he didn't know yet what had happened. At least, he would be somewhat prepared. However, when I looked in my purse, I couldn't find my phone. I paused, wondering if I had taken it out. I looked everywhere in the suite where I might have put it but didn't see it. When I recalled Edward and me saying good-bye at Fani's, I was positive I had put the phone back into my purse and closed my purse after he had punched in his cell-phone number. I was just about to call for Teresa to ask her if she knew anything, when Mrs. Newell returned.

"I want to check your pressure," she said, carrying her blood-pressure monitor.

"I feel fine," I said, "but I'm having trouble finding my cell phone. Do you know where it might be?"

"I'm sure I have no idea. People spend too much time on those phones, especially teenage girls. Everyone's babbling on one whenever I go to the mall. Everyone's private business is easily overheard, too."

She took my pressure and lifted her eyebrows.

"As I expected, it's higher than usual."

I could see in her face that she just loved being right.

"If you stay calm, it should go down."

"I'd like to know where my phone is," I said as she packed up her monitor to leave. "Would you ask Teresa to stop in, please?"

She sighed and dropped her shoulders, as if I were asking her to carry fifty-pound bags of potatoes up the stairway. Then she grunted and left. I waited and waited, but Teresa didn't come up. Finally, I went downstairs, thinking that maybe it had fallen out of my purse somehow and Teresa had located it. However, Teresa was nowhere in sight. I was about to go look for her in her quarters, when Señor Bovio emerged from his office and came down the corridor.

"Delia, why aren't you in your bedroom resting? Is anything else wrong? Why aren't you dressed?"

I didn't realize I had come down in my nightgown and was barefoot.

"Oh. Yes. I can't seem to find my cell phone," I said.

"Your cell phone? Yes, I took it earlier."

"You took it? Why?"

"It was part of the deal I made with your aunt, I'm afraid, and besides, you should keep focused now on the baby's birth. People will put crazy things in your head. I don't want you made nervous or overly excited again. We're too close, too close. Besides, you've agreed not to contact Edward, and you won't be seeing Fani Cordova."

"But there could be a time when I would need to call you or—"

"No, no. We won't let you out of our sight. Don't concern yourself anymore about that. Please, do what I ask, even if it seems foolish. Humor a worried grandfather." He widened his eyes and shook his right forefinger at me. "Mrs. Newell was not pleased with your blood pressure. That's the first time I've heard her sound so concerned about you. Now, please, go rest."

He patted my hand, stroked my hair once, and gazed at me with pleading eyes.

Maybe it was my imagination, but I could see Adan in his eyes. I nodded and returned to my suite. I would have to go to sleep worrying about my cousin Edward. I wasn't sleeping well these days, anyway. It was starting to get uncomfortable for me. I tossed and turned, waking often. Then, very late, close to midnight, I heard voices and footsteps in the hallway. Someone had come up the stairway. I remembered that Teresa had been preparing one of the guest suites not far from mine. Curious, I rose and went to my door. I listened for a moment, and then, even more curious, I stepped into the hallway and looked toward the stairway.

Just reaching the top was Stevens, Señor Bovio's driver. He was carrying two large suitcases, one in each hand. Coming up behind him was Mrs. Newell. She paused at the top of the stairway and looked in my direction.

"Why are you awake and out in the hallway?" she asked.

"I heard noise. Who has come to stay here?"

"I think it's pretty obvious," she said, nodding toward Stevens, who continued toward the suite. "I'm staying here now until you give birth. Go to sleep."

She walked on after Stevens.

She was moving in? There was nearly two months left. What about her husband, her own home? How could she be here day and night every day? I watched her enter the guest suite. Moments later, Stevens emerged. He didn't look my way. He walked as if he were in a trance, taking great care to step softly over the tiled floor, descending the stairway so quietly he could have been floating. Once again, it was very quiet. The hallway lights dimmed, and the spidery shadows crawled out from the corners and up the walls.

She was moving in? I wouldn't be able to take a deep breath without Mrs. Newell knowing about it now. Any other woman in my condition probably would be grateful to have such immediate and constant professional attention, but to me it felt like a collar being tightened around my throat.

I retreated to my bed and again tried to sleep. Just before morning, I did sink into a deep repose, but I heard the curtains being pulled open and felt the sunshine spill through the windows and over me.

"You didn't bathe last night," Mrs. Newell said, approaching. "Proper hygiene is even more important now. I'm running a bath for you."

"Not yet," I told her. "I'm tired. I want to sleep."

"Oh, you'll have plenty of time to sleep. A bath will even help you fall asleep again. Get up, please," she said.

When I didn't move quickly enough to satisfy her, she pulled my blanket away.

"The more cooperative you are, the happier you will be," she told me, blinking a smile.

She reached for my hand. Too tired to put up any resistance, I let her help me sit up.

"I guess I was right in regretting I had given permission for your little excursion yesterday. It was too much for you."

"No," I said.

"Please. There's no sense in debating about it. Look at you. However, what's done is done. Here are your slippers. I'll check the tub," she said, going to the bathroom.

I closed my eyes and nearly fell asleep again sitting up, but she was back quickly to get me moving.

In the bathroom, she pulled my nightgown up and over my head. I started to get into the tub when she stopped me.

"Wait."

She began to study my body and actually squatted to look at my legs. Suddenly, she squeezed my right calf, and I cried out.

"There's swelling here," she said, looking up at me with eyes of accusation. "Why didn't you tell me you had sensitivity? How am I supposed to do my duties if you don't follow what you've been told?"

"I didn't feel anything until just now."

She looked skeptical and then stood up. "Get into the tub," she told me.

I stepped in carefully and lowered myself, surprised at how hot the water was. When I mentioned it, she said I'd get used to it. My second surprise came when she took the sponge before I did and began to wash my body.

"I can do that myself."

"You can also twist and turn and injure yourself," she said, and continued. She made me raise my arms and then came around to run the sponge over my breasts. She paused to study them.

"Now what's wrong?"

"You need a larger maternity bra. Why don't you tell me when you have discomfort?"

"I didn't have any."

"Of course you did," she said, and continued to wash me.

I felt very foolish sitting in the tub and letting her go over every private inch of me, but she was working me over as if she were washing a car, turning and pressing my body until she dropped the sponge into the water and told me to get out carefully.

She held up a bath towel. I started to dry myself, but either she was impatient or she thought she had to be part of everything. She took another towel and worked on my back, rear, and legs.

"I'm going to have Dr. Denardo come look at your swelling," she said. "We must be very careful about potential blood clots. Thromboembolic disease is the leading cause of death of pregnant women in the United States," she recited.

"What is that?"

"A clot blocks an artery. If you die, naturally, the baby will," she added, without any emotion but making it clear that the baby was more important. "Get dressed, and get back into bed. I'll go see about your breakfast and call the doctor."

Holding the towels with two fingers, she dropped them into the hamper as if they were filled with disease and walked out. I stood there trembling, feeling she had handled me like a baby. I sensed that I was losing control of myself. She controlled what I wore, what I ate, when I ate, and when I slept. Soon, that woman would tell me when and how to breathe, I thought, and went out to get dressed.

Whatever she said to Señor Bovio about me put him into an immediate state of panic. He rushed up to my bedroom just as I had finished dressing.

"Please, get off your feet," he told me. "Dr. Denardo is going to get over here as soon as he can."

"I don't feel sick, *señor*. There's no reason for all this panic."

"There is much you don't know about yourself right now," he insisted. "You must follow Mrs. Newell's orders."

He stood there until I got back into the bed.

"I'm all right, Señor Bovio. Please."

His hovering over me with a look of deep concern was actually beginning to frighten me. When Mrs. Newell squeezed my leg, it did hurt. Was I really in some danger?

"You didn't do too much at Fani's yesterday, did you?" he asked. "Too much exercise, perhaps?"

"Oh, no, *señor.*"

"This is why it's good to have someone like Mrs. Newell on the job," he told me. He squeezed my hand gently.

Teresa entered with my breakfast tray. She looked more timid and afraid than ever. I couldn't imagine what Mrs. Newell had said to her. I hoped she hadn't blamed her for anything. Señor Bovio stepped aside, and she set up my breakfast on the bed table. He insisted on arranging my pillows himself and remained there watching me as if he half expected I might keel over with every new bite. Finally, he smiled, patted my hand again, and left.

Teresa had gone into the bathroom to clean up. I finished eating, although my stomach had tightened up because of my nervousness. Teresa took the tray.

"When you were told to prepare that guest suite, did you know that Mrs. Newell was moving into it, Teresa?" I asked.

"No, Miss. No one told me anything, and I don't ask questions," she said.

"She didn't yell at you for anything, did she?"

Teresa looked away rather than respond.

"Teresa?"

"She just told me I was to spend less time in here now. I have to look after her suite as well. Not that I'm complaining," she added quickly. "I have the time, of course."

"Why would she tell you that? You don't spend all that much time in here with me as it is."

"I don't ask questions," she told me, and left.

Maybe you don't, I thought, but I will. I rose to get dressed. How different this morning was from yesterday, I thought. Yesterday, although I was nervous, I felt excited and happy, looking forward to seeing Edward. What was I to look forward to now? The moment I stepped out of my suite, Mrs. Newell pounced as if she had been hovering in her own doorway.

"Where are you going?" she asked.

"I thought I would go out, take a little walk, get some fresh air. Is that all right with you?"

"No," she said sharply. "Are you really this foolish? Return to your room until Dr. Denardo arrives and examines your swelling. Stay off your feet."

"But it doesn't hurt when I walk."

She shook her head and stepped closer. "So, what does that mean?" she began in a very condescending tone. It was as if she were talking to a five-year-old. "That you should go and aggravate the problem until it does hurt, until it does get worse, until it does cause a serious problem?"

"I'm only going—"

"You're only going back to your room. Look at this stairway you have to descend and ascend. What if you cramp up out there and collapse? Who would be blamed for that, do you think? You, a child-mother, or me, a professional maternity nurse?

"Besides," she continued, "women can give birth at this point in a pregnancy, you know. There are more premature babies than ever. I'm going to take your blood pressure again in an hour, but I'd like you rested before I do, so go back to bed."

I hesitated. I wanted to be defiant, but I was also frightened.

She brought her hands to her hips and widened her eyes. "Do I have to call Señor Bovio and have him speak to you? I won't work here if my orders are disregarded," she threatened.

For a moment, I considered saying, "So what? Quit."

But then I thought about what this would do to Señor Bovio and all of our arrangements and bargains. Besides, both he and Dr. Denardo had shown how much faith and respect they had for Mrs. Newell. They wouldn't think much of me for driving her away. I really didn't have much choice. I turned around and went back to my suite, took off my special maternity shoes, and got into the bed. She didn't follow me to be sure, but exactly an hour later, she came by to take my blood pressure. It was still higher than she said it should be. She examined my swelling again, and again I jumped when she applied some pressure. Her face wasn't harsh and angry as much as it was now a face of concern.

"Is it worse?" I asked.

"Just continue to rest," she said, and left.

She had me so frightened I was afraid to move a

muscle. I concentrated on the swelling myself, anticipating some sort of pain. Whether it had been planted
in my imagination or not, I did not know, but I thought
my leg had begun to hurt without anyone touching it.

Horrible visions showing me losing my baby passed
under my closed eyelids, a streaming movie of my
screaming in pain, the doctor rushing to my side, the
baby being prematurely born and born dead. In Señor
Bovio's eyes, it would surely be as if I had killed his
son a second time. Ignacio would rot in prison, and
Señor Bovio and *mi tía* Isabela, with Sophia cheering
in the background, would send me packing off to
Mexico in some broken-down, smelly pickup truck.
I'd be dumped out across the border like some defec-
tive product.

I tried to sleep again and did nod off from time to
time, but mostly I lay there in a terrible nervous state.
Teresa brought up my lunch. I couldn't eat much of
anything. I thought I heard Señor Bovio and Mrs.
Newell whispering just outside my doorway, but neither of them came into the suite. Finally, late in the
afternoon, I heard footsteps in the corridor, and Dr.
Denardo came in with Mrs. Newell and Señor Bovio.

"Well, now," Dr. Denardo said. "A little complica-
tion. Let's take a look."

He examined me while Mrs. Newell stood behind
him smirking and looking exactly like someone who
would blame me. Señor Bovio was quiet and unmoving. Dr. Denardo took my blood pressure, too.

"Something's starting here," he said afterward. "But
we'll get right on it. Very good work, Millicent," he
told Mrs. Newell. She glowed. He turned back to me.

"I'm going to put you on a little bit of a blood thinner just to get rid of this. We'll watch you carefully. Just follow Mrs. Newell's instructions."

Tears came to my eyes.

"Now, now, don't get yourself upset over it. It's not that uncommon. Everyone's body is different, Delia. You'll be fine. Everything will be just fine."

He stepped away to confer quietly with both Mrs. Newell and Señor Bovio. Then he returned to my bedside to reassure me before leaving. Mrs. Newell followed him, but Señor Bovio remained.

"This is not your fault; it's mine," he said. "I should have known better than to let you go off and get into all that turmoil again. I was doing so well protecting you, protecting Adan's baby."

I looked away. I wanted to argue with him about it. Dr. Denardo didn't specifically blame anything for this. Señor Bovio had heard him say, "Everyone's body is different." This would probably have happened no matter what. I wasn't thinking so much about him blaming himself as I was about Edward and me causing it all to happen simply by meeting each other again, simply by daring to defy *mi tía* Isabela.

But resistance and defiance were seeping out of me. I felt like a blob of putty lying here. Everyone but me was shaping me, turning and twisting me to fit into a mold. And what could I do about it?

I had no money.

I had no home.

I really had no friends.

And I had no family.

That is, no family except for the baby forming inside me.

I was sure I felt him move, perhaps to reassure me so I would be strong for the fight that was yet to come.

And don't doubt it, Delia Yebarra, I told myself, *there will surely be a fight to come.*

8

The Only Game in Town

I thought I had been too restricted and confined before, but it was nothing compared to what followed after Dr. Denardo's visit. In an ironic way, I began to see myself as even more incarcerated than Ignacio, who was in prison. Now I was not to leave the suite to go anywhere in the house without first telling Mrs. Newell. Since the phone in my room still would not call out, and I didn't have my cell phone anymore, I could speak to no one but those who came to see me or who worked here, just like Ignacio in his prison. I could sneak about and use another phone in the *hacienda,* but for what? Señor Bovio wouldn't permit Fani to visit, and, of course, Edward was what Señor Bovio called persona non grata. For now, if he showed his face, it would be like looking at the face of the plague.

None of the other girls I had known at the private school had remained friendly with me after Tía Isabela had me transferred to the public school. They were fair-weather friends, anyway. I was afraid to make friends at the public school. *Mi tía* Isabela had forbidden me to do anything socially with anyone. There was no point in making friends, and I was ashamed for anyone to see where and how I lived at the time. I really didn't have anyone else who would or could visit me. Mrs. Newell had already prohibited Teresa from spending any time in my suite other than the time required to clean it and take care of my clothes, linen, and towels. These were the most difficult weeks.

Dr. Denardo stopped by more frequently and finally told me he was pleased with my improvements. The swelling had nearly disappeared, and my blood pressure had returned to an acceptable number, although according to Mrs. Newell, it was never where she would like it to be. She didn't build my confidence any, either, when she told me not to be too optimistic about myself yet.

"Doctors don't see patients as well as private-duty nurses, who spend more time and know their patients better," she said.

"I don't understand," I said. "How can a nurse know a patient better than the patient's doctor does?"

"Dr. Denardo is as good as any doctor under whom I have worked," she said, "but he has so many other patients. You can't expect him to pay attention to every little thing about you the way I do, the way any good private-duty nurse would, even with this so-called special attention he's giving you. Believe me, he is not doing anything for you that any other doctor would not do if you went to his or her office. Any special attention you get comes from me and me only."

I thought she was telling me all of this simply to make herself look more important, but it was still disturbing. Without having anyone with whom I could discuss these problems and fears, I felt even more alone. I began to sleep later and later in the morning, took frequent naps, and took far less care of my appearance. Some mornings, I didn't even brush out my hair, and whenever Señor Bovio suggested that he call in the beautician and the manicurist, I told him I didn't want them. I told him I didn't have the patience for them. When he looked surprised, I added that I couldn't sit still that long, and he nodded, thinking it all had to do with my discomforts from the pregnancy.

Dr. Denardo had warned me about depression. I was in my third trimester. Almost all of his patients start to feel sorry for themselves then, he said.

"They think they look so bloated and distorted, they are terribly self-conscious, and many withdraw."

I couldn't withdraw any more than I was, being practically locked away, so that warning didn't faze me. Everything about my situation, right from the beginning, lent itself to my becoming more and more depressed. I had no family to surround me with the joy of expectation. Instead, I had only the woman Fani had aptly named Nurse Diablo and an emotionally crippled older man. Why shouldn't I walk about with a long face?

I think Señor Bovio realized all of this, too. He couldn't have been more attentive. He continued to have Mr. Blumgarten show up to present me with new clothing, even though I pointed out that I wasn't going anywhere and it didn't look as if I would in the near future. I had enough to wear. The garments building up on the rack began to look silly to me. I practically chased the poor man out of my bedroom, piling the clothes on the bed to show him how ridiculous it had all become.

"You know it, too!" I screamed. "You just want to make more money."

He fled, and Señor Bovio promised not to bring him back.

He did bring me piles of new magazines, DVD movies, books, and even crossword-puzzle books in an attempt to make me happier about being so confined. And then, one night, he came in with one of the DVD movies in which his wife had acted.

"I have something very special to show you," he began. "Normally, it's painful for me to watch these now, but with you, I thought watching it might be different. This," he announced with some flair, "is one of my wife's films."

I had no idea why it would matter if I saw it with him, but I let him insert the DVD into the machine and sat with him as the movie began. Seeing Adan's mother in the film made me think more about him. I could see the resemblances in their gestures and facial expressions. Señora Bovio was a very good actress, too, and even more attractive than she was in the pictures of her I had seen. She had a beautiful voice and was quite sexy.

I was absorbed in the film, but from time to time, I looked at Señor Bovio and saw that he was staring at me with a soft smile on his lips.

"She was very beautiful," I told him, thinking that perhaps he was waiting for me to comment.

"*Sí*. She and I often sat here and watched her films together. Sometimes, Adan would be here as well, especially when he was just a little boy, but only if it was a film we thought it was all right for him to see," he quickly added. "And when she was off somewhere making another film, he and I would come in here to watch one of her previous movies. Although we have the entertainment center downstairs, we'd rather see the films in here. It helped us to feel she was close by. Just as I feel she is now," he concluded, and smiled. "You understand, I'm sure."

I nodded.

He looked around and closed his eyes. "I can feel her with us," he whispered. "With you. With our baby."

I said nothing, but his intensity made me a little nervous. He looked as if he actually did hear his wife's voice. Although I enjoyed the film, a good love story, I was happy when it ended. He sat there for a long moment, as if he expected to see it start again. Then he laughed.

"When Adan was little, he thought there were two different women. One was his real mother, the woman who was here with him, and the other was someone who looked like her and sounded like her. Rosalinda would laugh and talk about herself as if she really was someone else who was in the movie. When Adan was older, we teased him about it, but he stopped my wife in her tracks one night when he told her she would always be someone else to him when she was in a movie. He told her he would never like that woman. 'Why not?' she asked. 'Because that woman keeps her from being with me,' he replied. I think he was only twelve. For a while after that, I thought she might just give up acting. But of course, she didn't."

"She was very good," I said.

"Yes, this was one of her better films. I'll bring another around to watch with you soon. I hope you don't mind," he said. "I feel much more comfortable watching her films here and, as I said, especially with you."

"I don't mind, Señor Bovio."

He laughed at another thought. "For sure, Rosalinda would have tried to hide the fact that she had become a grandmother. She often told me it was very important, especially for an actress, to appear younger than she really was. 'When they start asking me to play some teenage girl's mother, I'll quit,' she vowed. She said there was a very negative attitude about older women in Hollywood. It bothered Adan, because she rarely encouraged him to join her on a press junket or any publicity event. After her death and even after her funeral, Adan didn't accept it. He told me he felt she was just away on another film. It took a long time for it finally to settle in. You know, we all have our own ways to stop the third death."

"*Sí*," I said. His words and memories brought me close to tears, tears for him and for Adan and tears of shame of myself for being so difficult now.

"I am sorry, *señor*. I know your pain goes deeply through your soul. You've lost the two people you loved the most in the world."

"*Gracias*," he said, and then quickly smiled. "Let's think of nothing but the baby."

"*Sí.*"

"Sleep well," he told me.

Nearly another week passed, but he didn't offer to watch another film, and I didn't ask for one. Perhaps it had been too painful for him after all, watching with me or not. He had obviously loved his wife very much and never stopped missing her, despite the stories about her affairs.

However, even though I tried to be happier for his sake, the boredom and tediousness of my days grew worse. I began to complain more and more about my confinement, until finally, after Dr. Denardo's next visit, I was permitted to take walks outside again.

"Mrs. Newell has done a very good job with you, Delia," he said. "We're back on track. Rest one more day, and then start your program of regular exercise. Millicent will begin training you in the breathing exercises, too. You've been a perfect patient," he said, patting my hand. "It's no secret that the first child for a woman is usually the most difficult." He smiled. "I have patients who swear they'll never have another afterward. Many don't."

I saw Mrs. Newell gazing at me over his shoulder. The expression on her face when he said that made me wonder. Was she included in the reference to such women? Was that why she never made another attempt at having a child? She knew all there was to know about pregnancy and birth, apparently. Was she so disappointed in herself, so angry at her own body, that she had forbidden herself to make another attempt?

Afterward, I chided myself for having any interest in her at all, but for the moment, as in the expression Adan had taught me, she was "the only game in town."

Getting anything personal from her was probably harder than getting government classified secrets, however.

I tossed away my interest and thought only about the next day. I couldn't believe how excited such a simple privilege was making me. I tossed and turned practically all night in anticipation, and I was very impatient in the morning, waiting for my breakfast. I knew Mrs. Newell wouldn't permit me to go walking if I didn't first eat her meager portions and nutritional concoctions.

Finally, I was ready to go out. I spent more time than I thought I would deciding what to wear and even took the time to brush my hair and apply a little lipstick. Then I put on a pair of earrings, decided they were too ostentatious, and chose another pair and another before settling on a pair. My face was a little bloated, but I didn't dwell on it. Nevertheless, anyone observing me would think I was going to some grand event. I imagined Fani teasing me, telling me I was hoping the handsome young pool man had returned.

With renewed energy surging through my body, I put on my newest pair of maternity shoes and stepped out of my suite feeling as if someone had unlocked a cell door. The moment I did, Mrs. Newell pounced, giving me the feeling that she had been waiting just outside her own suite, anticipating.

"Wait," she called to me, and walked slowly to me.

"What is it?"

"I don't want you going far," she said. "And I want you to return in fifteen minutes."

"Fifteen minutes? Why?"

"You've just recuperated from a scare. I don't want

a relapse under my watch. If we are to believe what you told us, you are in the seventh month now. This is the third trimester. You've been experiencing more changes in your own body, and I have explained to you how and why the baby has been moving, turning, positioning himself. In fact, from what I have observed and from my years and years of experience and numerous patients, I believe you might be farther along than even the doctor thinks."

"What does that mean?"

She blinked a smile. "It means that maybe you weren't as accurate as you think with your periods, or . . ."

"Or what?"

She took so long to reply that she made my heart race. It wasn't like her to hesitate. She usually said whatever she wanted whenever she wanted.

"Are you certain that the baby you are carrying is indeed Adan Bovio's baby?"

For a moment, the heat that came into my face felt as if it would burst into flames. I couldn't speak. She stood there with that sly, suspicious smile twisting her lips.

"What kind of a thing is that to ask? Of course, I am sure, Mrs. Newell. I had sexual relations only with Adan."

"I ask only the questions that are important. If you are not honest about it, we'll find out anyway. The baby will be more mature, more developed, even though apparently born earlier, and as you might know, there are scientific ways to determine who is really the father or, perhaps in this case, who is not. It would be better all around if you would confide in me.

I am a professional nurse and don't judge you by what is moral and what is immoral. I have my own opinions, of course, but how you live your life is your own affair."

"I'm glad to hear you say that," I told her. "Because sometimes you give me a different impression."

"Whatever. Do you have anything you wish to add to your story at this point? For the sake of the baby, if for anyone, that is."

"I have told you what you need to know and what is true. The period of time I have given is as accurate as it can be."

"Fine. Still, these are critical weeks and months. You never know what to expect. It's not an exact science. Nothing is, actually." She shrugged. "Babies, in my experience, drive the pregnancy, anyway. This baby might be moving faster to get out," she said, making it sound now as if my baby were the one who was feeling imprisoned.

"Get out?"

"All I'm saying is that this is not the time to be taking any chances at all. I'm sorry Dr. Denardo was so permissive."

"Permissive? All I want to do is take a walk! I'm not going dancing."

"Take your walk, but do it following my instructions," she snapped, slapping her hands together.

I actually flinched. Suddenly, her eyes grew smaller.

"Don't you have a watch to wear?" she asked, seeing my naked wrist.

"I do, but . . ."

"Take this one for now," she said, practically ripping hers off and handing it to me. I stared at it, and then she jerked it at me. "Take it."

I put it on.

"Can I go now?" I asked, but didn't wait for a reply. I walked toward the stairway.

"Fifteen minutes!" she shouted after me. "Don't make me come looking for you."

I turned. "I'm not an infant, Mrs. Newell."

She smiled. "No, you're not an infant, but socially mature and sensible women don't get themselves into these situations, Delia. The faster you understand all of this, the better off you will be." She turned off her smile as she would a flashlight. "I'm telling you that for your own good. I hope, you will remember."

"*Gracias,* Mrs. Newell. *Recordar es vivir.*"

"What?"

"To remember is to live," I said.

She smirked and walked away.

"One thing I know. I'll never forget you," I muttered under my breath as I descended the grand stairway.

I looked at her watch to see the time. Where could I go in fifteen minutes? By the time I rounded the corner of the *hacienda,* I would have to turn back. What kind of a walk would that be? I might as well just stick my head out of a window and take ten deep breaths. Where did she come up with fifteen minutes, anyway? Why not twenty, twenty-five? It was just mean of her. It couldn't be based on anything scientific, as she loved to say. It made me angry and defiant.

When I stepped outside, it was so beautiful I forgot all about her for a while, but as I approached my miserable fifteen minutes, I decided she would have to come get me. I kept walking. Of course, it was harder to walk quickly. I could feel myself waddling and laughed now at the way we schoolgirls used to poke fun at some of the young pregnant women back in my Mexican village. If any of them had heard us, they would stop, shake their heads, and tell us it wouldn't be long before we looked like them. Some had predicted we would blow up like balloons. We'd scream and run off, laughing, but our imaginations had been filled with visions of ourselves as budding young mothers. How did all of that happen, anyway? we had wondered.

None of us had any formal sex education. What we knew we had learned only from our own mothers or older sisters, those who had older sisters. Our teachers, priests, and elders were always warning us in one way or another, equating our sexual thoughts and feelings with *el diablo*'s temptations. Considering where I was now and what I was experiencing, I couldn't help but think they might have been right. Regardless of the gifts, the special attention, the promises for my future that Señor Bovio had lavished on me, I was not enjoying my pregnancy the way I knew a married woman back in my village had enjoyed hers. The coming of a new baby had been a rebirth for the entire family. There had been parties seemingly forever, and relatives would travel days over dirt roads to see the newborn, as if he or she had been born in a manger and given gifts by three wise men.

Mi abuela Anabela had loved to describe to me what a happy, pleasant baby I was. She had said my laughter was infectious and gave everyone a good feeling all day. For our family, I had been the best antidote to sadness or disappointment or hardship. Thinking about all of that, I looked forward to my own baby, who I dreamed would do the same for me.

Soon this would be over, I thought. Soon I would find some happiness in which to plant my seeds of hope for myself and my son. Like any prospective mother, I tried to envision what my baby would look like as he grew older. I saw Adan's face, of course, but I saw something of myself or perhaps of my own father in him as well. I envisioned him tall and strong and, of course, very intelligent. He would have to be with all of his heritage on both sides. He would become a great man. Maybe he would be the successful politician his grandfather Bovio had tried to be. Maybe he would carry forward all of the dreams and plans Adan and his father had once had for themselves. Of course, I would spend hours describing his father to him. It would be both sad and happy.

It was interesting that despite how all of this had happened, I could still see myself being a good mother.

"*Una mujer con un niño y ningún marido tiene que ser padre de la parte así como madre,*" Abuela Anabela would tell me when a young widow with children walked by. A woman with a child and no husband must be part father and mother. When I was young, I imagined the woman growing a mustache. Abuela Anabela thought that was very funny and told her friends, who laughed at me and hugged me. I was so confused.

But now I understood too well. I was determined that I would find ways to provide for my son. I wouldn't be so dependent on Señor Bovio and, of course, never depend on *mi tía* Isabela. I would want my son to know Edward. Perhaps, somehow, I could have him be my son's godfather. What would Tía Isabela do then? How could she keep her reputation in the community and oppose such a wonderful thing?

I wasn't as helpless as some thought, I told myself. I could still walk with my head high. I was still my father's daughter, and I had a proud heritage, despite our far poorer lifestyle. We were never a weak people. We found ways to survive and prosper, and, most important of all, we never stopped loving one another. That is, all of us except for Tía Isabela, and look at what her defiance and anger had brought her.

I was so lost in thought that I didn't realize how far I had gone, even with my waddling pace. I was nearly to the horse track. I had never been there, of course, nor had I met the man who cared for the two horses and maintained the stable. Right now, I saw him lead one of the horses, an Appaloosa with a frosty coat with white specks, to the corral and let him loose. Señor Lopez, the soybean farm owner my father had worked for, had had one just like it. He had even let me ride him once.

"Hello there," the caretaker called to me when he saw me approaching.

"Hi."

"I haven't seen you out and about lately," he told me. "I'm Gerry Sommer."

"I'm Delia," I said.

"Yeah, I know who you are. Teresa told me about you. How are you doing?" he asked, nodding at my stomach.

"Okay," I said.

"Not much longer, huh?"

I laughed. "I'm what you might say . . . exaggerated."

"Exaggerated?" He laughed. "Never heard it quite put that way."

"That's a pretty horse, an Appaloosa," I said, nodding at the corral.

"Oh, you know about horses?"

"A little. I once rode one just like him back in Mexico."

"He's just about fifteen hands and has a great temperament."

"Was that Adan's horse?"

He nodded. "He misses him, believe it or not."

"Oh, I believe it, *señor*."

"I ride him and give him exercise when I can. Adan was a good rider and a jumper."

"What's his name?"

"Adan simply called him Amigo."

I walked to the railing. "Amigo," I called, and he raised his head and looked at me. I remember Señor Lopez telling me that Appaloosas have eyes with an almost human look to them. Amigo certainly fit that description. Right now, his eyes were full of sadness, I thought. I smiled at him, called to him again, and suddenly, he started toward me.

"Well, that's something," Gerry Sommer said. "Sometimes he won't even come to me."

I reached out and touched him. He lowered his head and raised it.

Gerry Sommer laughed. "He likes you, all right. He's saying yes."

"Maybe someday I'll ride him," I said.

"Good. I could use the help when it comes to giving him exercise," he told me.

Suddenly, Amigo pulled back and turned to trot away from me.

"Hey," Gerry Sommer called to him. "Something spooked him," he said, and then we both looked behind me and saw Mrs. Newell charging in my direction.

"Uh-oh," I said. "I'm in trouble. That's the warden."

He laughed. "Can't help you there, Delia. I find it easier to get along with horses. Good luck," he said, and practically fled to the stable.

I started toward Mrs. Newell.

"Are you a complete idiot?" she began. "Do you think I'm going to waste my time on someone who refuses to listen to me? Give me back my watch," she snapped. "It was obviously worthless to let you borrow it." She held out her hand. "Give it to me right now."

I took it off and handed it to her.

"Did you even bother to look at it?" she asked as she put it on.

"I did, but I was having such a good time, and I felt—"

"And you go the stables? Didn't Mr. Bovio tell you not to go there? Weren't you warned?"

"I don't see why—"

"You don't see? You're the patient. You're supposed to be listening to me. I will not tolerate such disrespect. I will not work under these conditions. You're on your own. I'm packing up and leaving," she said, turning and walking away.

The shock of her anger and her decision sent a chill

up and down my spine. I felt as if my baby were twisting and turning every which way inside me. I had read that at this point in their development, babies could begin to hear. Perhaps he had heard my fear. Perhaps it was true that babies shared every emotion, every feeling their mothers had while they were still in their mothers' wombs.

I took a step forward, my legs trembling. Señor Bovio would be very angry, and Dr. Denardo would be as well. I never expected that she would do something like this. She was behaving more like the spoiled one now, having a tantrum. Of course, I would be the one to blame. Panic drained the blood from my face.

"Mrs. Newell!" I called. I called louder, but she didn't turn back. "Wait. I'm sorry."

I started after her, practically running, holding my stomach as I did. My whole body shook. I knew I was very awkward. I called to her again, but she didn't stop, so I tried to go faster and faster. And then, suddenly, I felt a horribly sharp pain in my groin, a pain so sharp it stole away my breath. I gasped, paused, and looked down, because I felt something. There was a thin trickle of blood moving in small jerks and turns down the inside of my left leg.

I screamed a scream louder than I thought possible.

Mrs. Newell finally stopped and turned. She didn't move until I squatted and fell over onto the grass, clutching my stomach.

Then she ran back to me.

Above me, the clouds seemed in a rush to part so that the sunlight could warm me and drive away the chill.

But the pain was not easing, and my stomach felt as

if it had turned into stone. I closed my eyes and mumbled prayers. I felt the tears streaming down my cheeks.

I sensed her kneeling beside me and thought I heard her say, "You fool."

And then, just before I lost consciousness, I was positive I heard Amigo neigh.

It sounded like a shrill cry of agony and accompanied me down a deep, long tunnel of darkness.

9

Little Adan

I drifted in and out but knew I was being carried and then driven somewhere. The moment I opened my eyes and became fully conscious of what had happened and where I was, I asked, "Did I lose the baby?" Or at least, I thought I had asked. No one seemed to have heard me. I saw I had been changed into a hospital gown.

I heard all of the movement going on around me and lifted my head slightly to see Mrs. Newell standing beside Dr. Denardo at the door of the hospital emergency room. Señor Bovio approached them and listened to Dr. Denardo. He had his head down the entire time the doctor spoke to him. I struggled to keep my head up to hear what they were saying, but there was a buzzing in my ears, and my neck ached too much. I looked to my right and saw that I was getting blood. Another nurse was working on me, and a technician was closing down an ultrasound machine.

I fought to raise my head again. Dr. Denardo stopped talking, and now all three turned to look at me. Dr. Denardo squeezed Señor Bovio's arm gently to reassure him and then approached me.

"Take it easy, Delia. How are you doing?"

"I don't know. I have pain in my stomach, and I feel so weak. What's wrong?"

"You're apparently suffering what we call abruptio placentae. It's very rare."

"What is it?"

"It's when the placenta comes away from the wall of the uterus. A pool of blood forms and clots in the space between the placenta and the uterus. Unfortunately, your baby can't get what it needs from you and is in some stress. I've kept you from going into shock, but I am afraid of renal failure."

"What does this mean?" I was so weak from the pain that I could barely phrase the words.

"It means I think we should do what we call a crash C-section. Your baby will be premature, but I believe he's developed enough to survive with prenatal care. We're moving you immediately to the operating room. It will be all right," he said, taking my hand. "I promise."

I didn't know if I was crying tears or not. I didn't think I had the strength even for that. The abdominal pain began to get worse and worse. I cried out, and he nodded at Mrs. Newell and a male nurse. I felt myself being rolled out of the room. Dr. Denardo walked beside me, and Señor Bovio, who had yet to speak, was somewhere behind us.

It was difficult enough to be put into such a situation with your family at your side, your loved ones praying for you and encouraging you, but I was being rolled along into the unknown alone. I could call to the spirits of my mother and my father and my grand-mother, but no one was there to hold my hand. Mrs. Newell marched along beside the gurney like some Roman centurion, never looking down at me, her back perfectly straight, her shoulders back, her neck stiff.

Like the gates of heaven, the operating-room doors seemingly opened by themselves, and I was passed through. Señor Bovio was stopped outside, but Dr. Denardo turned to him and smiled before the doors closed. In very quick, smooth motions, I was trans-ferred to the operating table, and the anesthesiologist went into action. I vaguely heard Dr. Denardo tell me he would rather give me general anesthesia than an epidural. I was too frightened and confused to hear his reasons. After that, I heard or saw nothing again until I woke up in the recovery room.

A pleasant-looking young nurse smiled at me. "How you doing, honey?" she asked.

"I'm cold," I said, and she added a blanket.

"It's not unusual. You'll be warm soon."

"What happened?" I asked as the events began to return to my memory. "My baby!"

"It all went very well. Your baby was taken immedi-ately to the NICU."

"What is that?"

"It's our neonatal intensive-care unit. It's where we place premature babies."

She checked the IV fluid.

"What is going into me?"

"You need antibiotics to prevent infections. We're

going to see if we can get you up in a while. Oh," she said, smiling at someone to my right. "Here's your doctor."

"Hello there," Dr. Denardo said, taking my hand. He wasn't smiling.

"My baby?"

"We're watching him carefully, Delia. His lungs aren't quite as developed as I would have liked them to be, but we're optimistic."

"Why did this happen?" I asked, and started to cry.

He didn't answer for a moment. Then he glanced at the nurse, who walked away.

"When you visited your friend, Delia, did you take any drugs, what you kids call recreational drugs these days?"

"No, *señor*. Never."

"You didn't bring anything back with you and take some occasionally, maybe because you were so bored and confined at the estate?"

"No, *señor*."

"Well, taking recreational drugs is one of the causes of abruptio placentae. Smoking is another, and I know you didn't smoke."

"I took no drugs, Dr. Denardo."

"Well, let's leave it at that," he said, finally smiling. "Whether you did or didn't doesn't change the situation now. You'll remain in the hospital for about four or five days. The baby will be here much longer."

"Does Señor Bovio think such a thing about me?" I asked, but Dr. Denardo didn't answer. "He must hate me," I said.

"He's all right. Nervous and concerned, but he's doing fine. You get stronger fast," he added. "I'm giving you medications for the pain. C-sections are really in the category of serious abdominal operations. It could take weeks, months, before you're back to any semblance of normalcy. Just listen to your nurses here and to your nurse when you're back at the Bovio estate."

"Mrs. Newell? She's staying with us?"

"I think we all agree. You guys need her more than ever now," he said, patted my hand, and walked away.

I closed my eyes.

The *ojo malvado* had struck again. Would I never be rid of the evil eye?

Whatever pain medication Dr. Denardo was giving me kicked in, and I dozed off. Each time I fell asleep, it felt as if I slept a whole day, when it was really only ten or fifteen minutes at a time. When the nurses tried to get me to stand and move, I folded in their arms, and they gave up. I realized I slept on and off for twenty-four hours. Once again, an attempt was made to get me up to take some steps. This time, I succeeded, with great difficulty, and everyone seemed happy about it. A few hours later, I was taken out of the recovery room and brought to what they called step-down. There were two beds in my room, but for now, no one was in the second.

Of course, I inquired about my baby's health whenever Dr. Denardo came to see me.

"When can I see him?"

"In a day or so," he said.

Although he was still as concerned about me as ever, I sensed a more formal air between us.

"I should be able to release you in two more days," he told me before leaving. "You'll be on some antibiotics, and I'll want to see you in my office in a week to check your incision."

I was going to ask if that meant he wouldn't be treating me at the *hacienda* anymore, but I held back the question. I thought it would make me sound spoiled or even sarcastic and ungrateful for all he had done.

It surprised me that Señor Bovio had not yet come by to see how I was doing. I even expected Mrs. Newell, but neither appeared. The next morning, however, I did have a visitor. I was shocked but very happy to see Fani Cordova come prancing into my room dressed in a pair of low-slung, stretchy, flare-legged jeans and a bright yellow sleeveless blouse cut so it showed her midsection. The blouse had a zipper opened to the top of her cleavage. She wore a pair of high-heeled shoes. With her hair flowing and her perfectly tanned complexion, she looked as if she had slipped off a magazine cover.

I was sitting up in bed with my legs over the side, considering demanding to be taken to see my baby. No one had yet offered to wheel me to the NICU, and Dr. Denardo had said I could see him in a day or so. When I asked the nurse, she said she would check as soon as she had a chance. Everyone seemed far too busy to care.

"Well," Fani said, laughing, "I guess you weren't lying about being pregnant after all."

"Does Señor Bovio know you've come to visit?" I asked quickly.

"He's the one who called and told me about all this."

"He did?"

"How else would I have found out? Nurse Diablo

wouldn't have called me. You look pretty bad," she added. "My mother has a friend who delivered her two children both ways, one normally and one C-section. She claims the old-fashioned way is better."

"I'm sure she's right."

"Have you seen your baby?"

"No, not yet. He's in the NICU. I'm trying to go now, but everyone's too busy. I can't walk that well yet since my crash C-section."

"Crash C-section? Aren't you the little doctor? Okay, what is that NICU thing?" she asked, taking a stick of gum out of her purse.

I explained it as well as I could. I had forgotten all of the machinery and technology the nurses had rattled off when I had asked about it myself.

"I don't know much about babies, period, much less premature ones," Fani said.

"He weighed less than four pounds when he was born."

"Less than four? I think this purse weighs five pounds," she said, bouncing it in her hands. "So, how long are you staying in the hospital?"

"Two more days. Will you help me go to the NICU?"

"Me?" She looked at the doorway. "How?"

"Help me into that wheelchair," I said, nodding at it, "and then wheel me there. It's just up one floor."

"I don't know," she said, shaking her head.

"Please, Fani. If you are really my friend, you will."

"Let's just call a nurse," she said, and backed up to the door. "Where are the nurses?"

"I told you. They are busy with other patients. It's

nothing hard to do, Fani," I said, getting up and going to the wheelchair. "Just push."

She looked at me and then went behind the wheelchair. "I'm sure I'll get in trouble for doing this."

"That shouldn't frighten you. It has never frightened you before," I told her, and she laughed.

"Where are we going again?"

"One floor up," I said, and we went to the elevator.

None of the nurses noticed us. They really were busy tending to patients. We went into the elevator and up. Signs directed us to the NICU. When we arrived, an elderly lady in a pink outfit was sitting behind the reception desk. She looked up, smiling.

"I'm here to see my baby," I said.

"Oh, yes, dear. What's his name?"

"Adan, Adan Yebarra."

She nodded, looked at a paper, and then looked up. "There's no Adan Yebarra, dear. We do have an Adan Bovio."

"That's him," Fani said quickly.

"Oh." The elderly lady looked at me. "You are his mother?"

"Doesn't she look like someone who gave birth recently?" Fani replied sharply.

"Let me call in to the nurse," she said. Her hand shook as she lifted the receiver. "Mrs. Cohen, I have Adan Bovio's mother here. Yes, I will." She hung up. "Just to the right of the doors, you will find an automatic sink. There's a soap dispenser. You have to wash for two minutes. The green light above the sink will go off after two minutes. Both of you."

"I'm not touching the baby," Fani said.

"You have to wash anyway," she replied.

"Whatever," Fani said. "It's easier to break into Fort Knox," she whispered in my ear.

I was too nervous and excited to care. The woman could have told me to put my hands in fire first, and I would have done it. Fani wheeled me in and turned me to the sinks. We then proceeded to do what we had been told.

"Hi," we heard Nurse Cohen say, and we turned. "I'm with Adan right now, Mrs. Bovio. You can come along. We're all very pleased with how he's doing. Don't be frightened by all the paraphernalia hooked to him."

I started to say I wasn't Mrs. Bovio, but Fani nudged me hard, and I stopped.

As the nurse led us past other pods and nurses attending to other premature babies, we heard bells and buzzers. She stopped at Adan's incubator and said, "Here he is."

"Wow, he is small!" Fani exclaimed.

I was unable to speak. The wires attached to him and then to monitors, the bandages around his tiny wrists, and the lines in his umbilicus all made him look unreal. I thought his color was good. His hair looked closer to my color than to Adan's, although I was positive it would change as he got older. He moved suddenly, but he didn't open his eyes.

"He probably thinks he's still inside you," Fani remarked.

I looked up at her. "*Sí.* Maybe."

Nurse Cohen shrugged. "That could be," she said. "Where he is and what is happening is about as close to being in the womb as we can get. On the other hand, he needs to feel your touch, too."

She showed me how to put my hands in to stroke his tiny hand and arm gently. He moved a little again, and then he looked as if he smiled.

"That's just gas or something, right?" Fani asked.

Nurse Cohen shrugged again. "Who am I to say?" she replied, and smiled.

"How much longer will he be in there?" Fani asked.

I was too occupied with studying every little part of him, his tiny fingers and fingernails, his feet and knees, and the features of his face, which were still in the process of forming. Even so, I was sure I could see Adan in him.

"It could be anywhere from four to six weeks. We can't release him until he's breathing well on his own and has gained enough weight. We have to keep monitoring him very closely to prevent infections, but I must say, he's off to a good start. Of course, you can see him every day," she added, looking at me.

I nodded.

"But you also have your own recuperation to get through," she continued. "Premature babies need a lot more care after they are sent home. You want to be strong and healthy for him."

"She's going to have lots of help," Fani said.

"That's fine, but a mother's care is always special," she told Fani.

I remained until I was feeling tired and uncomfortable, and then Fani wheeled me out and to the elevator. She could see my discomfort. I was due for a pain pill.

"I guess it will be a while before you go dancing, Delia," she said.

"There you are," my nurse cried when Fani wheeled me out of the elevator. "You have to tell me if you're leaving the floor."

"We couldn't find you," Fani said.

The nurse looked at her askance and indicated that she should wheel me into my room. I got back into bed and took my pills.

"Even though he's tiny, he's a beautiful baby, isn't he, Fani?"

She laughed. "*Sí*, Delia. Although I have dolls so much bigger that it's hard to think of him as a real baby."

"Oh, he's real, all right."

"Okay, you call me if you want anything. Oh," she said, returning from the door. "You probably don't know. Edward and your aunt had one helluva fight, apparently. He left college."

"What? Where is he?"

"I don't know. Jesse doesn't know, either. One day, he just upped and walked out. You come from one crazy family. Your cousin Sophia has already been asked to leave the College of the Desert. I heard she was caught stoned in one of her classes. Best thing that happened to you was your moving in with my cousin. Don't get him upset. He's your meal ticket as well as every other ticket."

I said nothing.

She smiled and fixed my blanket. "See you later, alligator," she told me, laughed, and left.

I stared up at the ceiling. I wanted to think more about all she had told me. I was very worried about Edward, especially, but I felt so exhausted, and the pill was starting to kick in. I fell asleep quickly and didn't wake up again until it was dinnertime. The nurse's aide brought up the back of my bed, and I was given my tray. Just as I started to eat, Señor Bovio entered my room. I held my breath in anticipation of hearing him express his anger. For a long moment, he simply stared at me.

"*Hola,* Señor Bovio."

"I didn't want to see you until you were strong enough to talk," he said, unsmiling. "How could you do such a thing, Delia?"

"What do you mean, Señor Bovio? This isn't my fault."

He shook his head and walked to the window.

"*Señor?*"

"I did everything in my power to make things easier for you, didn't I? I stood up for you against your aunt. I provided you with the best possible care." He spun around. "I put you in my wife's suite, my wife's bed!"

I started to cry. "Señor Bovio, the doctor—"

"Is as disappointed in you as I am," he quickly said, and returned to my bedside.

I looked down rather than up at him. His eyes were blazing with so much anger I thought they would burn my face.

"Why, *señor?*" I asked in a voice barely above a whisper.

"Why? Why? Dr. Denardo is a good doctor. I told you he was one of the best. He was so surprised at your condition that he had to get to the bottom of it, Delia. He insisted that the lab do the work, and I'm surprised you were so foolish as to think he wouldn't."

I looked up. "What are you saying, Señor Bovio? I

don't know what you mean, and you are frightening me."

"You should be frightened. Your blood had evidence of what you teenagers," he said, making the word "teenagers" sound like profanity, "call Ecstasy."

"No, *señor*. No, no."

"There wasn't much, I'll admit, but enough to show you had used it. Did you use it every night, every other night?"

"Never, *señor*. This is not true."

"You can't argue with scientific results, Delia. Were you not worried about our baby?"

I shook my head, my tears literally flying off every which way.

"Was this how you avoided being bored? You complained a great deal about it to Mrs. Newell. She told me she was ready to quit us, that you were so disobedient she couldn't deal with you anymore."

"That's not fair, not true. None of this is true, Señor Bovio."

"I should take no pity on you, Delia. You nearly killed my Adan twice," he said.

I felt all of the blood in my face rush out when he said that. My head felt ten times as heavy. The room started to spin. I struggled to remain conscious. I couldn't keep myself in a sitting position and fell back against my pillow, shaking my head.

"No, *señor*. It's not so. No . . ."

He leaned down to whisper in my ear. "You can come back to the *hacienda* to recuperate. I will do all I promised. I will get you what you need to go to a school, and you will go and live your own life, the life your fate decides for you. I don't want you returning to the hospital to see Adan while he is here struggling to live. Mrs. Newell will take care of you and see that you grow strong and healthy again. If you disobey her this time, I'll send you packing."

"These are all lies, Señor Bovio."

"Don't try my patience anymore, Delia. There's no point in your continuing to deny what you've done. Besides the laboratory results, I have Fani's confession."

"What? Fani? What confession?" I asked, looking up at him.

"She admits it's possible you took some of that drug when you were at her house for your secret meeting with Edward. Edward is not very stable these days. She says she couldn't deny that you brought drugs back to my *hacienda*."

I felt my lungs harden, my mouth get too dry for my tongue to move and form words. "I don't believe she said such a thing."

"You can continue to be friends with her. I don't care what you do with yourself now."

"Friends with her? She is lying if she said that."

"Yes, everyone is lying but you, Delia. The doctor and the laboratory are lying. I'm afraid your aunt Isabela was right about you, right about what I should and shouldn't have done. Maybe you should seriously consider returning to Mexico. It would be easier to keep your deceptions unknown, and you could start again. But not with my Adan."

"Nooooo."

"Whatever you decide is fine with me. As I said, I am an honorable man. I will live up to my part of this bargain we made, even though you have not been hon-

est with me. I do it for my son, who saw something
good in you. I do it for his memory. However, once
you are gone, you are gone," he said. He stood up
straighter and shook his head at me. "You make me
ashamed of myself, of how I shared my innermost
feelings about my wife and my son with you."

"Please, *señor*," I begged. "Do not think these terrible things about me."

"I won't think of them, Delia. It's my hope and
prayer that eventually I will forget them and you alto-
gether. But for now, we'll do as I said. The doctor tells
me you can be released tomorrow, since Mrs. Newell
will be attending to you, anyway. It's an unnecessary
expense to keep you here. Stevens will come by when
you are discharged and take you back. I am having
Teresa move you out of my wife's suite, of course, to
another bedroom in the *hacienda*. What clothes of my
wife's and things of hers, except the jewelry, of course,
that you have used will be moved out with you so you
can have something of a wardrobe. I have also asked
her to take your own things, the things you came with
to the *hacienda*, to your new room. Your aunt says she
has some things to send over as well. She doesn't want
them even in the help's quarters. Stevens will take you
for your doctor visits."

I felt as if I were sinking into the bed, disappearing.
Another urgent thought rose to the surface, however. I
reached for Señor Bovio's hand.

"Ignacio," I said.

He pulled his hand away. "You have betrayed him
as well, Delia. I can do nothing for him now."

He turned and started for the door. I tried to call
him back, but he was gone before I had even pro-

nounced his name. My crying brought back my pain. The nurse came in, ordered my tray taken away, and then, confused about why I was so upset, decided to give me some more pain medication. She thought it would be better for me if I slept. I thought it might be better if I slept forever.

Whatever she gave me wore off by the middle of the night. I woke with a start and looked around my room, dimly illuminated by the light that came from the hallway. Had I dreamed all that had happened? Was Señor Bovio really here, or was it a hallucination caused by the pain medication? How I wished that were true, but his words echoed too loudly in my brain.

I sat up to think. It was possible he had fabricated all of this, I thought. He had wanted me to go off and live an independent life without Adan Jr., hadn't he? Wasn't he always talking about it, suggesting it, telling me how he would make it all possible? He was going to buy me a car, pay for college, set me up with money. He knew I did not want to leave my baby behind. I had told him it would be too soon, and I had recently told him I would be better off out of the area. Surely, he was afraid that I would carry through with my plans.

The doctor and Fani were his allies and would say anything he wanted, as Mrs. Newell certainly would. The premature birth of Adan Jr. triggered this vicious new plan. How could I fight him? What could I do? *Mi tía* Isabela would even be on his side. She would see her revenge. What had happened to Edward, and what would happen to Ignacio and the Davila family? Look at me, I thought. I could barely get myself to the bathroom, much less do anything to help anyone else.

The thought of my having to leave and never seeing my baby again sent a sword of ice through my heart. I took deep breaths to keep myself from crying and crying. Then an idea came to me, and I went to the wheelchair. I wheeled myself to the door and gazed up and down the corridor. It was very quiet, the very walls looking asleep. I did hear some muffled noise coming from the nurses' station, but I saw no one. As softly as I could, I wheeled myself to the elevator, entered, and pushed the button for the NICU floor. When the door opened, I saw a corridor just as quiet and empty as mine. Again, I wheeled softly to the NICU doors. This late at night, there was no one at the reception desk. I went around to the intercom. After a moment, a nurse inside answered. It wasn't Nurse Cohen.

"I'm Adan Bovio's mother," I said. "Please, can I see him?"

She was quiet a moment and then said, "Yes."

The doors opened, and she met me and had me wash my hands.

"It's late," she said as I washed.

"I had a bad dream," I told her.

She nodded with understanding. "He's okay. Come along," she told me.

I dried my hands, and she pushed me to his pod. He was moving more than when I had first seen him. I put my hand in and touched his hand, and he turned his head in my direction so firmly even the nurse had to exclaim.

"They say a baby knows its mother," she told me.

"And a mother knows her child," I said softly. "Forever and ever."

I sat there gently touching him until the nurse

thought I should return. She had called down to my nurse, who was very upset at how I had snuck up.

"She's waiting for you just outside the door," the NICU nurse told me.

"Yes, thank you," I said. "Good-bye for now Adan. I will not lose you. I promise."

"Why would you lose your son?" the NICU nurse asked, curious.

"You'd be surprised," I said, "how easily we lose the ones we love the most."

She didn't respond.

She wheeled me out.

I didn't look back. I looked ahead. Whatever I had to do, whatever maze I had to go through, whatever challenges awaited me out there, I would meet and I would defeat.

Abuela Anabela would have it no other way.

10

We Lose the
Ones We Love

D r. Denardo stopped by in the morning to discharge me. He told me that Mrs. Newell was filling all of my prescriptions.

"Don't neglect the antibiotics," he warned. "You're still in some danger of infection. I'll see you in my office exactly one week from today. Mrs. Newell has the time for the appointment."

I listened but said nothing.

He noticed my silence, of course, and sighed. "I'm sorry for your troubles, Delia. I'm sure Adan Jr. will be all right despite everything."

"I did not take any recreational drugs, Dr. Denardo. I would swear on my parents' graves."

"Yes, well, we've got to think beyond all that now, Delia. Let's concentrate on your recuperation."

It was clear that he still didn't believe me or didn't want to believe me. He turned and walked out to sign the discharge papers. My nurse came in to help me dress, and then, when the time came, she got me into the wheelchair and took me down. No one suggested that I go up to my baby to say good-bye. It was as if the entire hospital staff had heard the stories about me. I could feel it in the air, see it in their faces. Stevens was waiting at the hospital entrance to the parking lot. He had brought Señor Bovio's limousine as close as he could to the entrance and then met me and my nurse. She helped me to the automobile and wished me luck, but she also looked as if she couldn't wait to get away.

"Comfortable, Miss?" Stevens asked.

Comfortable? When would I ever be comfortable again?

"Yes," I said. There was no point in complaining to Stevens.

I looked out at the hospital and up at the windows of the floor where I knew the NICU was, where Adan Jr. lay connected to all sorts of machinery. He knows I'm leaving, I thought. He feels it. I sat back and closed my eyes, dozing all the way to the estate. When we arrived, Mrs. Newell stepped out of the front entrance and waited. She made no effort to help me out of the car or up the steps. Stevens held my arm instead.

"You're downstairs now," she told me. "Toward the rear," she added, nodding at Stevens. I could see he looked surprised.

I was in no mood to say anything or even care. I had never been in that section of the *hacienda*, but I knew it was where Teresa stayed. She came down the stairs when she saw me enter and immediately asked how I was.

"I'm okay," I said.

"How frightening it must have been."

"I'm sure you have something better to do than stand here and keep her from lying down, Teresa," Mrs. Newell said. Teresa nodded and quickly walked off toward the laundry room. "I'll take her from here, Stevens," Mrs. Newell told him.

"Right," he said, let go of my arm, and left.

She held me at the elbow and firmly guided me down the corridor and around to the rear of the house. When we reached an opened door, she paused.

"This is it," she said. "All of your things are already hung up or in the dresser."

I entered the small bedroom. I would share a bathroom with Teresa, who was two doors down in another bedroom. The window in my bedroom looked out at the rear of the estate. At least I could see clearly to the stables, where I thought I saw Amigo grazing in the corral. Then I looked around my new room.

It wasn't a dirty or dingy room, nothing like the help's quarters at *mi tía* Isabela's estate. It was clean and simple, with two dressers, a double bed, a rocking chair with a standing lamp, a small chandelier at the center of the ceiling, and plain light-blue curtains on the two windows. There was a Spanish tile floor with a small oval dark-brown area rug by the bed. On the nightstand by the bed were a pitcher of water, my medications neatly lined up beside it, and a glass.

"Normally, you would be in the hospital at least another day or so," Mrs. Newell said when I sat on the bed. "So, except for your going to the bathroom, I'd like you to remain in bed or not go any farther than that rocking chair. I expect you will listen to me this time when I tell you what to do and what not to do," she added, smirking. "I'll have Teresa bring you the magazines and books still up in Señora Bovio's suite. Make sure you go to the bathroom, however, when you need to go. I don't do bedpans."

She went to my pills.

"You'll take one of these now. I have your schedule and will see to it that you follow it correctly, so pay attention." She handed me the pill and poured me a glass of water.

I took it and swallowed and drank. She put the glass down and started out, but then she stopped at the doorway.

"I'm sure you can get yourself undressed and into bed. Your nightgown is in the top dresser drawer." She stared at me a moment. "Have you experienced any leaking from your nipples?"

"No."

"You might."

"Shouldn't we use my milk? Adan Jr. could—"

"Of course not. Who knows what remains in your body?"

"Remains? But—"

"Do not concern yourself with what the baby will be fed and not fed. It's all well taken care of. Concern yourself with yourself." She blinked her usual smile and then said, "In a way, you're lucky this happened to you. I would have been long gone after you so blatantly disobeyed my orders and not here to help you recuperate."

I said nothing, but I thought that if being happy had anything to do with recuperation, I would never recuperate. She waited a moment and then left. Leaving the hospital, the trip home, and confronting all of this had exhausted me. That, with the effect of the pain pills, quickly put me to sleep. When I woke up, there was some lunch on a tray on the small table and a pile of magazines and books on the dresser. I laughed at the food I was now being given. There was a large cheese and ham sandwich, a Coke, potato salad, and a rather large piece of chocolate cake. Apparently gone was any attention to my so-called nutritional diet. Whether I gained too much weight was no longer Mrs. Newell's worry.

I was hungry and did eat most of it. Then, like some prisoner in solitary confinement, I began to walk in a circle around my small room. I knew that exercise was important, and I was determined to get as strong as I could as quickly as I could. Teresa was surprised to see me shuffling along when she came to get my tray.

"Hi," I said, happy to see a friendly face.

"Mrs. Newell sent me for your tray, but she said that after today, you have to go to the kitchen yourself for your meals."

"Good. At least she's letting me walk that far," I said. "I'm not afraid of making my own food and caring for myself, Teresa. I didn't have someone else doing that for me until I was treated like a member of my aunt's family and not one of her servants."

"I'm sorry for your troubles, dear. I'll help you as much as I can."

"Don't put yourself in any jeopardy for me, Teresa.

I've managed to cause harm to enough people as it is," I said.

"I'm sure you don't cause anyone harm, Miss."

She smiled, took the tray, and left. It amused me to know that part of my hard existence now was to be caring for myself. Did Señor Bovio and his favorite private-duty nurse really believe I had become that spoiled?

Back to walking, I thought, and circled the room until I had to go to the bathroom. Having so much time to myself permitted me to think more and more about what had happened. Why was Fani so two-faced? When I had first met her, she seemed quite independent and unconcerned about anyone's opinion of her. And what about all that business with her own parents? Why did she confide in me if she would betray me like this? These questions and my disappointment in her buzzed like angry bees in my brain.

Although I was still weak and even groggy from my pills, I decided to go out to the phone in the kitchen and try to call her.

The *hacienda* was very quiet. It was that time in midday when everyone could take a rest. I shuffled along and entered the kitchen. There was no one there, but a chicken was in a pot defrosting for the evening's meal. I didn't imagine it was for me. Of course, Mrs. Newell and Señor Bovio would have to be fed, I thought. I tried Fani's home number first, thinking she might still have not returned to college. To my surprise, she picked up on the second ring.

"It's me," I said. "I'm back in the Bovio *hacienda*."

"Good for you. I was just putting my stuff together. I'm driving back to Los Angeles; otherwise, I'd stop by."

"I don't want you to stop by, Fani."

"Huh?"

"Why did you make up that lie about me? Why did you say I might have taken drugs at your home?"

She was quiet for a long moment. I thought she was deciding whether or not to hang up on me. "Who told you that?" she asked.

"Señor Bovio."

"I didn't say that exactly," she said. "All I said when he asked me was that I couldn't swear one way or another about you."

"What?"

"I didn't know if you had done something with Edward when you and he were alone. I couldn't swear to your not doing it, could I? I knew he was doing some drugs at college."

"You never told me that."

"I told you he was depressed about Jesse and everything."

"But . . ."

"My cousin said the lab report on you showed some traces of X, so I just assumed that was where or how you might have gotten it. I told him I didn't search you before I brought you home. Besides, I didn't care if you did take it or not. I'm not going to say I haven't," she added, laughing.

"But he thinks that was the same as your telling him I did."

"I can't control what he thinks, Delia, especially after the doctor told him about your lab report. You don't have to put on this act for me. I told you that I don't care. It doesn't affect my feelings about you one way or the other. In fact, I don't know anyone who hasn't tried it, and I told you about your cousin Sophia being tossed out of college."

"That's Sophia. It's not me. And she wasn't pregnant at the time."

"I wouldn't say yes or no to that, either. I bet she's had an abortion or . . . two."

"I never took any drugs, Fani."

"Uh-huh."

"Your cousin is just trying to get me to leave my baby and go," I said.

"Delia, face it. Where would he be better off? Struggling in some Mexican cow town with you or as a Bovio living with Ray? He'll be treated like a little prince. Don't you want that? And besides, you want to get back out there in the playing field and find yourself a decent man, if there is such a thing. I have an idea for you," she said excitedly. "Try to go to a nursing school in Los Angeles, and you and I will be able to hang out together. It will be like old times again."

"You don't have children and then just desert them as if they were nothing more than some out-of-fashion dress, Fani."

"Really? You have a lot to learn about modern parents. In sociology class last week, the professor said there are now upward of fifty thousand new foster children a year here. If you want to think like that, you might be better off returning to Mexico. Families still mean something there."

"You're just bitter about your own family."

"Whatever. Look, Delia, you can do what you want. All I can do is give you some advice. If I were you, I'd grab what I could get from Ray and move on. It's going to end up being that way anyhow. You'll just skip all the turmoil and nastiness. You've been through enough of it, haven't you? Smarten up before it's too late. Ray's not going to want a public fight, either. Negotiate hard. There's a big payoff waiting for you, I'm sure."

"I cannot sell away my own baby, Fani!"

"So, don't think of it as selling him. Think of it as renting him to Ray for about twenty years or so. Didn't you tell me you felt you owed him something and that was what got you into this situation in the first place? It was truly as if you were giving him a gift. Delia's gift. Well, just continue thinking that way."

"I can't," I said, crying now.

"Rest on it for a while," she said. "Look, I've got to get my pretty little buns on the highway before the traffic gets too thick. I'll call you during the week. Maybe I'll come down again next weekend. I'll see what's doing on campus. There is this guy in my psych class who's been drooling over me. He's pretty good-looking, and he plays a mean guitar. I heard he was writing a song for me. Maybe he'll serenade me under my window tonight."

I was sobbing now but doing it quietly.

"Delia?"

"Good-bye, Fani," I said, and hung up.

I made my way back to my room and sat by the window, sucking back my tears. *Mi tía* Isabela's words when she had first visited me at the Bovio estate haunted me, especially when she had said: "No matter what Señor Bovio tells you, no matter how rich and expensive the gifts he lavishes on you are, make no mistake about it. He still believes his son is dead because of you. He thinks you bewitched him. If Adan hadn't come back for you, he would never have been on that boat that day, and if you hadn't lost control of the steering, he might not have suffered such a terrible accident. In the days following Adan's death, Señor Bovio muttered all these things to me repeatedly. And don't think his priest talked him out of them. There's no forgiveness in him. He has a bloodline that goes back to the Aztecs. He lives for vengeance. I know him through and through, Delia. You are in for a terrible time. Go home before you suffer some horrible fate."

Was this the horrible fate she had accurately predicted for me?

Mrs. Newell interrupted my thoughts. "It's time for your medication," she said.

"Is this the antibiotic?"

"Of course."

"It makes me tired, Mrs. Newell."

"It can, but you're not going dancing tonight," she replied, and opened the pill bottle to spill out a pill.

"Shouldn't I take it after I eat dinner? I have to prepare my own dinner."

She stood there glaring at me. "You don't learn quickly, do you? You're either very stubborn or very stupid. I haven't decided. Maybe you're both. If I thought you should take the pill after dinner, I would have you take it after dinner, wouldn't I?"

She held it out.

I plucked it from her palm and put it in my mouth, or at least that was what she thought. I drank some water, and she nodded.

"You can go prepare what you want to eat anytime you wish," she said. "You may even eat in the dining room if you want. Señor Bovio will not be home to-night. He'll be up at the hospital."

She flicked a smile and left.

I took the pill and put it back into the bottle. I would take it after I ate. It couldn't possibly make such a dif-ference. She was just showing me how much authority she held over me, I thought. *Let her believe what she wants,* I told myself, *until I'm strong enough to throw it back in her face.*

As time went by, ironically, what Señor Bovio and Mrs. Newell thought would serve as punishment served more to speed my recovery. My walking to and from the kitchen, my preparations of food, food that Teresa secretly enjoyed as well, and my work keeping my room clean all made me stronger faster.

When the week was up and I was told to get ready to go see Dr. Denardo, I was able to walk with straighter posture and a firmer gait. Stevens looked pleased to see me so much better and said so. Mrs. Newell did not go with me to Dr. Denardo's office. I was glad about that. I wanted to get there more to hear what he had to say about Adan Jr. than what he had to say about me. I hoped he would be willing to talk about him.

Naturally, he gave Mrs. Newell most of the credit for my good progress.

"You're healing well," he said. "I don't see any complications arising."

"And my baby?"

"He's gained weight," he said. "At the rate he's going, he might not be there as long as we first thought."

"Can you ask Señor Bovio to let me go visit him? Please," I pleaded. "The nurse told me premature babies like to have their mothers there."

"I'll speak to him," he promised.

"*Gracias,* Dr. Denardo."

"Keep doing what you're doing and listening to Millicent. She'll get you up and around as quickly as possible."

To get me out of the house, I thought. She's not helping me for me but for Señor Bovio.

Fani did not come home the following weekend as she had said she might. In fact, she never even bothered to call to tell me one way or another, or if she had called, I was never given the message. I tried desperately to keep myself occupied so I wouldn't think about the terrible situation in which I now found myself. I read, took my walks, and waited hopefully to hear Señor Bovio say I could go see Adan Jr., but he avoided me, never having his dinner when I had mine and never coming around to talk to me. Twice I went looking for him in his office, and twice Mrs. Newell intercepted me to tell me he wasn't home. He was away on business.

Finally, nearly ten days later, he did come to see me. I had just had my breakfast and was straightening up my room, arranging my clothes, and dreaming of the day I would walk out of the *hacienda* with Adan Jr. in my arms. Suddenly, I felt someone looking at me and turned to see Señor Bovio in the doorway. The mere sight of him filled me with renewed hope. Perhaps there was some shred of forgiveness and mercy in him after all. Maybe he had been convinced of how important a mother could be to an infant, especially one who had Adan Jr.'s special needs. I saw that he was carrying a briefcase and imagined he had stopped by on his way out to work.

"*Hola,* Señor Bovio," I said. I immediately sat at the small table, and he entered.

"I understand you're doing well with your recuperation," he began.

"*Sí,* Señor Bovio. How is the baby?"

"Adan is doing well. Dr. Denardo assures me he will be fine."

I smiled and waited.

He reached into the briefcase and produced a business envelope.

"I would like to keep this as simple as possible, and I have asked my attorney to write it up so it would be that way," he said. "I'm leaving it here for you to read and to sign."

"What is it, *señor*?"

Instead of replying, he continued to dig into his briefcase to produce another envelope.

"In this second envelope is a list of all that I am pledging to do for you. You will note that where there is money involved, there is actually a bank account and an investment account. This," he said, pulling a set of keys from his sport jacket's right pocket, "is one of the sets of keys for your new car. It will be delivered here as soon as Mrs. Newell or Dr. Denardo tells me you are well enough to drive."

I said nothing, nor did I reach for anything.

He went into his briefcase again and brought out a folder.

"I have asked my friends in the education department to recommend the best nursing schools, and they are all here, with an application for each one. I can assure you that all you have to do is fill out the application for the one you wish to attend, and that will be that. Some have housing for their students, but some do not. In the cases where they do not, should you choose one, I have access to apartment rental agents who will locate a good one for you.

"So," he concluded, "I am living up to all I promised despite what you've done."

"I did nothing, Señor Bovio. I spoke with Fani. She didn't say exactly what you said she had said."

He smirked. "Of course, she would tell you that. Do you think she's going to confess publicly to such a thing?"

"Why would she confess then to you?"

"I am not the public. I am her family, and I am not a threat to her. Besides, there's no point in arguing about exactly what she said and what she didn't say. There is other evidence that cannot be denied. Can you imagine what people would think of a young woman who would endanger the life of her baby just to enjoy a few hours of hallucination or whatever you young people call it?"

"I don't call it anything, because I don't do it, *señor.* There has been a terrible mistake."

"You're not listening to me, Delia. I am actually doing many good things for you, things I don't have to do, but I cannot forget Adan's feelings for you, so I continue to help you. Think about it. Here you are, a young girl who had to be rescued from the police for harboring a known fugitive, a young girl who took recreational drugs while she was pregnant. Who will step forward to help you if I don't?"

"You cannot do this. You cannot take a mother from her child, a child from his mother," I said. I tried to be brave, but my lips wouldn't stop trembling, and the tears wouldn't stop building in my eyes.

"It's done every day by our family courts," he said calmly and coolly. "You know already that I have great influence with the courts and the judges. Don't be a fool."

I lowered my head. His words were like lead weights piled on my shoulders.

"Take your time. Think about it all. I'm not throwing you out on the street, although your aunt is screaming for me to do just that."

I looked up quickly. "Tía Isabela? You told her this story about me?"

"She's the only family you have here. Technically, she has some legal standing."

"Family?" I laughed.

"She feels somewhat responsible, guilty herself."

"Guilty? Why?"

"It's no coincidence that her son has been heard to be doing drugs, too."

I shook my head, still in disbelief.

"He provided you with them, right? You can help him if you are willing to talk about that, tell her what you know about it, Delia."

"No, he did not give me any drugs. He would never do such a thing. He never took any drugs."

"You certainly are stubborn," he said, and suddenly softened his expression. "My mother was like that. My father was nearly bald from pulling out his hair sometimes." He thought for a moment, remembering, and then caught himself and firmed up his shoulders. "I have things to do, to arrange," he said. "Read what I brought you, sign what you have to sign, and keep up your recuperation so you can get on with your life as soon as possible."

"Can I go to the hospital and see Adan Jr.?"

"You can see him when he is well enough to be seen."

"But Dr. Denardo said—"

"Mrs. Newell will be in charge of his well-being."

"Mrs. Newell? You cannot hope to bring him up with a nurse for a mother, especially Mrs. Newell. You know she had a miscarriage and never wanted children after that, *señor*. Please, let me look after my son."

"He'll have a proper nanny when he is ready for her. Right now, he needs constant professional medical attention. See? You're not thinking of Adan. You're thinking of yourself; otherwise, you would be grateful for Mrs. Newell."

"But—"

"I don't wish to discuss it any longer, Delia. Read, and do what you should do," he said.

I watched him walk out and close the door behind him. My eyes went to the papers he had left behind. I didn't even want to touch them. I didn't want to move in their direction in any way, but I was curious and began to read what was in the first envelope, the one from his attorney.

There was a letter and a document. The letter was from his attorney, making the point that I had no means of supporting Adan Jr. It also made the point that Señor Bovio had a right to custody of his son's child. The attorney said that it would be easier on everyone, especially me, if I agreed to the assignment of full custody of Adan Jr. to Señor Bovio. There was a vague reference to my troubled background and current misdeeds that would have to be discussed publicly if it went to a formal hearing.

To me, it seemed as if the paper the letter was written on was so hot it burned my fingertips. I threw it down quickly and started to sob. Then I took deep breaths and went to the second envelope. The numbers actually frightened me, because they were so big. This was *el diablo* at his best. I was being set up with a two-hundred-thousand-dollar bank account and a half-million-dollar stock-and-bond portfolio. There was a checkbook with my name on each check, and there were a half-dozen credit cards already arranged in my name as well.

The folder had information and applications for nursing schools all over the country, the closest one being in Los Angeles. Someone had filled out most of the applications for me. I merely had to sign. I piled it all on the desk and pushed it away. Looking at it put me into a deeper depression.

I ate very little for dinner and went to bed early, but I kept waking up. I didn't get up until very late the next morning. Teresa told Mrs. Newell about me, and she came around to bawl me out for being lazy.

"You can't skip eating and just lie around all day. You will slow down your recuperation."

"I don't care," I told her.

"Well, I do. We do. We don't want another invalid in this house."

"Another? Who's the first?"

"Don't be stupid, Delia. A premature baby is a special assignment. I don't have time to baby you."

"I would never want you to do anything that has the word 'baby' in it," I said defiantly.

She smiled. "Suit yourself. If you insist on becoming a mental case, you'll be shipped back to that clinic. I won't be back."

"Good," I said.

She walked away, but her words lingered in the air.

She was right, of course. I would just defeat myself by sulking and falling into deeper depressions. I returned to eating well and walking.

Señor Bovio did not pressure me to sign the papers, however. They lay where I had first placed them. I was sure he felt so confident about it that he had no concern. What choice did I have?

A week later, I actually seriously considered signing the papers. I was a young woman without any means. How could I battle such a rich and powerful man? The faster I got my hands on my money, the faster I could work at finding some way to get Adan Jr. back. I went to the kitchen and prepared some breakfast. I had a doctor's appointment in two days. I felt confident that he would approve of my driving, and I would then have Señor Bovio deliver my car.

Teresa entered and smiled at my robust appetite.

"I'm glad you're feeling so much better," she told me. "I guess I know why you're so happy."

"Oh? Why?"

She looked at me askance. It made my heart thump harder and faster.

"What is it, Teresa? What's happening?"

"It's the baby, Miss," she said. "That's all I meant."

"What about the baby?" I pushed my food away and stood up. "What?" I screamed.

She brought her hands to the base of her throat. I saw that I had frightened her and quickly calmed myself.

"What are you saying, Teresa?"

"I thought you knew. I thought you had seen him. He's home. He's been home for two days."

11

Farewell Dinner

Just as I reached the top of the stairway, Mrs. Newell stepped out of what I knew to have been Adan's bedroom. She closed the door behind her softly and turned. When she saw me standing there, catching my breath, she froze into the demeanor of a security guard, folding her arms under her breasts and sending a steel rod down her own spine. Her face turned to chiseled granite, and she walked purposefully straight at me.

"What are you doing up here?" she demanded. "Your quarters are downstairs. Mr. Bovio does not want you wandering around up here."

"My baby is here!" I exclaimed, shocked at her complete disregard of that fact. "Why didn't you tell me he had been brought home?"

"The baby is still in a fragile state. No visitors are permitted."

"But I'm not a visitor!" I cried. "I'm his mother!"

"And I am his personal nurse. Right now," she said with an icy smile on her lips, "his well-being, his life, literally his every breath, are dependent on me and my expertise. The only reason he is not still in the NICU is that I am here to care for him. I sleep in the room right beside his, so I am with him whenever it is necessary, day or night. No mother could attend to him any better. Now, turn yourself around and go back down those stairs to where you belong."

"I want to see my baby."

Her neck seemed to metamorphose into marble right before my eyes as she lowered her arms slowly and put her hands on her hips.

"Didn't you hear me? I said there are no visitors permitted yet," she declared.

"And I said I am not a visitor. I am his mother. You can't keep me from seeing my own baby," I told her, disappointed by the weak sound of my own voice. I started around her, and she seized my arm, her fingers like pincers.

"The door is locked. There is no point in your walking over there, and if you make noise and wake him out of his desperately needed sleep, I'll call Mr. Bovio, and I'm sure he'll have you forcefully removed from the premises entirely. Furthermore, when visitors are permitted, no one will enter that room without proper preparation. He's too vulnerable to disease yet." She paused, releasing her grip on my arm and folding her arms again under her breasts. "Is there something I'm telling you that you don't understand?"

"Yes. I don't understand why a mother would not be permitted to see her own child."

She smiled again. "Believe me, Delia, there are

dozens, hundreds, maybe thousands of mothers who are not only prohibited from seeing and being with their own children but who don't care, selfish women who are happy that someone else is doing what they should be doing."

"I'm not one of them."

"We'll see," she said.

I looked past her at the door. If it were truly locked, there would be no point in my trying to get into the room.

"If you really do care about that baby," she said, her tone not harsh as much as condescending, "you wouldn't challenge me and what I'm doing, especially after what you have put him through with your misbehavior."

"I didn't do anything!"

I started to cry. My forearm ached where she had grabbed it. She simply stared, unmoving, her eyes turning into two steely gray balls.

"This is very mean, very cruel."

"Please. Save your breath," she said. "I'm immune to such dramatics."

"You mean you are immune to such real feeling," I threw back at her, turned, and descended the stairway, my heart feeling as if it had fallen into my stomach.

Coming from the kitchen, Teresa glanced my way and then quickly disappeared down the hall. I returned to my room to think. I hated myself for being so weak and retreating. At the moment, I was even having trouble keeping my eyes open. Maybe I'm being poisoned somehow, I thought. Maybe they're killing me slowly with those pills. After all, it was Mrs. Newell who had filled the prescriptions.

Back in my room, I sobbed for a while until I did fall asleep. When I woke up, it was late in the afternoon. I rose, still groggy, and washed my face in cold water. I gazed at the ceiling, thinking. I was sure that above me, Adan Jr. waited, longing for his mother's touch. I had to get up there to see him. I just had to.

Señor Bovio's envelopes and papers lay on the table. I decided I would have to be clever now. I took the paper that would assign him custody of Adan Jr. and started down the hallway.

The house was quiet. The descending afternoon sun cast long shadows in the living room and down the hallways. Maybe I was imagining it, but I thought I could hear the faint cry of a baby. I gazed up the stairway and then headed for Señor Bovio's office. He was sitting behind his desk, talking on his phone, with his chair turned so that his back was to the door. I waited until he finished his conversation, and then I knocked on the opened door, and he turned to me quickly.

"Ah, Delia. How are you?"

"I'm very upset, Señor Bovio. I was never told that Adan Jr. was brought home."

"*Sí.* I pushed Dr. Denardo a bit on that, and he relented only because of Mrs. Newell's presence. For now, it is better that she be the only one to be with him, to care for him. It is still a little critical, although Dr. Denardo assures me he will be fine. Neither you nor Adan need any additional excitement at the moment."

"I'm not that kind of excitement for him, *señor.* I'm his mother. Surely, you know that a baby has a need for his mother's touch, especially at this time. It will only help him get stronger faster. Besides, *señor,* I can give him the milk he needs. Breast-fed babies are healthier. Surely—"

"He is being breast-fed," he said.

"What? How?"

"I have hired someone whom Mrs. Newell recommended. We can be sure he is getting good mother's milk."

"But not his own mother's milk!" I cried.

He didn't reply. Then he nodded at me. "Have you signed the paper? Is that why you brought me the envelope?"

"I brought it to ask you to have your attorney add something before I sign it."

"What?"

"It doesn't provide for me to have any visiting privileges after I leave the *hacienda.*"

"You don't need that."

"I'd like it nevertheless, *señor.* Then I would be more inclined to sign it," I added. I tried to sound as firm as I could.

He thought for a long moment and then reached out. "Give it to me, and I'll see to it," he said.

"*Gracias, señor.*"

I handed it to him.

"Have you chosen a nursing school?"

"I am thinking about one of the schools in Los Angeles."

He didn't look happy about that, but he nodded.

"Give me the application as soon as possible, and we'll see to what you need."

"*Gracias, señor.* I have one more favor to ask of you."

"What is it?"

"Please, please, ask Mrs. Newell to permit me to see Adan Jr. It's torture for me to know that he's just upstairs and I am unable to see him."

"When she feels he's ready for that, she will tell me. Don't annoy her or do anything that would cause her to resign," he warned. "She was on the verge of doing that just before you had your episode and nearly lost our baby. I won't stand for anything like it."

"But—"

"I have some other news for you. Better news," he added. "I have made some headway with the future of this boy, Ignacio Davila."

"You have?"

"*Sí*. His situation is finally before someone who has the power to help, but it must be done very carefully, subtly, so as not to stir up a hornet's nest. Do you understand what I'm saying?"

"*Sí, señor.*"

I understood all too well what he was saying: I must do exactly what he wanted, or else.

"But surely, my seeing my baby—"

"I'm very busy, Delia. Please, have patience. I'll have this document for you tomorrow to sign. Then I will release the funds, and you can start to move on with your life more intelligently." He reached for his phone. "Do we have an understanding?"

I nodded. It was my plan now to play along. My chance would come later, I thought, and maybe he was telling the truth about Ignacio this time. A little more hopeful, I left his office and decided to take a walk outside. I headed directly for the stables. Now that I had given birth, no one cared about my being around the horses. I saw Amigo and Señora Bovio's horse in the corral, but Gerry Sommer didn't appear until I was almost there. He stepped out of the barn and hurried in my direction.

"Delia, how are you? I couldn't get much information about you out of anyone here."

"I'm not surprised. I'm much better. I have my last doctor's visit day after tomorrow," I said.

"That's great. What are you going to do then?"

"I'm not sure yet. I would like to go to nursing school. Adan Jr.'s been brought home from the hospital," I told him, and looked back at the house. "I want to wait to see how he is before I decide anything."

"Home from the hospital? That's nice. I didn't know. Like I said," he added, "no one tells me anything."

"Me, neither, I'm afraid. How's Amigo?"

"You know," he said, looking at the horse, "sometimes I think that horse is part human. He was not the same after you collapsed out here. Look at him." He nodded toward the corral laughing. "He's anxious for you to get over there."

When I approached the corral, Amigo stepped close enough for me to reach out and touch him.

"He knows who's good people," Gerry Sommer said, coming up beside me.

"Where do you ride him when you do?"

"Oh, there's a trail back there. It goes off the Bovio estate and through the wash, a gully for runoff whenever there's a big rainstorm."

"And then where does it go?"

"Well, if you kept going, you'd end up in what's known as the Indian Canyons of Palm Springs."

"Is it far to the city of Palm Springs?"

"Maybe two miles," he replied. "It was one of Adan's favorite rides, especially in the cool evenings. I went with him a few times. There's a riding academy not far from the canyon, and they have some trails along it as well."

I looked in the direction he had indicated. Perhaps Adan and I would have taken that ride, I thought.

I watched Gerry Sommer water and feed the horses. He talked about Adan and the time he would spend caring for Amigo, exercising him, and brushing him down.

"Adan and Amigo were as connected as I've ever seen a horse and its owner," he told me. "That horse has been in mourning ever since. You're the first thing that's brought some life back into him, Delia. Come around as much as you want."

I promised I would.

The following morning, after my breakfast, I tried again to see Adan Jr., and again, as if she were waiting for me to do just that, Mrs. Newell appeared to turn me away.

"Didn't you understand what I told you yesterday? Are you really this stupid?"

"I was hoping . . . please, Mrs. Newell," I begged. I thought that begging might satisfy her enough to grant me some time with my own baby.

"I told you. When I believe it's safe for him to have visitors, I will permit it, but not until then," she said, and went into Adan's room, locking the door behind her.

I stood there debating whether or not this was the time to challenge her, to pound on the door and scream. I had no doubt, however, that Señor Bovio would support her and do just what she threatened and throw me out.

Later that afternoon, Señor Bovio came to my room with the revised document. I read it and nodded.

"Would this mean I can visit him now?" I asked.

"Of course not. That's a medical decision, not a legal decision," he replied. "Are you signing it?"

"It's still a very big decision, *señor*," I said. It was my only bargaining point. "Would you be kind enough to let me sleep on it a day or so more?"

"Why? It won't change anything," he said. I didn't reply, and he relented. "Okay. Two days, and that's it," he told me. "I mean it, Delia. I won't be played like some fool. After that, I'm taking back all that I have offered you. I'll go forward with the court action, and you will find yourself all alone out there. I imagine you might have to return to Mexico. I don't mean to sound as if I'm threatening you, but you have to be made to understand what will be. The choice is in your own hands now, but as I said, the clock is ticking."

He left, closing the door behind him.

I sat with the paper in my hands, his words lingering in the air. Even though I had no intention to obey such a legal document and all this money lay in waiting for me, it was still difficult to sign it. I came from a line of people who never gave away their children despite how close to starvation they might be. There was nothing stronger or more meaningful than family. It had destroyed my grandfather's spirit when Tía Isabela turned on him, and he had disowned her. Abuela Anabela never failed to remind me of it and to express her hope that somehow my going to live with her would eventually bring her back to her family, even though they were long gone. That return would keep them from the third death.

Whether she owed him a favor or she was still looking for some way to get revenge on me, Tía Isabela showed up at the Bovio *hacienda* the next afternoon. I had just returned from my last visit with Dr. Denardo, who had given me a clean bill of health and told me to resume normal activities.

"I understand you're thinking about going to nursing school. It's a good career, and we need nurses," he said. "You have a nice opportunity. I would seize it," he added, clearly implying that I should do as Señor Bovio wanted.

I was sitting quietly in my room, thinking about all of this, when Tía Isabela suddenly appeared in the doorway. She wore a blouse and skirt that looked almost too plain for her. Her hair was tied back but not as severely as I had seen it done, and she wasn't as heavily made up. She actually looked tired, even a little old. It surprised me as much as anything else to see that she had left her house and was being seen in public like this.

"When I first came here," she began, "my husband had a housekeeper who believed that God rained children down on us as punishment for original sin. She actually believed it, and I suppose when she saw the way Sophia behaved, even as an infant, she was convinced it was true."

She came into the room and looked around.

"Quite a come-down from Señora Bovio's luxurious suite," she said.

"I was never that comfortable up there, anyway," I said.

"I imagine not. It was probably like sleeping with a ghost, but I warned you."

She plopped into a chair and for a long moment looked too tired to speak.

"You know that Sophia was thrown out of school and Edward has run off from college?"

"I heard. Fani Cordova told me."

"Fani," she said. "It doesn't surprise me to hear that. She probably enjoys spreading bad news, especially where it concerns me. I never liked that girl, and she knew it." For a moment, she ran her gaze over me like someone looking for concealed weapons. "Well, despite all you have done—"

"I did nothing," I said quickly. "It's not true."

"Whatever. It doesn't matter now, does it? I understand Ray has made you quite an offer. You'll be as rich as Señor Lopez. Wouldn't your parents be surprised?"

"He's buying my son."

"Buying your son," she repeated. "It's his grandson, isn't it?"

"I'm his mother. Maybe you don't know it, Tía Isabela, but a mother is more important."

"Please, spare me the canned lectures about parenthood. My husband used to go on and on about it. Think, Delia. What could you offer your son now?"

"Family," I said. "Love."

"Right. I don't know why you're being so stubborn about this. You see what raising children brings you. Sophia is still trying to drive a stake through my heart, and now Edward has run off, wasting all that I've done for him and all of his opportunities. If I died tomorrow, my children would barely blink."

"I would never have such a relationship with my child. I would never permit him to be as self-centered as Sophia or drive him away as you have done with Edward."

"No? You don't think he'll grow up self-centered, the way Señor Bovio would spoil him, despite you?"

"I won't let that happen. I'll take him away from here first."

"Please, Delia. Get real, already. He'll never permit it, and you'll end up in a bad place. He's too powerful for you."

I looked away. Her words were like nails pounded into a coffin. Just like death, the truth about what she was saying couldn't be denied.

"He's described to me in detail what he's offering you. I think he's nuts, myself, but I can't believe you're actually procrastinating about it, risking that he'll take back his offer and have you thrown out."

I couldn't stand hearing it, especially from her.

"Why have you come here, Tía Isabela? You don't really care about what happens to me, do you?"

She sighed. "Ray pleaded with me to come talk sense into you. He sounded as if he was on the verge of losing his patience."

"He's losing his patience? My baby is upstairs, locked in a room. I am not permitted to see him."

She shook her head as if it wasn't a big thing.

"It's my baby!" I cried.

She closed and opened her eyes. "You had better think hard about all he is offering you and not make this last big mistake. I came for you as much as for him. It's the last thing I will do for you, Delia."

She stood up.

"Get out with something while you still can. That's what I would do."

"Maybe that's why I shouldn't," I said.

She reddened. "I'm really tired of you. You won't see me again."

"Is that a threat or a promise?"

She shook her head. "You know what, Delia? I hope you don't take Ray's offer. I hope he does me a favor and gets rid of you, has you deported or something."

She turned and walked out, her footsteps echoing off along with her, the threats lingering in the air like the odor of something dead.

Not long afterward, Teresa came to my room carrying a dress. She told me Señor Bovio had asked her to invite me to have dinner with him that evening. He had called her from one of his commercial properties and asked her to bring me this dress of his wife's to wear. It was one I had not seen. It looked like one of the ones that hung with the tags still on them in the closet, never worn.

"He said to tell you he has a nice surprise for you," she said. "Dinner will be at seven tonight, Miss."

"A surprise?"

"That's all I know, Miss. Oh. He said you should be sure to bring the signed document with you."

"I see. Thank you, Teresa."

She smiled. "I hope there's truly good news for you, Delia."

"Thank you," I said.

I was on pins and needles waiting for this dinner and this surprise. Did it mean Ignacio would be freed? Whatever the surprise, it was clear he expected me to give him what he wanted first. I read and reread the revised statement. It simply said that I had visitation privileges, but I had to call and arrange for the visits first. If there was any doubt in my mind before, it was clear now that Señor Bovio expected me to be out of his *hacienda* very soon.

I put on the dress. It had a very pretty off-the-shoulder white bodice and a red ankle-length skirt. It fit well. I didn't have the right shoes for it and laughed at myself for even caring. However, I brushed and pinned my hair. I imagined that he didn't want me to look like the poor lost soul I was. I didn't mind. If I looked good and held on to some of my dignity and pride, perhaps he would be more forthcoming. I was determined to bring up Adan's name and see if that would get me anywhere with him, too.

He was already at the table in the dining room when I arrived at seven. He looked quite dapper, more like the Señor Bovio I remembered. It was almost as if all of the terrible things that had happened since were just bad dreams. At any moment, Adan himself would come in behind me, and we would sit at the beautiful table and talk about wonderful things.

"You look very nice," Señor Bovio said. "I knew that dress would fit you now."

"*Gracias, señor.*"

I sat, and Señor Bovio offered me some red wine. When I hesitated, he smiled.

"You don't have the same food and drink restrictions now, Delia. Enjoy."

I nodded, and he poured me a glass.

"I can see, by the way, that Mrs. Newell did a very good job of keeping your weight down. Despite what you've been through, you have nearly regained your beautiful figure."

"Perhaps she should work more with people who are obese," I said, and he laughed.

"No, no, she is a top maternity nurse. But no more about her."

He sat back and waited for Teresa to serve us our salads and leave. Then he lifted his fork and smiled.

"Tomorrow, Stevens will be outside at ten A.M. to take you to see someone I know you have been waiting a long time to see."

He kept his smile, waiting for my response. My thoughts ran wild for a moment.

"Ignacio? He is out of prison?"

"No, not out of prison yet, but I have arranged for you to see him."

I started to shake my head.

"It's okay," he said.

"He wants to see me?"

"He doesn't know what he wants or doesn't want right now. He's in prison, and it's not a country-club prison, believe me."

"But—"

"I thought it would please you, Delia," he said. "Don't you want to see him?"

"Yes, of course, but . . . was he told that he had to see me?"

Señor Bovio lost his smile. "Do you want to see him or not?"

"Yes, *señor,* very much."

"Then I wouldn't ask so many questions. These things are not as easy to arrange as you might imagine.

It will lead to his release faster if the people who are in a position to arrange it believe he can be a successful man out in public again. He has, I understand, not been an ideal prisoner and has not been interested in seeing anyone, even members of his own family. You could do him some good."

"*Sí,*" I said, still feeling ambivalent and confused. There was something going on here that I didn't quite understand.

"Dress simply, and don't bring a purse. It's easier if they have less to search."

"Search?"

"They won't let you into the visitors' area without being sure you're not bringing in weapons, drugs. You could be strip-searched, Delia. This is a maximum-security prison."

"*Sí,*" I said, now growing frightened.

"I don't know exactly why, myself, but I was told to tell you not to wear a wire bra. Maybe women hide things in them. You have a sports bra, I know. Wear that."

"*Sí,*" I said.

"You signed the paper?" he asked, eating and nodding at the envelope.

"*Sí, señor,*" I said.

"Good. We're having prime rib for dinner." He leaned toward me. "Mrs. Newell would never permit you to have it when you were pregnant. Too fatty, but it's very tasty. And wait until you see our dessert."

He put his fork down and reached for the envelope. I watched him open it and look at the paper. Then he smiled at me.

"You have done a wise thing," he said, "both for yourself and for Adan."

I said nothing. Teresa served us our meal, and Señor Bovio asked me about my choice of nursing schools and then began to talk about Adan Jr. as if he were already old enough to consider college himself.

"Too many young people think only about the social scene and not enough about their education. They choose to go to this school or that, not because of the school's success in studies but because of football or basketball or whatever. If a parent or a guardian is to do a good job with a young man, he should guide him to make the right choices for the right reasons."

I just sat listening and eating. After a while, he grew quiet himself and just ate and looked off as if he were sitting by himself. In fact, when Teresa came to clear off the dishes, he looked around as if he had just realized I was there with him and we had just eaten.

I heard a door slam, and we both listened to the footsteps descending the stairs. Moments later, Mrs. Newell appeared in the dining-room doorway.

"How is he?" Señor Bovio asked.

"He's doing fine, Mr. Bovio." She looked at him, and he nodded at the envelope. Then she turned to me. "In two hours, you can come upstairs for five minutes," she said. "First, I'd like you to wash your hands, and I want you to put on the robe I have for this purpose. If you are doused heavily in perfume, I'd like you to wash it off."

"No, no, I'm not," I said. "Why am I limited to only five minutes?"

"You can appreciate what I went through with her

these past months," she told Señor Bovio instead of responding. "It was constantly like this, questioning every order I gave, making me work harder."

"I don't mean to make you work harder, Mrs. Newell. I—"

"Considering what you have done to this child," she said coldly, "and how difficult you have made it for him to survive, I would think you would be grateful for even two minutes."

I started to speak but stopped myself. If I said anything more, I might not be able to see Adan Jr. at all. Señor Bovio hadn't raised a syllable in my defense. He looked away, in fact.

Mrs. Newell didn't say another word. She went into the kitchen to get her own dinner. I looked at Señor Bovio, hoping to hear him promise me more.

Instead, he said, "I'll go in with you."

I wondered if he thought I might scoop up Adan Jr. and run out of the house, but then he smiled and added, "When we brought Adan home, Señora Bovio and I sat at his side for hours and hours, marveling at his tiny features, his every move. It meant more for us to be there together. After all, we made him together. Aaah," he exclaimed when Teresa came out with a rich chocolate cake. "The dessert I promised. Nothing is too rich for you now, Delia." He smiled gleefully.

I thought to myself that when *el diablo* smiled, he surely smiled the same way.

Two hours later, he was waiting at the door for me. I was so nervous that I was trembling. He knocked softly, and we heard the door unlocked. Mrs. Newell looked at us and stepped aside, directing me first into the bathroom, where she had special soap she wanted me to use and the robe she wanted me to wear. I did everything just as she directed, terrified that I'd make some small error and she would send me away before I saw Adan.

Finally, I was able to approach the crib and look at my baby. To me, he looked absolutely perfect, his face fuller. I didn't see myself in him as much as I did Adan. For a while, all I could do was stare in wonder. Then, slowly, almost like someone bringing her fingers close to a candle's flame, I reached down to touch his little hand. His eyes fluttered open, and I would swear forever that he looked up at me and smiled.

Then and there, I vowed I would not leave him behind. Señor Bovio could have me sign a thousand documents, give me tons of money, and lavish the most expensive gifts on me, but none of it, nothing, would keep me from my baby.

Suddenly, I felt Señor Bovio step up beside me, his body touching mine.

"Adan," he whispered, "has come back to us."

My heart fluttered. I looked up at him, and in his eyes, I saw the madness of love Adam surely had for Eve, the same love that would enable him to defy God's commandment and deport him and Eve forever from Paradise. Like a dark, heavy shadow, Señor Bovio loomed over me and my baby.

"It's time," Mrs. Newell declared.

"But surely it hasn't been five minutes," I protested.

"Surely it has," she said, stepping closer.

I looked at Señor Bovio. He nodded, took my arm, and turned me toward the door.

When I looked back, Mrs. Newell was leaning over

the crib, blocking Adan Jr. from my view. I heard him cry and started to turn back, but Señor Bovio kept me moving forward and out of the room.

I knew then that my baby was the paradise from which I was being driven away.

12

Ignacio

I pleaded outside in the hallway.

"Didn't you see him smile when I touched him, *señor*? Couldn't you see how a mother's touch brought him happiness?"

Señor Bovio continued walking toward the stairway. I caught up with him and grabbed his arm to get him to stop and turn around.

"He knew it was me, *señor*. He grew inside me. My blood is in his veins. He—"

"It was the dress," Señor Bovio said, leaning down to whisper to me.

"*Qué*? What?"

"The dress." He smiled. "That dress you're wearing was the dress she wore the day we brought Adan back from the hospital. The dress," he whispered again, and continued toward the stairway.

I stood looking after him, my mouth open but my

tongue unable to form a single word. Behind me, I heard the door being locked.

I followed Señor Bovio, but he hurried off to his office and closed the door before I could get to him. I knocked on it, but he didn't answer.

"*Señor,* please, listen to me."

I waited, but there was only silence, and the door was locked.

Frustrated, I hurried back to my room to take off the dress. I couldn't get it off fast enough. His comment frightened me so. What madness was this now? Was he just confused, overwhelmed by emotion? How much could I blame on a man's sorrow over the loss of his only son? Whom could I tell all of this to, anyway? Tía Isabela? Fani? Edward, who had run off? Dr. Denardo? Who would listen to me or believe anything I said now?

Undressed, I sat in a daze until I was too tired to think or keep my eyes open, but the image of Adan Jr.'s face settled over my eyes the moment I closed them to search for sleep. It brought me to tears. Then I remembered that I would be seeing Ignacio the next day, and I began to think only of that.

In the morning, I put on the dress I had worn when I had first come to *mi tía* Isabela's home, a dress Ignacio had seen me wearing. I was surprised at how tight it was in the waist and bosom, but I wore it anyway. I looked for Señor Bovio. Teresa told me he had already left the house. Mrs. Newell went up and down the stairs quickly, avoiding me.

As I went out to the car, I think I was as nervous as I had been that first day I had arrived in Palm Springs. My stomach was doing flip-flops, and my heart wasn't racing as much as it was ticking loudly like some old grandfather clock. Stevens said good morning and smiled at me. At least someone acknowledged my existence, I thought. I got into the car and practically curled up in the corner, terrified of what awaited me.

What would Ignacio do? Would he even come to the visitors' area to see me? Would he want to greet me with a kiss or a slap? Not that long ago, we had risked our lives together in the desert, and he had nearly lost his life to protect me. He had rescued me a second time when he appeared at my old house to reveal that he was still alive. I had been days away from marrying a man I did not love, trapping myself in a life that would be a kind of prison, too. We had made promises to each other then, promises that were perhaps too great for me to keep.

As the limousine took me to him, I admitted to myself that I couldn't place all of the blame on Sophia for having alerted the police. Ignacio's father hadn't been wrong, either. I had blundered and made it possible for her to do it, knowing all along that she was crouching like a cat in the bushes, waiting for an opportunity to do me harm and to do the Davilas even more harm. Ignacio had put so much trust in me, so much faith and love. I was sure that he had spent many lonely hours in his prison cell berating himself for being so gullible. I was not his favorite person.

And yet I wondered if the love we had once had for each other, a love that had seen us through such a dangerous and painful time, was strong enough to survive all of this. Would I see a flicker of it in his eyes or only hate and anger? What sort of weak defense could I put up for myself, anyway?

More important, I wondered now why Señor Bovio really had arranged for this. Why was it suddenly so important? How did it fit into his plans? What did he expect would happen? Somewhere inside me, in a place where my skepticism and distrust lived, I felt we were being manipulated. I had missed so many signs and warnings before. I was probably missing one now, too.

The guard at the entrance had my name on a list. We drove in and parked. Stevens told me he would wait in the car. The prison walls, fences, and barbed wire looked intimidating. I had read about prisons and seen them in movies, but this was the first time I would be in such a place. So nervous that I couldn't feel my legs moving, I walked to the first booth practically in a trance and again gave my name. The guard opened a door, through which I walked to another door and another security checkpoint. The guard there was older and friendlier. He showed me the way to the visitors' reception area. There was another guard there, with a dog that was brought close to me to sniff for drugs. I was told to pass through the door, where a female security guard took me to a private area. I thought this was where I would be strip-searched, but she only patted me down and showed me into the visitors' room.

It was a large room, with rows of tables and chairs evenly spaced. There were already families visiting inmates, wives and even children. Guards were stationed at every corner, and one walked slowly through the aisles, watching the conversations. I saw television cameras in the ceiling. I was directed to a table to wait.

"How long will it be?" I asked.

"Not long," the female guard said, "but sometimes

the inmate decides not to come. I'll let you know immediately if that is the case."

I thanked her and found I was holding my breath. A young woman sitting two tables to my right smiled at me. The inmate she was visiting had yet to arrive, too. I couldn't help but wonder how many times she had been there and how long the person she loved would be in prison. Surely, it must be even more difficult for people like Ignacio and me, people who have lived outdoors so much of their lives, to be locked away in this concrete and metal world, I thought. It nearly brought me to tears, but one thing I didn't want to do in front of him was cry.

So much time passed, or seemed to pass, that I began to believe he wasn't coming. Perhaps Señor Bovio wanted me to experience this rejection as a way of ending my request for him to do something for Ignacio. That made sense to me. I now anticipated the female security guard returning without him. She did enter the room, but she didn't come to me. She went to greet another female visitor, and then, a minute or so later, Ignacio walked through the door.

His hair was cut so close he looked almost bald. I thought he was somehow bigger, wider in the shoulders, even taller. He paused for a moment when he saw me and then walked slowly to the table. He said nothing, and I said nothing. Then he sat, folded his hands, and looked down at them.

"Why did you come here?" he asked, still not looking at me.

I wasn't sure if he hated me so much he couldn't look at me or if he couldn't look at me because he was ashamed of being there, of my seeing him so trapped.

"For the very same reason I wrote to you, to try to get you to believe me when I said I did not arrange for you to be arrested. It was my cousin who told the police."

He raised his eyes to look at me. "I know all about you, about your love affair with the rich man who died on the boat and your being pregnant and living in his father's home."

"Yes, but—"

"While you were writing to me, promising all those things, telling me to have hope and come back to you, you were going to fancy parties and having this affair. You played me for the fool."

"No."

"Do you have a baby?"

"I do and I don't," I said.

He snapped his head back. "What's that mean?"

"My baby's grandfather made me sign a paper to give him custody."

"You gave away your baby?"

"You don't understand, Ignacio. I have nothing. *Mi tía* Isabela hates me and won't help me. *Mi primo* Edward has run away from college and has not been able to help me. He has his own problems. I have no one, no money, and—"

"Why didn't you just return to Mexico?"

"Listen, listen," I pleaded, leaning over the table.

Out of the corner of my eye, I saw the security guard study me closer, so I backed away a little.

"I'm going to have a lot of money. Señor Bovio has promised to help get you out of here soon. Maybe—"

"Maybe what, Delia? You have a different life now. You're a true *norteamericana*."

"No."

"You will live in a grand *hacienda,* have rich friends and soon a new man. When I get out of here, where am I going? Back to ten dollars an hour, maybe. I'm not going to let you fill me with new promises, Delia. I am stuck here. These promises are like pins in my heart now. I don't want to believe in anything or anyone anymore.

"A man almost killed me here yesterday. You know what the fight was over? It was over a CD he said I stole. Life is not very valuable here. People kill each other for the simplest reasons. I'm just trying to survive. I don't want to hear about money and futures.

"You look very good, prosperous," he added bitterly. "You have a *patrón,* no? It was probably very smart of you to get pregnant."

"I did not plan this, Ignacio. Please don't think such a thing of me. Things just happened. You don't know what my life was like when I returned from Mexico. Tía Isabela—"

"I don't want to hear how hard your life was, Delia. Look at where I am."

I nodded, the tears now flooding my eyes so thickly that looking at him was like looking through gauze. My face softened him a bit.

"Why did you come here? What is it you want from me, Delia? Forgiveness? A blessing? You don't need any of that. At least, you don't need it from me."

"I do," I said.

"That's too bad, then. I'm all out of forgiveness. They drum it out of you here," he said. "Sometimes I feel as if I no longer have skin. I have a hard crust. I have to be like a lizard, especially when my mother comes here and cries the whole time, and my father just sits and stares like a man who has been robbed of his soul."

"I'm so sorry, Ignacio." I wiped a fugitive tear away quickly.

"You used to worry so much about the *ojo malvado*. Well, in here, no one worries about the evil eye. It's satisfied enough. Look," he said, sounding more like the Ignacio I had once known. "I'm not important anymore in your life. We have different borders now to cross, Delia. You're in a different world. You can't return to mine, and you shouldn't, anyway. Just forget me, and I'll forget you. Think of our lives before as if it was all a dream and nothing more."

"I don't want to do that, Ignacio."

"*Sí,* but what we want and don't want doesn't really matter, Delia. At least, not for me. Stay with the grandfather," he said, and started to rise.

"No, I can't. He doesn't want me to stay, anyway. He wants only his grandson."

"My father wants grandsons, too. Right now, I can't imagine why anyone would want to bring another child into this world. *Adios, muchacha.*" He started away.

"Ignacio!"

He did not turn back. He walked with his shoulders turned in, his head down, and disappeared through the doorway. The tears broke free and streamed down my face. I sucked in my breath and looked at the security guard, who was smirking and shaking his head at me. He looked as if he thought both Ignacio and I deserved every moment of our agony.

Ignacio was right about this place, I thought. Forgiveness and love were as locked out of it as the inmates were locked in. I got up and quickly left. Stevens was asleep behind the wheel when I reached the car. I knocked on the window, and he jumped up and looked at me, surprised.

"Back already?"

I nodded and got in. He said nothing more. He could see I wouldn't talk. I felt as if I were shrinking in the backseat. Before we reached the Bovio estate, I would probably disappear. I didn't, of course, but we drove out and rode in heavy silence all the way back to the *hacienda*. Señor Bovio was at the foot of the stairway, talking with Mrs. Newell, when I arrived. They both looked at me, and then she hurried up the stairs as he approached to greet me.

"So? How was your visit with your old boyfriend?"

"Not good," I said.

"Not good? Why not good? Look at what you are trying to do for him? Wasn't he appreciative? Doesn't he still want you to be his wife? You told him Adan was well taken care of, didn't you? You explained our arrangement?"

I looked at him more closely now. Was this his hope? That I would go off and start a new life with Ignacio, who would probably not want another man's child to raise? All of it suddenly made sense.

"None of that matters to him, *señor*. Ignacio is a very bitter young man. He does not see his life and mine joining ever again."

"Well, that's ingratitude if I've ever seen it. He should count his lucky stars that he has a woman like you willing to care for him." He thought a moment. "Well, maybe after you have gone to school and become a nurse . . ."

"I do not think any of that would matter to him now, *señor*."

"Then good riddance to him," he said angrily.

"Can I see my baby now?"

"No. Later, maybe. We'll see what Mrs. Newell says," he said sharply, and walked toward his office.

I looked up the stairway and saw Mrs. Newell looking down at me. I never thought I could hate someone as much as I hated her at that moment. I never thought I would wish someone dead, but I prayed that the evil eye would turn its attention to her for a while. She must have seen the anger in my face, fire coming from my eyes. She turned and disappeared quickly down the hallway. As I started toward my room, Teresa stepped out of the kitchen and called to me.

"Delia, you had a phone call while you were away," she said. "Fani Cordova would like you to call her back. She said you know her number."

"Fani? *Gracias,* Teresa."

Perhaps Fani had news of Edward, I thought. I needed some good news. It was the last bright light left in my stormy, gray sky. I hurried to a phone.

"Yes, I've seen him," she said when I immediately asked if that was her reason for calling me. "He's back from his self-destructive rampage. He looks as if he lost twenty pounds and won't say where he's been."

"Did he—"

"Ask about you?" She laughed. "Yes, it was practically the first thing he asked. Didn't he call? I told him you would probably be able to talk to him and see him now."

"No," I said, my happiness balloon losing air.

"Well, I imagine he will, or maybe . . ."

"Maybe what?"

"Maybe you can see him. I'm inviting you to come to Los Angeles. I have my own apartment here, you know. There's a terrific party this weekend, and there's a good chance Edward will be there, especially if he hears you're coming."

"I don't know. I'm not exactly in a party-going mode," I said, and told her about my visit with Ignacio.

"You went to see him in prison? Wow. That's cool."

"It wasn't so cool, Fani."

"Look, you're tired. It's not your fault. You can't just roll over and die, Delia. I heard the doctor gave you a clean bill of health."

"How did you hear?"

"My cousin, how else? I called him to ask how you were doing. Didn't he tell you?"

"No."

"I wondered why you didn't call me. Have you been given your car yet?"

"No."

"Don't worry about it. I'll send a car for you. It's time you got out, got back on your feet, Delia. Put some color in those cheeks. If everyone sees you depressed and sad all the time, they will think you really are mentally disturbed."

"Is that what Señor Bovio thinks?"

"Who cares what he thinks? Are you going to come or not?"

Perhaps Fani was right, I thought. Perhaps I should try to improve, not only my mental state but my looks. Moping about like this did me no good. How would I ever get back on my feet and fight for my son? And then there was the wonderful possibility of seeing Edward. He would know what I should do.

"Yes, I'll come," I said.

"Great. Don't worry about anything. I have clothes for you, too. I don't want you dressing like some old lady. Just bring yourself. I'll have you picked up Friday at noon. My last class is at one, so I'll be at my apartment by the time you arrive." She laughed. "It'll be like a resurrection, the resurrection of Delia Yebarra. I love it."

I nodded to myself. She still enjoyed running everyone else's life, but for now, I didn't care. Maybe she would do better at running my life than I obviously had been doing.

After I hung up, I marched down to Señor Bovio's office to tell him about Fani's invitation. He shrugged, barely looking at me.

"You're free to go anywhere you wish, Delia. Where is the application for the school?"

"I'll give it to you later, *señor.*"

"Good. I just arranged for your money's release. You can write a check anytime. See," he said, "I knew you would realize it's all for the best. You have your whole life ahead of you. And Adan has his."

It was on the tip of my tongue to correct him, to say he was not Adan. He was Adan Jr. But I just nodded and left him.

Later, I did give him the application when I joined him for dinner. He was in such a good mood that I felt guilty for being even slightly depressed. A part of me wanted me to hate him for what he was doing and what he had done, but another part of me continued to see his resurrection, too. And then I thought that Mrs. Newell wouldn't be there forever. In fact, she probably wouldn't be there much longer. I would wait her out. Things would be very different then. He would realize how important a mother was to a child, and didn't he want the best for his grandson?

As Abuela Anabela used to say, *con paciencia, se gana el cielo.* With patience, you can win heaven. And that's what Adan Jr. was to me, heaven.

Nevertheless, the waiting was difficult. Mrs. Newell did not agree to another visit after dinner. She said the baby was too fragile to be disturbed. She thought it was a mistake to start any visits this soon. It did me no good before to point out that I was his mother and not a visitor, so I didn't even mention it.

I retreated to my room and tried to occupy my mind with thoughts about Edward and the weekend in Los Angeles, but nothing could stop me from breaking into tears every few hours. I was happy to fall asleep, but I woke up in the middle of the night because I thought I heard a baby's cry. I listened hard, but it was very quiet. Could I have wanted so much to hear Adan Jr.'s voice that I imagined it, or could I somehow have heard him, even this far away?

I got out of bed, put on my robe and my slippers, and tiptoed out, down the hallway to the stairs. The house was always kept dimly lit. I stood at the foot of the stairway, listening hard. I did hear a baby's cry. I wasn't imagining it. Slowly, I climbed the stairs and then paused at the top. It was just as dimly lit up there. I listened again. Now I was positive I heard the baby crying. Why wasn't Mrs. Newell attending to him? I inched my way along the shadowy hallway wall and saw that the door to Adan's room was open. It was as dark in there as it was in the hallway.

Of course, I expected Mrs. Newell to leap out at me at any moment, but I continued to the room. When I looked inside, I froze. Sitting beside the crib, Señor Bovio, in his robe and slippers, had his head in his hands and was sobbing softly. Adan Jr. moved his arms and cried. Just as I started into the room, Mrs. Newell appeared, coming from the bathroom. She was in a nightgown, but there was something very different about her. She looked as if she were in a daze until she felt my presence and turned sharply to look at me.

"What's wrong?" I asked. "Has something happened to my baby?"

"It's none of your business," she said, and closed the door in my face.

All I could do was stand there, terrified, my whole body shaking. Adan Jr.'s crying stopped, and it was silent, so silent I could hear the thumping of my own panic-stricken heart.

"Please, let me see him!" I cried, and knocked on the door. I might have been there for minutes, I wasn't sure, but suddenly the door opened, and Mrs. Newell, now back in her uniform, stepped out.

I backed away.

She closed the door behind her.

"What is it? Why is Señor Bovio crying? Why was Adan Jr. crying so hard?"

"How dare you pound on this door like that?"

"I wasn't pounding. What is happening?"

"This sneaking around and violating of my rules will end here and now," she said instead of replying.

"I won't leave here until I find out what's going on. I want to speak with Señor Bovio. *Señor!*" I called. "Please!"

She shook her head calmly when he didn't come to the door.

"Yelling like that won't do you any good now. You might as well pack your things tonight. I assure you, you'll be leaving tomorrow."

"I won't. I won't leave my baby. You have no right to tell me what to do."

"No, it is you who have no rights anymore, Delia, especially when it concerns the baby. Have you forgotten? You signed them away. Señor Bovio will have to choose between you and me, and whom do you think he will choose, Delia?"

"I don't know what you're doing, but I know you're taking advantage of his sorrow. You're a sick woman," I said, gathering my courage.

"Am I? Who's been in trouble with the law? Who nearly lost her baby because of drugs? Who signed away her baby for money? Whom will people be more inclined to believe, you or me?"

"I won't—"

"Won't what? Please stop wasting my time. It's very late. Go to sleep. Enjoy your last night here. There's a motel I can recommend, by the way. It caters to illegal immigrants. You'll be right at home. Good night," she said. She turned and went back into Adan's room.

I heard the door being locked. I debated whether to pound on it again and again until Señor Bovio came to his senses, but I decided not to make a scene that could disturb Adan Jr. and give her more ammunition to shoot at me.

I've got to get help now, I thought. I've got to get her away from my baby. Somehow, I've got to make Señor Bovio see what is happening and why it is wrong for him as much as for Adan Jr.

I had no idea how I would do it, but I knew this was my sole purpose for living now.

I returned to my room to pray and call on the spirit of *mi abuela* Anabela to return to me and help me.

"Give me the strength; give me the wisdom," I begged.

I closed my eyes, but I slept for only minutes on and off. I was exhausted when the morning light shattered the darkness and pulled the stars back into the sky. Somehow, however, I reached down deep and gathered the energy I needed to rise and dress and go face the enemy.

I knew that the enemy wasn't simply Mrs. Newell or *mi tía* Isabela or *mi prima* Sophia.

It wasn't simply the *ojo malvado,* either.

The enemy was my own fear, my own weakness.

There was so much first to defeat in myself before I could defeat the rest.

But I would do it. On the graves of my family, on the memories of my parents whom I cherished, on the very essence of my own soul, I pledged and swore that I would save the baby I had nearly lost once. I would win back the respect of my ancestors.

And in doing so, I would save all those I loved.

13

Fani

Señor Bovio was already at the table dressed for work. He had finished eating his breakfast and was simply sitting there, staring down, not even reading his paper. I stood there for a few moments, waiting for him to realize that I had entered the dining room, but he didn't look up.

"*Señor,*" I said.

He raised his gaze from the table and turned slowly to me. For a moment, he looked as if he had completely forgotten who I was. Then he blinked, and his expression changed to a look of sternness, anger.

"Your car is outside, all registered and insured," he said.

"My car?"

"It's the last part of our agreement, isn't it? It was delivered last night after dinner, a brand-new Jaguar. Now, you must pack your things and go."

"Go where?"

"I have sent your application in. You'll start nursing school next semester. Here is the name and address of the man I have employed to set you up in your apartment near the school," he said. "Take it!" he shouted when I didn't move.

His loud voice made me jump. I reached for the slip of paper but continued to shake my head.

"*Señor,* I don't under—"

"You can let Fani know she doesn't have to send a car for you. I'm sure she'll be happy to help you settle yourself, too. She likes doing things like that."

"But *señor,* please listen to me. Last night, I went upstairs—"

"No," he said. "Don't bother arguing. Mrs. Newell is very adamant about it. You've disturbed her too much, and I cannot lose her right now. Adan needs her. I need her."

"You need her? What is she doing to you, *señor*? Please listen to me."

"Good-bye," he said. "There is no more discussion to be had."

He rose and started out.

"Adan would hate you for this!" I cried. He stopped in the doorway but didn't turn for a moment. "He would, *señor.* I know he would."

"No, Delia," he said, turning back to face me. "You do not understand. I hear his voice in this house."

He looked at the ceiling as if he could hear him that very moment. Then he smiled at me.

"This is all for the best now. Go live your life, and make the best of yourself," he said, and walked out.

I felt myself falling into a panic. Once I left this

compound, I would need a small army to get me back in to see my own baby. But what could I do about it now? I had signed the papers, and he had delivered on all his promises. For a few moments, I actually turned in a circle. I wanted to go back upstairs to see Adan Jr. before I left the *hacienda*. I was sure I wouldn't be permitted to do so. Mrs. Newell would stop me. Teresa, who had overheard the discussion, looked at me with so much pity in her eyes I had to turn away. I looked at the front door, having the urge to run out and scream, and finally just walked back to my room to get my things together. I found two suitcases in my room and imagined Mrs. Newell had told one of the maids to bring them.

I was trembling so badly as I packed that I thought I would faint. Where would I go now? Certainly not back to *mi tía* Isabela's *hacienda*. With my suitcases in hand, I stood dumbfounded in my room. I had such an empty feeling deep in my stomach when I thought about walking out that door and leaving my baby behind in this mad turmoil, but what choice did I have? I had been stupid to think I could play along and find a solution. Tía Isabela was right. I was out of my league.

Unable to think of anything or anyone else, I called Fani and got her on her cell phone as she was going between classes. I don't know how she understood what I was saying. I was crying so hard.

"Look, I don't have much time, Delia. This is all fine. I'll let Edward know you're coming. Take down my address. It's easy to find it," she said. "And I will help you get settled. Don't forget to bring the information my cousin gave you. Here's how you get here."

I fumbled with a pen and scribbled down the directions to her apartment in Los Angeles. She wisely made me repeat it twice. Despite how easy she made it seem, it still sounded confusing to me. I didn't know how I was holding myself together.

"I don't know what I'm doing. I can't think," I told her.

"Calm down, Delia. You'll get into an accident or something, and that won't help anyone. Don't worry. If you get lost, call. This is going to be so much fun for you. Stop crying. Relax. I'll help you with everything. Everything will look different tomorrow. You'll see. You'll soon be enjoying your money just like I do," she predicted, laughed, and hung up.

No one was waiting to say good-bye to me when I walked out carrying my suitcases. I was sure that all of the employees, including Teresa, were afraid of getting on Señor Bovio's wrong side. How ironic this was when I thought about the way I had been greeted and viewed when I had first arrived here. I was like a goddess who had been brought back to earth, statues of her smashed.

I stood near the foot of the stairs and looked up, half expecting to see Mrs. Newell glaring down at me with satisfaction. I went to the doorway, paused for a moment to say a little prayer for Adan Jr., and stepped outside. I hadn't even wondered about the car, but there it was, a brand-new silver Jaguar sedan.

I put my suitcases into the trunk and stood looking up at the *hacienda,* imagining Adan Jr. lying with his eyes open, expecting me to return. The images put a heavy weight on my chest. I took deep breaths to keep myself from collapsing. Then I got into the car and started the engine. I was moving like someone in a trance, going through the necessary motions.

The guard stepped out when I reached the gate. He was the one who had been there when Edward had tried to come see me. He stepped closer when I stopped. He looked into the car closely. *Mi dios,* I thought. He was checking to be sure I had not kidnapped my own baby. I wondered if Señor Bovio had given him those orders.

Satisfied, he stepped back and opened the gate for me. I drove out slowly and turned to the left, vaguely remembering the directions that would take me to the freeway and into Los Angeles. I must get to see Edward, I thought. He'll know what I should do. Edward. That thought filled me with some new hope and helped me to relax.

As I approached the boundary of Señor Bovio's estate, I was able to see the stable and the corral. Amigo was standing in the corral looking my way. He was nodding his head and pawing the ground as if he wanted to come charging after me.

"I'll be back," I promised him. "I'll be back."

He disappeared from my sight when I made another turn, and not long after, I was well on my way to Los Angeles. Driving actually calmed me down. Fani had given me very simple directions to follow, and a little more than two hours later, I was parking in front of her apartment building in downtown Los Angeles. I got out my suitcases and entered the lobby, where a doorman greeted me.

"I'm here to visit Estefani Cordova," I said.

"Delia Yebarra?"

"Yes."

"She's expecting you. Take the elevator to the third floor. It's apartment three C," he said. "You need help with your suitcases?"

"No, I'm fine, thank you." I wanted to add that there wasn't much in either of them.

He came around his desk to push the elevator button for me. When the doors opened, I thanked him again and got in. I couldn't imagine that this was typical student housing. It was clearly an expensive place to live. Everything looking new and clean, with the hallway on the third floor covered in what looked like a brand-new dark-brown carpet. Before I reached the door of 3C, Fani opened it.

"Jake called up to tell me you had arrived," she said, holding out her arms to embrace me. "Told you that you would find it easily."

"*Gracias,* Fani."

She held me out at arm's length and smiled. "Don't look so frightened. You're away from Nurse Diablo, aren't you?"

"But I'm away from my baby, too," I said.

"Don't worry. You'll get to see him plenty, I'm sure. Come on in. We'll get you settled in the second bedroom. Edward is coming over in about an hour."

I paused to look around. It was a large, beautifully decorated apartment.

"Do other students live like this?"

"No, stupid. We own this apartment. Daddy bought it when I decided to go to USC. Don't worry. No one from my family comes to use it. This way," she said, and led me down a short hallway to a very pretty bedroom with a king-size bed, new light-pink carpeting, and white velvet drapes.

"There's no view to speak of," she said. "This is the city, and we're not high enough, but I'm not complaining."

"No. I would not complain."

"Here's your bathroom. I've stocked it with everything you need." She turned on the bathroom lights. It was marble and tile, with a large shower stall and tub. "That tub has power jets. You can bubble up and relax for hours. Good place to bring a boyfriend, too," she added, smiling.

As soon as I started to blush, she added, "You're perfect, Delia. College guys secretly love shy girls. It's their egos. They have to be in charge. *Hombres machos*," she said, laughing. "They're easy to fool, believe me. Most of the boys you'll meet are pretty immature, actually, especially if you compare them to someone like Adan Bovio, but you'll find someone who fits for a while, I'm sure."

"I'm not rushing to find anyone, Fani."

"No, but they'll be rushing you when they set eyes on you, Delia. I'll have to admit, Nurse Diablo did a good job with your recuperation."

"Only to get me on my feet faster so she could get rid of me. You don't know what went on there."

"Oh, I want to know. I want to know everything, of course. Get yourself settled in first," she quickly added, as if she were afraid I might start to tell her the details. "We'll have some wine and cheese and crackers while we're waiting for Edward. Look in the closet. Go on, look."

I looked at her suspiciously and then slid the doors open to see a half-dozen outfits hanging. There were still tags on them.

"This is for me?"

"Of course."

"But when did you get all of this?"

"Oh, now and then," she said cryptically.

"How did you know I would come here?"

"Where else would you go? And even if you hadn't, I would have brought it all to you wherever you were in Los Angeles. I'm pretty sure I have your size, but the tags are on them, so we can exchange anything we have to exchange. Pick out something for tonight, and we'll deal with the rest later. We're close to the same shoe size," she said, nodding at the rack of shoes to match the outfits.

I was still amazed. Despite what she had just said and what she had done, she had sounded surprised that I was coming when I had called. I told her so.

"I didn't think you would be leaving the Bovio *hacienda* this soon. You have lots of time before the nursing-school semester begins."

"I didn't think I'd leave, either. As I told you, he threw me out, but—"

"Get refreshed. Pick out something to wear," she insisted. "Then we'll talk more about it."

I looked at the clothes again.

"You spent a lot of money."

"So what? What's it for? My father is feeling so guilty about what's going on between him and my mother and what it supposedly is doing to me that he rains dollars down in torrents if I just make a small suggestion. He's paving his way to forgiveness." She laughed.

"It doesn't really bother you?"

"I don't think about it long enough for it to bother

me. I'm not going to get depressed and sick over my parents. You have to be the same. We've got to think of ourselves, Delia. You have to learn how to spell 'ME' in capital letters all the time. By the time I'm finished with you, I'll have a smile so deeply planted in your face people will think you're the Joker's sister."

"Who?"

"From *Batman.* The Joker? Forget about it," she said when I didn't register understanding. "You'll get the point eventually. Freshen up. We've got some living to catch up with, or you do, I should say. I've been having quite a good time."

"And school?"

"A minor inconvenience," she said, laughing again. "Oh, it's so good to see you here, Delia. Look how far you've come from that first day you entered the private school and hovered in the shadows your cousin Sophia and her friends cast over you like a fishnet. You're a woman, and she's still a spoiled brat."

"I know nothing about her."

"What's to know? Supposedly, your aunt is working on getting her into another school. I don't know what for except to get her out of the house. She happens to be in L.A. now, too, you know. She's hanging out with her friend Trudy Taylor, who goes to a community college here."

"Has Edward seen her?"

"I don't know. Ask him when he comes, if you want."

"What is he doing?"

"I don't think he knows yet himself. He's living in some crummy hotel. I don't know why. Maybe he's punishing himself. I don't know that much more about him and what he's been doing than you do, Delia."

"You know how terrible things became for him after we met at your house. *Mi tía* Isabela was very angry and made all sorts of threats."

"Right, and it wasn't long after that when he left college and went wherever, so she has no one to blame but herself. Go freshen up," she said, and left me.

I stood looking around. The room was very nice, and it was very kind of her to buy me all of these clothes and things, but I couldn't help asking myself, *What am I doing here? I belong with my baby.*

I heard Fani put on some music. The phone rang. She was laughing loudly. It would be difficult to be depressed here, I thought. Maybe that was a good thing. Nevertheless, without much enthusiasm, I unpacked my basic things and put them in the dresser drawers. Then I went into the bathroom to shower and fix my hair so I would at least look alive when Edward arrived. I was very nervous about seeing him, afraid he would not be as friendly or care as much about me as he once had. Perhaps he blamed me somehow for his new trouble.

I looked for the most conservative outfit to wear from among the clothes Fani had bought for me, but everything was more her style than mine. I had never worn skirts so short, I thought as I tried them on and looked at myself in the full-length mirror on the wall beside the closet. What would Edward think of me? But I didn't want to insult Fani, either. I couldn't decide what to do.

There was a black satin minidress with boots to match, a sequined T-shirt dress I couldn't imagine myself ever wearing, a purple silk halter dress that was cut so low I felt half naked, and a petrol silk layered minidress. Nothing went more than an inch or two below my knees. One orange and black outfit looked as if it came from a cheerleader's costume. She had bought me a pair of designer jeans and a strapless gray tube top with a jeweled black centerpiece. Both were very tight. I could imagine someone saying they were painted on me. I was about to take these off, too, when Fani came in.

"Perfect choice!" she cried. "I was hoping you'd wear that. How about me coming up with the right size, too? I've got an eye for fashion."

"It's too tight, Fani."

"Nonsense. That's exactly the frame of mind you have to get yourself out of, Delia. You're free now, really free. Look at yourself," she ordered, and turned me around to gaze at myself in the mirror. "You're a very sexy-looking chick. I think I might even be a little jealous."

"Jealous of me? You wouldn't trade places for even a second if you had to live my life," I told her.

She shrugged. "Yesterday doesn't matter. Only tomorrow. C'mon," she said. "Let's do what we used to do, sip wine and talk."

She took my hand and led me out of the bedroom to the living room. She poured me a glass of wine and sat on the sofa. There was a plate of cheese and crackers on the table.

"Okay, now tell me all of it. Ray actually threw you out?"

"*Sí.*"

"I didn't understand what you were babbling about."

"Last night, when I went to Adan Jr.'s room, I found

Señor Bovio crying very hard by the crib. Mrs. Newell was there just letting him cry and cry. I thought there was something wrong with my baby, but she wouldn't let me see him."

"Did you ask Ray to let you see him?"

"She shut the door in my face. I was so shocked that I couldn't speak for a few moments. Then I cried for Señor Bovio and pounded on the door. She came out and told me I would be thrown out of the house. You should have seen how evil she looked, how happy."

Fani shrugged and sipped her wine. "She won't be there forever."

"It was very strange, Fani. Señor Bovio was sitting by the crib crying so hard."

"That's not strange, Delia. You didn't know him and Adan that long. They were more like brothers than father and son. Sometimes I thought Ray believed Adan was literally part of his body, especially after his wife was killed. At the funeral, they were never more than an inch apart, and they held each other so long at the gravesite that people were bawling openly. I thought my chest would explode. I've never seen grown men that devastated. You fell into the middle of all that and were barely there long enough to . . . to get pregnant!"

"I thought he was in there alone, but when I started to enter, she appeared in her nightgown. I think she was upset about my discovering her there while Señor Bovio was crying so hard. It's not right," I said, shaking my head. "Something is very, very wrong. She's taking advantage of your cousin's grief. Señor Bovio's maid Teresa told me some stories about her. There was a couple who fired her because of the way she behaved. Do you know she acts as if she's the one who's pregnant, following the same diet?"

"You're getting yourself all worked up, Delia."

"How can I not? I'm no longer there to stand in her way," I cried, the tears coming into my eyes.

"Great," she said, grimacing angrily. "Dwell on it night and day. You'll get yourself sick and be utterly worthless to your son and to everyone else, including me."

"I'm worthless to him now," I said.

She sipped her wine. She remained angry for a moment longer and then suddenly smiled, as if she could turn her emotions on and off like a faucet.

"Okay. First, we'll get you settled in, get you into some sort of a life so you can get yourself mentally stronger. Until you start at your own school, I'll make you part of mine. You will go to everything I go to here. Then, when you're stronger, you and I will pay my father a visit and ask him to look into things for you, check up on Ray and the nurse and see about your baby."

"Really? You would go to your father?"

"Why not? He'd do anything I ask him to do, especially now."

"*Gracias,* Fani."

"*De nada,*" she said. "It's great being able to speak in Spanish, too. Most of the boys we'll meet can barely speak English. Whenever we want to talk about them in front of them, we'll speak Spanish."

I had to laugh. It felt good to let myself go, even for a split second or two.

"That's better," she said.

The phone rang.

"That's Jake telling me I have a visitor, I bet, and we know who that could be," she added, winking.

My heart began to thump. She picked up the phone and nodded at me.

"He's coming right up. I've decided to let you two talk in private. I have to run out to do an errand, anyway," she said. I didn't believe her, but I did want to be alone with Edward.

We heard the door buzzer.

I stood up.

She opened the door, and Edward looked in at us. He was in a sea-blue short-sleeve shirt and jeans and looked much thinner to me. His hair was longer and not nearly as neatly trimmed as he always had kept it. Of course, he still wore his eye patch.

"Edward the First!" Fani cried, and hugged him. He didn't hug her back. He continued to stare past her at me. "Well, I can see you're happy to see me," she said.

He looked at her. "Hello, Fani."

"Well, I'm not going to stay here and be ignored," she said. "I have something to do."

"Some boy's heart to break?" Edward said.

She laughed. "How did you know? I'll be back in an hour or so." She grabbed a light-pink jacket with a white fur collar off the rack at the door. "There's wine, cheese, and crackers or something stronger in the cabinet, if you want. Have fun, you guys," she added, and walked out.

Edward stood there looking at me. "You look good, Delia."

"I don't feel good, Edward."

He nodded, concerned. "Fani told me about all the complications with your pregnancy. I'm sorry about that."

"Did she tell you that they insist I had drugs in me and that was what caused my near-miscarriage?"

He shook his head. "I'm sure they made it up."

"Señor Bovio said there was proof from the hospital's lab tests."

"When you are as powerful and as rich as Ray Bovio is, you can get whatever proof you want from anywhere you want," he said.

I looked down, nodding, and finally he came to me to hold me.

"Poor Delia. What a big disaster coming to America and your American relatives have been for you." He kissed my forehead, and then we both sat on the sofa.

"Where have you been, Edward? I know you left school. When I saw you at Fani's home, you seemed okay. You told me you were thinking of law school. What changed?"

"I wasn't as over Jesse as I thought I was, but let's not talk about me just yet. Tell me what's been happening at the Bovio estate."

I described how Mrs. Newell had treated me during my pregnancy and the emergency that had led to Adan Jr.'s premature birth. He listened quietly, thoughtfully, and sipped some wine. I couldn't help but start to cry when I described my baby and how little I had seen of him.

"First," Edward began, "if she is such a good maternity nurse, how come she didn't see you were having trouble?"

"I didn't know myself until it was too late."

"You're not a nurse, not yet, and this was your first pregnancy. Second, you know I didn't give you any drugs. Did Fani?"

"No, Edward. And I've read about these drugs. I had none of those symptoms. At least, none so strong I'd think anything of them."

He thought a moment. "Something is very wrong here. Tell me again about this bargain you made with Señor Bovio."

I described all of the arrangements. He asked to see the documents that listed the money I was given. I watched him study everything. Just having him take interest in me and being near him reassured me.

"Yes, he's apparently given you quite a lot of money, Delia. It's all in order. And this paper you signed giving him custody has been recorded in family court. I'm sure Ray used his influence to get it all moving faster than it normally would. It's official."

"I did not want to give up my baby, Edward."

He nodded. "I have a friend whose father is an influential attorney here in Los Angeles. I'll discuss it with him."

"You will?"

He folded it all and put it back into the envelope. "I'll try to see him tomorrow."

"*Gracias.* Are you returning to school, Edward?"

"Probably."

"I'm sorry about you and Jesse. I know how close you two were."

"It's not uncommon for people who are close to grow apart when they move on, go to college or work or something. I just took it a little harder than he did. Maybe a lot harder," he admitted.

"Where have you been?"

"I wanted to be alone, travel, discover more about myself and in the process make my mother feel bad," he added with a smile. "She had her lawyer make some moves on me after I had disobeyed her and seen you. At the time, I didn't care, but I've come back, and now I have my own lawyer. My father did some things for Sophia and me that she cannot change, and I think she's finally realized it."

"What about Sophia?"

"I saw her the day before yesterday. She's worse than ever, a time bomb waiting to explode. She's into everything, drugs, sex, and rock and roll," he added. "My mother can't do much about that, either. Sophia turned eighteen last month. How long are you going to stay with Fani?"

"Until I get my own apartment. Señor Bovio gave me this," I said, showing him the information.

"Rental broker. He's lined up some places near your school. The nursing school isn't far from here. Maybe we'll get an apartment together," he said.

"Really?"

"You'd like that?"

"Oh, very much, Edward."

"I'll take care of this," he said. "Don't depend too much on Fani. She likes to toy with people."

"I know."

"I'll move as quickly as I can on everything."

"*Gracias,* Edward."

He took another sip of wine. "What about your boyfriend, Ignacio?" he asked.

I described my visit at the prison and Señor Bovio's failure to deliver on the promise he had made.

"Can't blame Ignacio for being bitter, and I'm sure that place isn't exactly a walk on the beach. Sorry about all that, Delia."

"I should have told you everything."

"Water under the bridge now. Let's just think about the future." He finished his wine and stood.

"What will I do if your friend's father says I can do nothing now about my baby, Edward?"

"Let's wait to see before we get too depressed about it, Delia. There might be a good case for proving you were coerced into this."

"But what if there's not, Edward? What could I do then?"

He shrugged. "The question is not what could you do, but what wouldn't you do, Delia. Is there anything you wouldn't do?"

"Nothing, *nada.*"

He nodded and started for the door. I followed him. He turned back to me at the door.

"Would you return to Mexico? You could live very well with the money you have."

"You mean, with Adan Jr.?"

"Yes."

"I would."

He thought a moment. "Well, maybe that will come to be someday," Edward said. He leaned over to kiss my cheek and waved the slip of paper with the broker's information. "I'll get right on this and see about finding a place as soon as possible. I don't like you being under Fani's influence too long."

"And the lawyer?"

"I'll speak to him in the morning. Don't worry, Delia. Things will change for the better."

"I pray so, Edward."

"Pray for both of us," he added. "I'll call you later."

I stood in the doorway as he walked down the hall to the elevator.

"Wash that solemn look from your face, Delia Yebarra. Remember what you told me your mother told you," he said. "*La esperanza enciende mañana.*" Hope lights tomorrow.

"*Sí*, Edward. I remember."

He pointed both thumbs up and went into the elevator.

And my heart felt as if it had returned.

14

Blind Date

"**W**here's Mr. Wonderful?" Fani asked as she came into her apartment and saw that Edward was no longer there.

"He went to look into some things for me," I said.

"Well, is he coming back?"

"I don't know."

"Is he taking us to dinner or not?"

"He didn't mention it."

"I thought he said he was. Where did he go? What's he doing for you?" she asked.

"He is going to see about my apartment. I gave him the information Señor Bovio gave me."

"I told you I would do that."

"I know, but . . ."

"But what?"

"He and I might room together," I said, and her eyes nearly exploded.

"Edward wants to take an apartment with you? Interesting. Did you get any more out of him than I did? Where did he go? Where has he been all this time? What did he do?"

"He didn't say where he went, exactly, Fani, but I think he did a lot of thinking about himself, and he's going to be all right now. I'm sure if he wants to take an apartment with me, he wants to return to school."

She moved her lips around as if she were rinsing her mouth with something as she thought.

"Okay, forget about him for now," she said, moving to the phone. "I have a blind date on the hook for you, a friend of a guy I've been tormenting. This guy's father owns a chain of movie theaters. We'll go out with them tonight. It's a big night around here."

"A date tonight? But I just arrived, Fani, and I'm—"

"Don't say something stupid like you're too tired or anything, Delia. You're here now, where everything's going to be different. There's no one laying down any rules on you, no restrictions. We're going to have fun," she declared with the same sort of authority Señor Bovio had when he was carving his words in cement.

She held up her hand before I could respond, went to the phone, tapped out a number, and smiled at me.

"Hello, Larry," she sang. "Did you talk to Cliff about tonight? Good. Come get us in . . ." She looked at her watch. "An hour, and prepare to spend a lot of money on us." She laughed and hung up. "He's been trying to get me to go out with him for weeks. I could practically hear him panting through the phone. You don't have to change or anything. I like you in that, but now I'm going to have to pick out something sexier for me. C'mon. We'll talk in my bedroom."

I felt like a balloon on a string and followed her.

"So," she said, pulling off her blouse and undoing her jeans, which I thought were as tight as mine. "What else did King Edward have to say?"

"He wanted to know how I was and what had happened at Señor Bovio's *hacienda*. He didn't believe they had found any trace of any drugs in me at the hospital," I said.

She picked out another pair of pants with sequins running down the sides and a pullover with a deep V neck. She was so concerned about her clothes I didn't think she had heard anything I had said. Then she turned.

"How's this?"

"You always look nice, Fani."

"Very diplomatic," she said, and laughed. "What were you saying?"

"Edward didn't believe they had found traces of drugs in my blood."

"So?"

"He felt very sorry for me. He wants to help me with Señor Bovio."

"He shouldn't keep you thinking about all this. That doesn't help right now. He just loves wallowing in misery. He's become such a drag to be around. Actually, now that I think about it, I'm glad he's not hanging with us on your first night here. You should have seen him when Jesse started with someone else. He was all doom and gloom. It was like being with an undertaker burying smiles and laughter daily, even after I arranged for you two to meet. Nothing helped."

"I'm sure he was in emotional pain. They were very close, Fani."

"Very close. I can tell you this," she said, brushing out her hair. "I'll never let anyone get me down like that. If I'm not good enough for him, he's definitely not good enough for me."

She turned to me and shook her head.

"He should be a good example for you, an example of how you can drag yourself down so far nothing can help. You've got to relax, Delia. I told you I'll speak to my father for you. That will do tons more than anything Edward does. Ray will come to his senses after a while. He's just going through his mourning period, and for now, the baby is a breath of fresh air. Let him have it for a while. You know the baby will get the best possible care. And anyway, you had better think hard about this. If you get the baby back, you'll have to hire someone to help, won't you? It's the same thing. Most of the time, someone else will be with him. I mean, you still want to become a nurse or something, I imagine. You can't bring your baby with you to class."

"*Sí,* I do want to be a nurse, more than ever. I am very interested in medicine and helping people. While I was at Señor Bovio's, I read as much as I could. I even read about this drug they accused me of taking. It can be very dangerous."

"So's too much milk," Fani said, laughing.

"But I want my baby to be with me, too," I said. "He belongs with me. He should be with his mother, not some stranger."

"Oh, brother. Okay, okay. I promise. I won't wait. In fact, first chance I get, I'll speak to my father tomorrow. Does that make you happy?"

"*Sí,* it does. *Gracias,* Fani."

"Good. Let's not talk about any of that for a while. Let's concentrate on having a good time."

She started on her makeup.

"You should try this lip gloss. Here," she offered. "Go on, take it, Delia. You're not going to turn into a pumpkin or something. It's not a sin to look attractive and sexy, either. In fact," she said, "it's a sin not to."

"Where will these boys take us?" I asked, putting on the lipstick.

"Beverly Hills. There's this very expensive restaurant I have wanted to go to. We'll eat and then go dancing and have some fun."

"Dancing, too? I hope I don't fall asleep."

"You won't. I'll give you something to help you stay awake if you need it," she said.

"A drug?"

"A boost. Don't be such a . . . such an Edward!" she cried.

I thought a moment. "When I told you what Señor Bovio said you had said, you told me you couldn't be sure Edward hadn't given me something."

"That was then. This is now. Believe me. He's a changed man, Delia. Fun to him now is reading the obituaries. In fact, now that I think about it, I'm not so sure you should jump into rooming with him. You could stay here with me as long as you want. You probably don't even need your own apartment. There's plenty of room here."

"*Gracias,* but I don't want to insult him."

"Insult him? What about insulting me?" she muttered. "All right. Forget about it for now. Fun. That's the only order we have."

When she was satisfied with how she and I looked, we sat in the living room and waited for our dates. She saw that I was very nervous. I hadn't gone on what could be called a date since the day Adan was killed.

I told her, and she said it was like falling off a bike.

"You get up as soon as possible and start riding again, or you won't ever. You're taking it all too seriously."

She continued, "Now, let me give you some advice on how to behave with a college boy."

"How to behave with a college boy?"

She laughed. "It sounds like a college subject, I know. Actually, I can teach a class in the subject."

"Why does any girl have to learn such a thing?"

"Why? I'll tell you why," she said, looking angry. "Most of the guys around here and everywhere on all college campuses, for that matter, think that every girl is looking for an intense, marry-me relationship. I admit some girls are, but most just want to have a good time. So, my first advice to you is to be as nonchalant as possible. Don't act as if the guy you meet is another Mr. Wonderful so fast. Make him work for your attention, and give him the strong impression that you are an independent person. Once he knows you can take him or leave him, he'll relax, and you'll have a better time. Get it?"

"I think so," I said, and wondered if this was how it was for all young women in America. I certainly had none of these feelings when I was with Adan. She seemed to read my mind.

"That could have been your problem with Adan," she said, pointing at me. "He was a very sensitive, compassionate guy. He probably felt sorry for you and gave you more attention than necessary."

"I don't think that is true, Fani."

"Of course not. You're like every other damsel in distress here. You want to be thought a goddess."

"No, that's not true, either. Besides, you once told me he was head over heels in love with me, didn't you? You told me you even thought of him romantically but gave up when you saw how much he cared for me."

"Whatever," she said. "That game is over. You're in a new game now."

"This is not a game, Fani."

"Sure it is. All of life is," she said. She leaned toward me. "There are winners and losers, period. Be a winner, Delia. It's easy to be a loser, and you're well on your way. Take charge of yourself, and don't depend on poor Edward to come to the rescue here. He has enough trouble figuring out how to rescue himself."

Her words fell like stones on my budding flowers of hope.

"Edward said he would call here later."

"Well, we can't wait around for him, can we? He'll leave a message. All right, Delia?" she insisted.

I nodded.

"And another thing," she said. "You'll find that these boys just love talking about themselves. From minute one, they'll be out to impress you and try to make you feel lucky they're spending any time with you. If you like him well enough and want to be with him, give him the impression that he's right. If you don't, act bored."

"How do you know all this?"

"Natural instincts. I was born girl-smart. My father says I even teased the doctor and wouldn't cry until he caressed my rear more softly."

She expected me to laugh, but my mind had drifted back to Edward and his asking me what would I not do to get my baby back. I thought I would make a deal with the devil, but now I wondered why I had to make deals with anyone. Adan Jr. was my baby, my flesh and blood.

"Hello?" Fani sang at me. "I was trying to be funny, Delia. Oh, brother. Don't sit there with such a dark, brooding look on your face. Brighten up!" she ordered. Just then, the phone rang. "They're here. Good!" she cried, and went to the phone to speak to the doorman. Then she checked her hair and toyed with mine and rattled off her instructions again before we heard the buzzer.

She paused at the door, turned to me, and said, "One more very important thing, Delia. Obviously, these boys don't know anything about you. No one you will meet knows anything about your giving birth recently, so don't dare mention it. That's a turnoff."

Before I could say anything, she opened the door and screamed, "Larry, what took you so long?"

"Long?" a tall, lean, dark-brown-haired boy said. He wore a light-blue sweater and jeans and had a thick gold necklace drooping under his Adam's apple. I was surprised Fani had called him, because he wasn't very good-looking. His nose was thin and long, his mouth was weak, and he had a soft, round chin. He grimaced and looked at his watch. "I got us here as fast as I could." He tapped the face of his watch and held it up. "We're actually a little early, Fani."

"Oh, are you? Well, I guess us girls are just a little overanxious," she teased.

The boy beside Larry stepped forward. He was a good four or five inches shorter, broad in the shoulders, and better-looking, with blue eyes, light-brown hair and high cheekbones. He wore a dark-blue shirt open at the collar and jeans.

"Oh. This is Cliff Alexander," Larry said. "He's a freshman from North Carolina, so don't expect to understand anything he says when he talks."

Cliff elbowed Larry in the ribs rather sharply. Larry rubbed his side and groaned.

"Pleased to meet you," Cliff said, jabbing his hand toward me like a sword.

Fani froze a smile and widened her eyes at me. I took his hand.

"I'm Delia Yebarra," I said.

"Yeah, I heard," Larry quickly chimed in. "From Mexico. *Cómo Estefani*?" he quipped.

"You're such a genuine idiot, Larry," she replied. "That's why I like you."

He laughed, and she and I stepped out of the apartment.

"Larry said Fani told him you just arrived here in Los Angeles and will be going to nursing school. Is that right?" Cliff asked me on the way to the elevator.

"Yes," I said.

"My aunt's a nurse in a VA hospital. She hates it," he added. "She says it's too depressing. Maybe that's not the best career for you."

We stepped into the elevator.

Fani looked at me with an expression that said, *See?*

They think they know everything. They can even run your life after meeting you for a minute.

"Then why does your aunt still do it?" I asked him. I saw Fani liked that quick comeback.

He shrugged. "She's unmarried, almost fifty. What else can she do?"

"She can work in a supermarket packing groceries," Fani said, and Larry laughed.

The door opened. As we walked out of the lobby, Cliff reached for my hand.

"You're too pretty to be a nurse," he said.

Fani was listening and turned on him. "Maybe that will make her patients get better faster. Ever think of that, Clifford?"

"I'm just Cliff," he said.

"No one is just anything," Fani told him, and he actually blanched.

Would I ever be as confident of myself around people as Fani was? Maybe if I was, what had happened to me and my baby wouldn't have happened. Maybe Edward was wrong. Maybe being around Fani was good for me. She reached out and pulled me forward.

"We'll sit in the back," she told the boys as we stepped up to Larry's late-model black Mercedes sedan.

Nobody poor went to college around here, I thought, and then recalled Fani telling me that Larry's father owned a chain of movie theaters.

Contrary to what Fani had said about college boys, Cliff at first was interested enough in me to ask many questions about Mexico instead of talking about himself. I could see from the way Fani was looking at me when I answered that she didn't want me telling too much about my background. She made the point of telling him that I was living with my very rich aunt in Palm Springs, even though I wasn't now, of course. She told him I had inherited a lot of money.

"So, don't even begin to think of her as some poor immigrant," she warned. "She can probably buy and sell all three of us."

I was shocked at her exaggeration, but Cliff looked impressed. Once we arrived at the restaurant and were at our table, he began to talk about himself and his family. It seemed important to him to make sure I understood he was from a wealthy family, too. I could see Fani was growing bored with the conversation.

"Tell me, Clifford," she asked. "Is your nurse aunt your father's or mother's sister?"

"Father's," he said.

"So, why doesn't your moneybags father just give her money so she doesn't have to continue nursing and be depressed?"

"Maybe she doesn't really want to leave nursing," I answered for him. I saw he was embarrassed by her question. "Everyone complains about the work he or she does."

"That's probably it," Cliff said, and smiled at me. "You're very smart, Delia."

"For a Mexican immigrant," Fani added, and he started to protest that he didn't mean anything negative. She broke out in laughter, but I could see he was upset with how she was teasing him in front of me.

Fani winked. Later, in the bathroom, she told me I had him wrapped around my finger already.

"If you want him, he's yours for the night," she said. "He's what is known as smitten. You can bring him back to my place. You have your own bedroom."

"What? No, no," I said. "I don't want that."

"Soon you will, Delia. Don't make like the Virgin Mary. You might not find anyone better than this guy. He's not as bad as most of them, and he's rather good-looking. If you toss him back into the sea, I might just reel him in myself."

"No, Fani. It's too soon for me."

"No, it's not too soon for you; it's too bad for you," she said. "How are you doing? Can you stay awake, or do you want this?" She showed me a pill.

"I'm awake."

"Okay. Let's get you in the groove, then."

We returned to the table. After we had dinner, Fani told Larry to take us dancing at a club she knew downtown. He knew it, too. It was a college hangout. Despite what I had told Fani in the bathroom, I was feeling very tired. I just didn't want her to know it and push that pill at me. When we got to the club, I knew I wasn't very good on the dance floor, but Cliff didn't seem to mind. Actually, he was eyeing other girls and showing off.

Fani moved closer to me to shout over the music. "Pay more attention to him. You're losing him."

"I never had him," I replied, and she laughed.

Suddenly, I stopped dancing. There, not more than ten feet away from me, was my cousin Sophia. *Mi tía* Isabela would be outraged if she saw how she was dressed, I thought. She had on a very low-cut, tight blouse, a bare midriff, and pants tighter than mine, cut so low they left little to the imagination.

"What's wrong?" Cliff asked.

I shook my head and moved closer to Fani.

"Sophia is here," I told her.

"She is? Where?"

I nodded in her direction.

"So she is. I'm not coming here anymore. They let anyone in," she joked, but continued dancing with Larry. She was teasing and tormenting him by drawing very close to him and then pulling away. He was a bad dancer, gangly and awkward, but he was trying very hard to impress her, which only made her laugh more and tease him more.

"I want to sit for a while," I told Cliff. He looked as if he might stay out there and dance by himself, but he reluctantly followed me to the table.

"What's wrong?" he asked. "I thought we were having lots of fun out there."

"It's been a long day for me," I said. "Traveling, moving to a new place . . ."

He nodded but didn't look very sympathetic. His gaze went everywhere else, and occasionally he smiled at some girls who smiled back.

His behavior, the whole scene, brought back memories of Adan and how calm and mature he had been. I was lucky to have been with him. Fani was wrong to tell me he had been with me only because he had felt sorry for me. He had wanted to be with me. We hadn't had to prove anything to each other. We had already known who we were.

I was so lost in my memories that I didn't realize

Sophia and her friend Trudy had approached our table and were standing right beside me.

"Well, look who's here," Sophia said. "Surprise of all surprises."

Cliff looked up at her. "Who's here?" he asked.

"This is my cousin you're with, Mommy Delia."

"Huh?"

I looked up at her.

"How come you're not home with your baby, Cousin Dearest?" she continued.

"What baby?" Cliff asked.

I looked for Fani. She was still very much in Larry's spotlight and hadn't even realized that Cliff and I had left the dance floor.

"I heard you were thrown out of college," I snapped back at Sophia, hoping to get her off the topic quickly.

"It was boring. But let's not talk about me. Is your baby with you?"

"I don't get it," Cliff said, leaning toward me. "What baby?"

"She's got a baby. Didn't she tell you? She was also in a nuthouse for a while."

He shook his head. "Is that true? What does that mean, nuthouse? You have a baby?" Cliff asked. He grimaced as if it were something disgusting.

I felt myself falling into a panic. Fani was still distracted. Sophia's friend Trudy was rattling off stories about me, weaving the story of Ignacio, Adan's death, and my pregnancy together so fast it made Cliff's mind spin. He was sitting back with his mouth open. Sophia was smiling gleefully.

And then suddenly, she broke into hysterical laughter and pointed at me.

"Baby hungry!" she screamed.

I looked down at the tight, strapless gray tube top I was wearing. In my haste to find something to wear, I had forgotten to put some pads in my bra. My nipples were leaking, and it was showing through. Cliff's eyes widened in amused surprise. The scene Sophia was making stopped some dancers near us, who turned to look. It finally attracted Fani, who stopped dancing, too.

Embarrassed, I shot away from the table and rushed toward the ladies' room, Sophia and Trudy's loud laughter trailing behind me. Inside, I got into a stall and stuffed tissue into my bra. I was sobbing so hard that I didn't hear Fani knocking on the stall door.

"What is it? What's going on?" she shouted.

I caught my breath and opened the door, turning to show her.

"Wow. You know, I never saw that happen."

"I have. Many times," I said. "I don't know why I forgot it could."

"Take off the top. I'll wash it out and use the hand dryer."

"I want to go back to your apartment, Fani," I said, wiping the tears from my cheeks. "I don't want to stay here."

"Okay, okay. First things first, Delia. Take it off, and let me fix it. You don't want to walk around out there like this, do you?"

I sucked in my breath and did what she asked.

"You'd better give me that bra, too. It's damp. Just stay in here. I'll fix things. It's actually a very funny situation," she added.

"How is it funny?"

"Clifford Carolina or whatever his name is sitting

there in shock. He looks like he's going to faint. He's telling Larry what happened, and Larry keeps going, 'Huh? Huh?' This is a blind date Clifford will never forget. Give me a few minutes with all this," she added.

I closed the door, put my arms around my naked breasts, and sat on the toilet seat. Moments later, I heard Sophia and Trudy come into the bathroom.

"Doing laundry now, Fani?" Sophia asked. "Where's Mommy Delia?"

"She's in there," I heard Trudy tell her. She came to my stall and tried to open the door.

"Better stay in there, Delia. Everyone's talking about you on the dance floor. You've made a wonderful first impression in Los Angeles," Sophia said. Trudy laughed. "I can't wait to tell Edward about this leaking of information."

"Leave her alone, Sophia," Fani said.

"I thought you weren't going to protect her anymore. I thought after what happened with Adan, you hated her," Sophia snapped back at her. "Why are you with her, anyway?"

"Get out of here, Sophia. What I do and don't do is none of your business," Fani replied.

I heard the hand dryer go off and on.

"Oh, really. Well, Trudy and I might just steal away your boyfriends."

Fani laughed. "Sophia, you're such an idiot. You think we care about them?"

"Yeah? Maybe I don't care about the boys. Maybe I care about something else, something you can give me and better give me."

"Forget it, Sophia," Fani said.

"You owe me. I spied on my mother for you."

"Shut up, Sophia!" Fani shouted.

"I'm not going to shut up," Sophia replied. "Trudy and I would like some X now, and don't say you don't have any."

"You had better get away from me, Sophia," Fani told her.

I stood up in the stall. I felt helpless, half naked, but I wanted to hear more. Why would Fani want Sophia to spy on *mi tía* Isabela? What was this about X?

"We can make quite a scene if we have to," Sophia said. "Think you want all that attention? Think Mommy Dearest in there wants it? Maybe it will get back to your parents, and they won't be so generous anymore."

Fani was quiet. I heard the hand dryer go off. No one spoke. And then I heard the door open and close. Fani knocked on the stall.

"It's all clear. I've fixed this pretty well, too," she said.

I unlocked the stall and looked past her.

"Where is she?"

"They left. Forget about her. Here, put this back on. It's all right for now," she said.

She handed me my bra and top. I got dressed as quickly as I could.

"Why did she say she spied on *mi tía* Isabela for you?"

"That was back when Adan was thinking about asking you out again. I wanted to be sure Isabela wouldn't embarrass him. Forget it."

"That X she mentioned, isn't that the drug they accused me of taking?"

"It's very common around here, especially with younger people. It's as easy to get as popcorn. Only an idiot like Sophia has trouble getting some for herself."

"So, you have this drug? Is that what you offered me earlier? Did you give it to her? I told you I have read about it, what it can do."

"Stop being such a worrywart, Delia. I'm trying to help you have a good time, and all you do is think about the dark side of everything. C'mon."

Other girls came into the bathroom, but none seemed to be paying any attention to me. I looked in the mirror. There was still a faint stain around my breasts, but it wasn't going to be that noticeable when I left the bathroom.

"Are we going back to your apartment now?" I asked.

"It's still early," Fani said. "I don't want your first night here to be a disaster, Delia. You've got to start a new life."

"Why is it so important to you that I start a new life so quickly, Fani?"

"Larry told me about a party," she said instead of replying. "Let's at least stop by for a while. Maybe you'll meet someone nicer than Clifford."

"I'm just so—"

"Just come along," she said, and pulled me toward the door.

I stepped out with her, terrified of facing a crowd of people looking at me and laughing. Instead, all I saw was what I had first seen when we came in, a crowd dancing, laughing, drinking. Fani leaned toward me.

"See? You're already forgotten. No big deal. Let's salvage what we can of the night."

I followed her timidly back toward our table. Larry was there, but Cliff was not.

"Hey," he said. "Everything all right?"

"Peachy keen. Where's Mr. North Carolina?"

"He went off with that girl who made a big scene with Delia."

"Sophia? Well, I'll be," Fani said. "I wonder what she offered him."

Larry smiled lustfully. "You could make the same offer. I'm interested."

"Don't blow your gaskets, Larry. The night is young. Let's go," Fani told him. "We need a change of scenery right away."

"Aye-aye, commander," Larry replied, saluting and standing up quickly.

Fani looked at me and shook her head. "What an idiot," she whispered. "We'll lose him before the evening's over."

"When is it over?" I asked.

"When it's over," she replied.

We followed Larry through the crowd and out the front door.

"Where are we going?" I asked.

"A secret party thrown by one of the fraternities. They do this once in a while, rent a house for a weekend. Since it's out of the area and away from the college, they have more freedom, if you know what I mean."

She started to get into the front seat with Larry.

"We don't want him to think he's just a chauffeur," she whispered, "even though that's all he really is."

"Where is this secret party?" I asked.

"Hollywood Hills," she said. "Here. This will give you the energy you need for the night."

She handed me a pill.

"Is this—"

"Just take it. You don't have to worry about complicating a pregnancy now, and I guarantee you'll have a better time. Go on, take it, Delia," she insisted. "You need something to get you out of your funk. Go on!"

I pretended to put it in my mouth, and then I crushed it between my fingers and let it dribble to the car floor. Minutes later, with the radio blasting, we were winding down city streets and weaving our way to the secret party.

And the ending of an evening that would be the true beginning of a new life.

Only it wouldn't be the new life Fani Cordova had envisioned for me.

15

Overdose

We could actually hear the music, laughter, and loud conversation from the bottom of the hill, where we had to park because there were so many cars on both sides of the road. I couldn't imagine why the people in the homes we walked past hadn't already called the police. Fani laughed when I wondered aloud.

"Who says they haven't?" she told me. "The police are probably chasing parties like this all over the city tonight."

Larry thought that was funny, too. I saw him pull her aside and whisper something. A moment later, she handed him what looked like the pill she had offered me.

"How are you feeling, Delia?" she asked.

"I'm okay."

"Just okay?"

"I'm not tired, if that's what you mean," I said, afraid she would realize I hadn't taken the pill. "I might even dance with Larry," I added, so she wouldn't be suspicious, and she laughed.

"Thatta girl," she said, putting her arm around me. "We're going to light up this city together."

We marched on to the party house.

As we walked up the driveway, I saw people dancing on a side patio. The music was spilling out of every open window, and when I looked up, I saw there were people dancing on a second-story balcony as well. Inside, the furniture had been shoved against the wall. In the center of the living-room floor was a large keg of beer. Apparently, some of the partygoers had jumped into the pool at the rear of the house. They were wearing towels around their waists, and some girls were in their bras with towels serving as skirts.

Everyone was dancing and shouting, waving his or her arms in the air. To me, it looked like bedlam, but Larry was very excited.

"Let's get into this!" he screamed.

"Go ahead. We'll be right behind you," Fani told him.

He shrugged and joined two girls dancing nearby. I thought they looked as if they would dance with any warm body, but he obviously was flattered when they accepted him. He looked our way, smiling and dancing close to the girls to make Fani jealous.

"He's such a goofball," she said. "See what I meant about these college guys? It's like shooting fish in a barrel!" she shouted in my right ear. The music was so loud that no one could hear anyone without shouting.

Why, I wondered, did she think this was any fun? To me, it seemed as if everyone was trying too hard to prove he or she was having a good time. If this was the world she wanted me to embrace now, I couldn't see her ever being happy with me. I would never be able to room with her for a long period of time, I realized.

"You want some beer?" she shouted.

I shook my head.

"Let's get some beer," she insisted, and led me to the keg.

"One kiss per glass," the fat, curly-black-haired boy at the keg told her. He was dripping wet and wearing a towel that looked soaked through.

Fani seized his towel at the waist and threatened to pull it off him.

"Give us the beer if you know what's good for you," she said, raising her other hand with her long fingernails out like tiny knives.

"Take it easy," he said, quickly pouring two cups.

She handed me one, and we wove our way through the mob of wild dancers toward the rear of the house, where the patio doors were thrown open.

What would this house look like in the morning? Who would rent his home to such a crowd? I wondered.

The music piped out was loud enough for the party-goers to dance on the patio down by the pool, where we could see boys throwing one another into the water and some girls screaming and being thrown in as well.

"Wild, huh?" Fani said. She looked at me. "You didn't take the pill, did you?" she asked. Before I could reply, she laughed and shook her head. "You're going to be a challenge, all right, Delia, but one way or another, I'm going to get you to loosen up and have a good time. You were rushed too quickly out of your youth. I'm bringing you back."

She downed her glass of beer, tossed the cup, and joined a group dancing to our right. She beckoned for me to join her, but I wandered off to the right to watch some of the havoc at a safe distance. I found a place to put the cup of beer and then sat on a wide railing that ran along the back patio.

Despite the loud music, the screams and laughter, and the partygoers dancing close by, I was able to close my eyes and focus back on Adan Jr. I thought about his little face when he turned toward me and the way he reacted to my touch. Surely, in his baby mind, he was wondering where that touch was and when would it return. My heart ached thinking about it.

"Delia?" I heard, and turned to see Cliff. He had come up the small grassy hill between the patio and the pool below. He looked out of breath, his hair wild and his shirt wide open. "Thank God I found someone I know," he said. He was gasping for breath.

"What is it?" I asked, standing.

"It's your cousin," he said. "Something's really wrong with her."

"Where is she?"

"We're over there," he said, nodding toward the *casita.* I could see a small group near the small guest house.

"What do you mean, something's really wrong with her?"

"She went into convulsions, and then she passed out," he said quickly. "Her girlfriend is hysterical. I don't know what to do."

I looked for Fani. She was really into her dancing

and had found a boy she appeared to like and was no longer paying any attention to me. There was no way she could hear me shouting. I looked at Cliff. He was in a genuine panic.

"Someone's got to do something, and fast!" he screamed.

"Let's go," I said, and I hurried after him down the hill and toward the *casita*.

As we drew closer, I could see Sophia lying on the patio floor. It was hard to believe, but a few girls and some boys were actually dancing around her as if the whole thing were a big joke. For a moment, I wondered if it could be. Was this all an act to get me there and embarrass me further? How could the others be so nonchalant about someone being unconscious? I saw Trudy off to the side being consoled by another girl.

"Get the hell out of the way!" Cliff shouted at the dancers. They looked at him and parted but continued to dance.

I knelt down beside Sophia and touched her face. She was burning up. I remembered reading about the symptoms of an overdose of Ecstasy and knew what this could mean. Trudy came closer. I looked up at her.

"How much of that Ecstasy did she swallow?" I asked.

"All of it," Trudy said. "She said one pill didn't do anything for her. What's the matter with her?"

"She's going into hyperthermia," I said.

"What's that?"

"Her body temperature is very high. Very high!" I shouted.

Incredibly, none of the other partygoers paid any attention to what I was saying.

I felt for Sophia's pulse.

"Her heartbeat is too fast. I'm sure her blood pressure is way up, too. We've got to get her to a hospital quickly," I said.

"Oh man, oh man," Cliff chanted. "I'm going to get into so much trouble. This isn't the first time I've been around something like this. My parents will kill me."

"Go get Fani," I told him.

"Hey, I can't have anything more to do with this. I don't even know her, really," Cliff said, nodding at Sophia and backing away. "She's your cousin, not mine. You guys take care of it."

Before I could respond, he turned and walked off to disappear in the crowd.

"We've got to get her to the hospital!" I screamed at Trudy. She seemed incapable of moving. "She could die!"

The music seemed to get even louder. The laughter and screams around me put me into more of a panic. Was everyone insane? Couldn't anyone see what was happening? I stood up and reached for the nearest boy, seizing his arm.

"Hey!" he complained.

"Help us get her into a car!" I shouted at him. "She has to go to a hospital."

He looked at me and then down at Sophia. "She's just drunk."

"No. She took drugs. She's dying," I said. The girl beside him shrieked and put her hand over her mouth as if she had to shut herself up.

"Wow," he said. "I ain't going to any hospital with

you," he warned. "I could get thrown out of college over something like this."

"We don't need you to go to the hospital. Just help me get her there. Please, get her feet," I said.

I knelt down and lifted under her arms. Sophia was no lightweight, and I struggled.

I looked to the other boys, who were now watching, hoping one of them would step forward. Finally, as I stumbled back, one of them did. He was stocky, so holding her was no effort for him.

"Where are we going with her?" he asked, looking as if he might drop Sophia if I didn't answer very fast.

"Trudy, show us where your car is. Quickly!" I said.

She nodded and led us around the side of the house. The boy complained when he saw how far down the road Trudy's car was parked.

"I'm going to get a hernia," the boy holding her at the legs said.

I told Trudy to rush ahead and get the rear door opened. When we got there, the boy was very clumsy about putting Sophia into the rear. He bumped her shoulders and her head. I got in from the other side and guided her onto the seat. As soon as she was fully in, the stocky boy closed the door and walked away as if he had simply helped someone load his or her car with groceries. Trudy, still in a panic, was just standing there stupidly.

"Get into the car and drive," I ordered.

"Where?"

"The nearest hospital!" I shouted. How could she be so stupid?

"I don't know where that is. I don't live here, Delia."

"Just drive down the road, and we'll stop at the first place we see people to get directions."

She got in and started the engine. I felt Sophia's face again. Her skin was so hot that it was difficult for me to hold my fingers there. Her pulse was still very, very fast. She's actually going to die in this car, I thought. Despite all she had done to me, the horror of such an event sent cold chills through my body. I sat back and lowered her head to my lap. Trudy drove erratically. She was crying as she was driving.

"Be careful!" I screamed when she made a turn too close to the side of the road and went over the sidewalk. The moment I saw a lit storefront, I shouted, "Park there, and get directions. Quickly!"

She did as I said. I was worried she wouldn't understand the directions well enough to follow them, but when she came out, she said it wasn't far. She simply had to follow this street, and then she would make a right turn on the fifth street. She kept repeating what she had been told, babbling now. The only thing I thought was in our favor was that according to Trudy, Sophia had passed out just before Cliff had come for me. She wasn't unconscious that long.

When we arrived at the hospital, I thought it was better for me to rush into the emergency room for help. I told Trudy to stay in the car with Sophia. A nurse and an emergency-room attendant listened to my quick report, and moments later, two attendants wheeled out a gurney and loaded Sophia onto it. I told Trudy to find a place to park the car, and then I followed them into the emergency room.

Trudy never came in. Later, I realized she hadn't looked for a place to park the car. Instead, she had driven away.

Such were the friends Sophia considered her dearest, I thought, and actually pitied her.

Not long afterward, a policeman came into the waiting room and beckoned to me. My heart began to pound. Sophia had been in the emergency room for almost a half hour. I had given the admittance nurse as much information as I could, including *mi tía* Isabela's name and telephone number, and she had told me to wait in the lobby area.

"I need to speak with you, Miss," the policeman said.

He looked very young, I thought, but he also looked very angry.

"Where is this party you mentioned?"

"I'm not sure," I said. He pulled his head back in disbelief. "I'm not from here, and I don't know the streets. It was up a hill. I was too frantic to pay much attention to anything but getting her here, sir."

He grimaced. "Did you give your cousin the drugs?"

"No, sir," I said, astonished at the question.

"Are you carrying any on you now?"

"I never had any," I said, and rushed out a description of what had happened at the party.

He looked at a clipboard on which I could see some of the information I had given the admittance nurse.

"This is the address where you are now staying?"

"Yes, sir."

"And this is the name of the person who lives there?" he asked, pointing to Fani's name.

"Yes, it is."

"And this is your aunt's address and phone number?"

I nodded. "How is my cousin?"

"The doctor will speak with you as soon as he can. In the meantime, don't leave this area. Any drug overdose is a very serious situation."

"I understand," I said.

He didn't look satisfied. "I'll be back in a while," he said, and left.

When I turned to go back to my seat, I saw the way the other people waiting were looking at me. No one smiled. I lowered my head and sat. At the moment, I was too tired and numb to feel anything, even fear. I wondered if Trudy had returned to the party to tell Fani or if Fani had met Cliff and he had told her. Surely, she was looking for me by now and would seek out anyone who knew me.

Almost another forty minutes went by, and still no one came to speak with me. I went to the admittance desk and asked the nurse there if she knew anything about Sophia. I told her how long I had been waiting.

"When the doctor is able to speak with you, he will," she told me. She looked as angry as the policeman.

Why were they angry at me? I wondered. Did everyone assume I had given Sophia the drugs?

This time, when I returned to my seat, I closed my eyes and leaned back. Despite the lights and the noise around me, I was so exhausted, both physically and emotionally, that I actually fell asleep. I had no idea how much time had passed, but I woke up when I felt myself being nudged and looked up at Tía Isabela.

For a moment, she seemed to loom above me like

some imaginary giant whose head brushed the ceiling. Her eyes rained down rage and disgust. She was dressed in a black pantsuit, with her hair pinned back severely. Although she was wearing her usual ton of makeup, she looked pale.

"Was this meant to be your little revenge?" she asked.

I sat up quickly. "No, no," I said.

"First, you nearly kill your own baby with this stuff, and then, you nearly do the same to Sophia?"

I felt my throat close. Of course, everyone would believe such a thing, I thought. I just kept shaking my head.

"The police are involved now, and this time, I am not going to do anything to save you, and neither is Ray Bovio."

"I did not do anything!" I cried.

"She nearly went into acute renal failure. People, especially young people, have died from this junk. You could be charged with attempted murder."

"I gave her nothing, Tía Isabela. When I heard what was happening to her, I got her girlfriend Trudy to drive her here. I—"

"You knew what would happen to her. You knew what this drug could do."

"No. I did not even know she was at this party. Please, listen—"

"No, you listen. You should have taken my advice and used the money I gave you to return to where you belong. If you had, you would have your baby."

I stared at her, speechless. She was right. I lowered my head, the tears now streaming down my cheeks. I was too tired to fight or to argue.

"You're a bigger disappointment to me than I ever imagined you would be, Delia. There was a time when I thought you would make me proud, when you would achieve some remarkable things for a girl from such a backward, poor place, but all you have done is prove my initial instincts correct. All you have done here is bring pain and misery to anyone who has had the least to do with you. Don't you move. The police will be seeing about you now." She turned and walked away.

I put my hands over my face. I didn't want to look at any of the people nearby who had heard the things Tía Isabela had said to me. Soon afterward, the policeman who had spoken to me returned. He had a man with him who was wearing a dark gray sports jacket and a tie. He looked much older.

"This is Detective Boyton," the policeman said. "He is with narcotics."

"I'd like you to come out to my car to talk, Delia," Detective Boyton said.

"I did not do anything bad," I moaned.

"We're not arresting you for anything yet, Miss Yebarra," Detective Boyton said. "But we do need to talk to you about all this, and this isn't the place for it. Are you resisting my request?" he asked when I made no effort to move.

I was just in a numb state. "No, sir," I said.

They led me out. I looked toward the emergency room and saw Tía Isabela in the hallway speaking with a doctor. She glanced at me and turned her back.

"How long have you been in the States, Delia?" Detective Boyton asked after I was put in the rear of the sedan. He and another detective he introduced as Lieutenant Danbury sat up front.

I told him.

"So, you just arrived in L.A.?"

"Yes, sir. Today."

"And this . . . Estefani Cordova . . . she invited you to stay at her apartment?"

"Yes."

"Okay. Tell us what happened tonight," Lieutenant Danbury said.

I described the events as accurately as I could.

"And this boy's name is Cliff Alexander? He attends USC?"

"Yes."

"Your aunt tells us you had another incident with the drug known as Ecstasy. During your pregnancy?"

"I did not take this drug. I don't know why the hospital said so."

"Uh-huh. So, you don't know how your cousin got this drug tonight?"

I hadn't seen Fani give her anything in the bathroom, so I didn't want to accuse her. She could have gotten it from someone else, perhaps at the wild party.

"No, I did not see anyone give her the drug."

"Okay. For now, we're going to let you return to this address you've given us, Delia. If you intend to leave it, you must call to let us know. Here's my card with the phone number to call," Detective Boyton said. He handed it to me. "We're going to investigate everything you've told us. If you're leaving something out or not telling us the truth, this is the time to speak up. Once we leave you and begin this investigation, you won't have another chance."

"I did nothing wrong," I said, now growing more

angry than afraid. "I tried to help her. If I hadn't gotten her here, she would have died."

"Okay. You can return to the hospital or to this address. We'll possibly be stopping by to see you tomorrow or calling you to come to us. Why you kids fool around with this stuff is a mystery to me," Lieutenant Danbury said. "It's like rolling dice with death."

"I do not fool around with drugs. I am telling you the truth," I said.

"Okay, you can go."

I reached for the door handle, and he added, "You know, your legal status here might come into question. Your own aunt is suggesting that."

I didn't respond.

"There'll be no question about it if you're involved with drugs, Delia," Detective Boyton emphasized.

I was trembling so hard now that I didn't think I had the strength to open the door. Once I was deported, my hope of ever seeing my baby again would probably die. I fumbled with the handle. Lieutenant Danbury got out and opened the door from the outside for me.

"Remember, Delia," he said as I started back toward the emergency room, "if you leave that address, you had better call us."

I nodded and continued walking, even though I couldn't feel my legs under me. It was as if I were floating now, drifting along in a body that had turned into air. Maybe I'm dead, I thought, but when I looked up, my heart began to beat again. Edward was standing in the emergency-room doorway, waiting for me. I rushed to him, and he embraced me.

In a hysterical flood of words, I told him as much as

I could about the evening and what his mother and the police believed.

"Easy," he said. "Take it easy. We'll get it all straightened out."

He led me to his car in the parking lot. When I was inside, I calmed down enough to ask him about Sophia.

"She'll live," he said dryly. "She was close to being in serious trouble, however. My mother should be kissing your feet and not sending the police after you. You really don't know how she got the drugs, then?"

"When I was in the ladies' room, I heard her ask Fani for it, but I didn't see Fani give it to her."

"Well, we need to have a little talk with Fani. She never came here?"

"No. I don't even know if she knows I'm here. She didn't see us leave that party."

"Let's try her cell phone," he said, and called. He was directed to her answering service. He thought a moment and then said he would take me to where he was rooming. "It's not much, but you need some sleep."

"I have to tell the police if I don't go back to Fani's."

I showed him the detective's card. He took it and called to explain who he was and where I would be for now.

"Don't you want to go back to see about Sophia?"

"No. We'll check on her later. It's going to be a while before she's talking, anyway."

We drove to a small hotel where he had a room. He insisted that I take the bed and he would sleep in the cushioned chair. I didn't have the strength to argue about anything. Minutes after my head touched the pillow, I was asleep. When I woke up, I was alone. I saw that it was a little after one o'clock. I went to the bathroom and washed my face, and then I heard him come in. He had gone for some coffee and sweet cakes for me.

"Did you call the hospital?"

"Yes. She's a lot better. My mother is at the Peninsula Hotel in Beverly Hills. She'll probably make use of this trip to go shopping on Rodeo Drive," he said.

"What about Fani?"

"She called this morning, shocked about it all. She claims she spent most of the night looking for you and finally went home with some guy named Larry. She thought you might have gone off with someone named Cliff. She said she didn't know anything about Sophia. No one told her anything at the party. That's her story." He looked at his watch. "We'll see her soon. We have to go to the police station. She's been told to appear, and so have you. We have to be there in an hour."

"Oh, Edward, what will happen to me?"

"If I have anything to say about it, you'll get a medal," he replied. Then he smiled. "Don't worry. I've called my friend's father, Mike Simon. We have an important attorney on it for us. He'll be there. He's been looking into the family-court matter involving your baby as well this morning, so cheer up."

Was it possible to be hopeful after all of this?

"*Muchas gracias,* Edward."

"*De nada,*" he said, and laughed. "Having you to look after has given me a reason to get back to business myself. So, thank you, Delia."

I hadn't thought it would ever be possible to laugh again, but I did, and so did he.

An hour later, we were at the police station. Fani came hurrying over to us the moment we entered.

"What is all this?" she asked. "Did you say something to the police about me? Why was I called down here?"

"She didn't say anything about you, Fani. Take it easy. I have Curtis Simon's father meeting us here. In fact, here he is," he said, turning to greet a short, rotund man with a Santa Claus beard to match.

"Hey, Mr. Simon. Thanks for helping us," Edward said, extending his hand.

"Who's Delia Yebarra?" he asked, looking at Fani and me.

Edward introduced me.

"All right. From here on, no one but me says anything to anyone. We'll make this go away quicker that way, understood?"

"Yes, sir," Edward said.

"What about me?" Fani asked.

"You might want to call your own attorney," Mr. Simon said. "From what I know of this, I can't represent you both."

Fani's forehead creased as she pursed her lips. "What does that mean?"

"Maybe nothing," Mr. Simon said. "I can only advise you to contact your attorney or have your parents do so. Let me go talk to these guys," he added. "Then we'll talk."

He went into the station.

"You'd better tell me what you told these policemen last night," Fani said.

I went through it as best I could.

"Did you give the drugs to my sister?" Edward asked her.

"No," Fani said firmly. "Is that what she's saying?"

"I don't think anyone from the police have spoken with her yet, but will she say that?"

"Who could tell what your sister will say? She had better not implicate me. I know enough about her to get her in bigger trouble."

"I'll bet," Edward said. "Everyone, just relax. Go call an attorney, Fani. Mr. Simon is probably right."

"Where am I supposed to get an attorney?"

"You'd better call your father."

"Damn it," she said. She looked at me. "Why didn't you come to me last night before you rushed off to the hospital? We could have done this without getting the police involved."

"I tried to get your attention, but you were too involved, and then when I saw how bad she was, I thought she belonged in a hospital right away. I asked Cliff to tell you what had happened."

"I never saw him. All I knew was that I couldn't find you."

"The point is, Delia saved her life by moving quickly, I'm sure," Edward said.

Fani pouted a moment and then relaxed her shoulders. "Cliff's in there," she revealed. "I saw him enter the station just before I did. I'm sure he's doing and saying everything he can to save his own rear end."

"Go call your father, Fani," Edward suggested more strongly.

She nodded and looked at me. "I'm just trying to help you adjust to a new life, Delia. I was there for you. You had better be there for me." She walked away.

"She surely gave Sophia the drugs," Edward muttered. "That guy Cliff Alexander might implicate her somehow, and if you said something that confirmed it . . ."

"She's not wrong, Edward. She wanted to help me. She was the only one I could turn to when Señor Bovio threw me out. I can't hurt her. Besides, I really did not see her give Sophia drugs. I can't say I did."

"Girls like Fani don't need someone to hurt them," Edward said. "They do a good enough job hurting themselves."

Before we sat, Mr. Simon came out and asked me to accompany him to a room where Detective Boyton and Lieutenant Danbury were waiting.

"I'll do all the talking," Mr. Simon said. "You speak when I say you speak. Look to me before answering any questions, understand?"

I nodded. The two detectives were at a long table waiting for us. Mr. Simon and I sat across from them.

"Okay, Delia," Lieutenant Danbury began. "Most of what you've told us has checked out."

"So, that's it?" Mr. Simon asked.

Both detectives smiled.

"Not so fast." Lieutenant Danbury looked at his notebook. "Cliff Alexander claims that it wasn't until you had an embarrassing accident at this dance club and went into the bathroom that he saw Sophia Dallas with any pills. She had them after she came out of the bathroom you were in."

"Can he say without doubt that Sophia did not have the pills before she went in?" Mr. Simon asked.

Neither detective responded to him.

"He says she said she got them in the bathroom," Detective Boyton said.

When the detectives spoke, they looked directly at me, as if Mr. Simon weren't there.

Mr. Simon turned to me. "Did you see anyone hand Sophia Dallas any pills, Delia?"

"No, sir."

"Did you speak to or have any contact with Sophia in the bathroom?" he asked.

"No, sir. I was in the stall waiting for my clothes to be dried."

Mr. Simon did not know why, so he raised his eyebrows, but he did not ask the detectives. He turned to them.

"Are you accusing her of selling drugs to Sophia Dallas?"

"You know we're not," Lieutenant Danbury said. "We're trying to find out who did, however."

"So, why don't you ask her outright if she has any definitive information about that?"

"Do you?" Detective Boyton asked me.

I looked at Mr. Simon. He nodded.

"No, sir," I said.

"Not in the bathroom or at the party?" Lieutenant Danbury asked.

"She's answered you," Mr. Simon said.

"How did you get the drugs you used when you were pregnant?" Lieutenant Danbury asked quickly.

Mr. Simon nodded at me.

"I did not get any drugs then. I do not know why the hospital said I took drugs."

"If you're protecting someone, you could be in just as much trouble," Lieutenant Danbury said.

"She knows that," Mr. Simon said. "Anything else?"

"This investigation will continue," Lieutenant Danbury said. He made it sound like a threat.

"Well, we hope so. We can't let this sort of thing go on and on," Mr. Simon said. Although his words should have made the two detectives happy, his tone obviously angered them.

"Okay, that's it for now," Lieutenant Danbury said.

We got up and left the room.

"I hope you were telling the truth in there, Delia," Mr. Simon said before we met Edward.

"I did not see Sophia get drugs, Mr. Simon."

"Okay."

"What happened?" Edward asked, rushing over to us.

"Nothing for now. They don't have anything to implicate Delia on this. Maybe her friend is in trouble, but that's not our problem."

"What about her other matter, Mr. Simon?" Edward asked.

He looked at me and shook his head. "The lab report is authentic, Delia, and from what I've seen of the paperwork, you pretty much have made this custody matter irrevocable."

"What does that mean?" I asked.

"It means I don't think I can do much about it and would only waste your money trying. Your baby will remain with Ray Bovio, his grandfather," Mr. Simon said. "Talk to you later, Edward," he added, and left me feeling as if I had just been on a roller coaster.

"Edward," I began, but he put his finger on my lips.

"Don't despair," he said. "We're not done yet."

I had no idea what he meant, but I followed him out of the police station like someone clinging desperately to the last drops of water in the desert.

16

A New Crossing

Before we did anything else, Edward wanted us to return to the hospital to see how his sister and his mother were doing. Despite the bad feelings between him and his sister, she was still his sister, and no matter what his mother had said and done, Tía Isabela was still his mother.

Back in my Mexican village, Señora Porres, who would make predictions with the authority of a biblical prophet, often said, *"Vale más una gota de sangre que un arroba de amistad."* A drop of blood is worth more than a gallon of friendship. Beware of those who seem to turn against their own brothers and sisters, she would warn. In the end, they'll turn on you instead. Family was too strong. No matter how hard Edward might try, he couldn't deny it, either.

By the time we arrived at the hospital, Sophia had just been moved from intensive care to a private room.

Her vital signs had stabilized. Tía Isabela was on the phone in her room when we arrived. When she saw me with Edward, her eyes widened, but she did not stop talking to whoever was on the phone. Sophia looked smaller in the hospital bed somehow and suddenly very young. I could see in her face that she had been told how close she had come to dying and had been seriously frightened.

Tía Isabela hung up the phone and turned to us. "That was Ray Bovio," she said, looking directly at me. "After this, if he never sees you again, it would be too soon."

"Now, just a minute, Mother. Before you say another word that you will regret," Edward began, holding up his hand, "the police know that Delia had nothing to do with what happened to Sophia. In fact, if there is anyone he should think of avoiding, it might be his cousin Fani Cordova. If you told Ray Bovio anything else—"

"I didn't have to tell him anything," Tía Isabela said. "Once he heard there were drugs involved, he came to his own conclusions."

"Which are deliberately incorrect. By now, you also know that if it weren't for Delia, Sophia might not be alive. Mother, did you manage to get that little detail into the conversation?"

She didn't reply. She just turned away to look out the window.

Edward walked to the bed and looked at Sophia. "I bet you feel like a little idiot now."

She turned away, but Tía Isabela turned back to us.

"If you two have come here to gloat," she started to warn, "you had better just walk out of here and—"

"No, Mother. We don't need to gloat. I'm happy you're going to be okay, Sophia," Edward continued. "When you grow up someday, you can thank your cousin. She remained at the hospital, concerned about you, while your so-called best friend ran off. I don't imagine she's been around today, either, has she?"

Sophia looked at me and then looked away again.

"She doesn't need this now, Edward," Tía Isabela said in a softer tone of voice. "Anyway, she's already heard all of that from me. I think, or at least I hope, this has opened her eyes wider."

"Good. We haven't been much of a family," Edward said, more directly to his mother now, "but whether we like it or not, this is it. We're the only family we have."

Tía Isabela raised her eyebrows with surprise. "Well, I'm glad you realize that," she said.

"I realize it, but that includes Delia," he said. He turned back to Sophia. "The police will be back to see you, Sophia. I hope you will do the right thing and tell them only the truth."

"She will be coming home with me as soon as she is able to do so," Tía Isabela quickly interjected. "We're not going to remain here and deal with any police. She doesn't remember anything. Someone obviously slipped something into her drink. It happens often at these sorts of parties. My lawyer is already handling it."

"Whatever story you come up with is fine, as long as it doesn't implicate Delia," Edward said firmly. "Otherwise, it will open up a whole other can of worms."

Neither Sophia nor Tía Isabela replied. Edward looked satisfied and winked at me.

"All right, Mother, I might not see or call you for a while," he continued. "I just wanted you both to know that we're happy Sophia is going to be all right. Let's go," he said to me, and turned toward the door.

"What do you mean, you might not see us for a while? Where are you going?" Tía Isabela asked.

"We're going to do what we have to do," he replied. "Let's leave it at that."

"I have no idea what that's supposed to mean, Edward."

"It's better you don't," he replied.

I had no idea what he meant, either, but I was afraid to say another word. I nodded at Tía Isabela and at Sophia and quickly followed Edward out of the room. He was walking quickly down the hallway.

"Where are we going?" I asked.

"To get your baby back," he said.

"But you heard what Mr. Simon said. How will we do that?" I asked when we stepped into the elevator.

"You'll tell me," he replied.

"Me?"

"Yes, you, Delia, but I have a few things to arrange first for afterward."

We went from the hospital to a bank and from the bank to a brokerage house, where my recently acquired portfolio was being held. Edward helped me make arrangements to get to my money whenever and wherever I wanted. He thought it wise for me to carry a considerable sum of money as well, so we withdrew nearly four thousand dollars. He said he wanted everything as far away from Señor Bovio's control as possible as quickly as possible. After all of that, we had lunch and talked.

"As you can see from the way my mother gets things done, what's just and right is often forgotten, so don't think anything will change for you in that regard, Delia. What I think should be done is the only thing to do now."

"I'm frightened, Edward," I told him, "and not just for myself. I'm frightened for you as well. The more you have to do with me, the more trouble you get into, especially if we do what you are suggesting."

"You're doing me a favor by letting me help you," he replied. "I haven't done anything I consider worthwhile in my life for some time. In fact, this might be the very first thing."

"Are you really sure we should do this, Edward?"

"Do you want your baby to be with you?"

"*Con todo mi corazón*. With all my heart," I replied.

"Then it's settled," he said, slapping his palm on the table. "Let's go."

Despite his confidence and determination, I couldn't stop the trembling inside me. We drove back to Fani's apartment so I could get my things and my car. Edward thought we should use my car, since it was bigger than his sports car. Fani came to the door as soon as we stepped off the elevator and started down the hallway.

"Where have you been?" she asked. She looked at Edward. "What's going on?"

"Sophia's doing better. Thanks for asking," he replied dryly.

"I know how she's doing. I called the hospital. What are you doing?" she asked me.

"I've got to get my things," I said.

"Why?"

I didn't answer. I hurried into the bedroom and quickly took off the clothes she had bought for me. I changed into my own clothes, closed my suitcases, and came out. She and Edward were still standing near the doorway.

"Thanks for not saying anything that would get me into trouble," she told me. To Edward, she said, "Thanks for advising me to get an attorney, too."

"Then you did give my sister the drugs?" Edward asked, pouncing quickly like a prosecutor in a courtroom.

"I didn't give her anything, Edward. She took what she wanted while I was doing something for Delia in the bathroom. What happened afterward was not my fault, either. I'm not and never have been your sister's keeper."

"We'll discuss all of this some other time," he said, taking my suitcases.

"Are you moving in with him already?" she asked me. "Because I'm not chasing you out."

"What she does now isn't really your business, Fani."

"Oh, really? You're both sick," she said angrily. "You probably do belong together."

"We know we don't belong here with you," he retorted, nodded to me, and started out.

"You're making a mistake, Delia," Fani said.

"I've made so many. One more won't matter," I told her.

"I'm the best friend you could have. The best friend you ever will have!" she shouted after me as soon as I walked out. Edward gazed back at her, and she shut the door.

"I've never trusted Fani," he said. "She lives in another dimension."

When we stepped into the elevator, I told him I couldn't help feeling sorry for Fani because of what was going on between her parents.

"What's going on?" he asked, and I told him what she had confided in me.

"So, she had you believing she was telling you a big family secret, is that it?"

"Yes."

He didn't say any more until we had put my suitcases in the trunk of my car.

"Now, let me tell you something about the Cordovas that's not such a big family secret. Her father has had a mistress for years and years. Everyone knows it. She knows it. She made all that up about his being gay," he said. He looked up at her apartment window. "Maybe not just to get your sympathy. Maybe it was how she could live with it." He shook his head. "This whole world is one big soap opera. Let's get out of here, Delia. While we still can."

He drove, and I sat shivering with my thoughts, feeling like someone who had just come through an icy rainstorm but was not heading toward sunshine. There was quite a bit more thunder and lightning looming ahead. Sunshine was still a distant dream.

We fell into heavy traffic as we started back toward Palm Springs. It was stop-and-go for miles and miles. Finally, Edward decided we should pull off to have some dinner and wait it out.

"We don't want to get there too soon, anyway," he said. "There's no point in rushing."

I was too nervous to have any sort of appetite, but I ate to pass the time. He could see how tense I was and reached across the table to put his hand on mine.

"It's going to be all right, Delia. We can do this. Besides, there is clearly no other way," he stressed.

I smiled. At least, I would pretend to be brave.

Afterward, the traffic did lighten up. We made better time and went directly to his home. Of course, Tía Isabela was still in Los Angeles. He gathered up what he said we would need. He had black clothing for me to wear. I rolled up the bottoms of the pants and tightened the belt around my waist. He decided we should put black shoe polish on our faces.

"After all," he told me, "we're going behind enemy lines."

Later, in the wee hours of the morning, we drove to the Indian Canyons, parked my car where it would be unnoticeable, and began our trek through the canyon, where I had explained we could approach Señor Bovio's estate and enter undetected. As we walked over the desert floor, we heard the coyotes moving and howling in packs just to our right. The stars were so bright in the dry desert atmosphere, the terrain so stark, only sparsely peppered here and there with cactus or brush, that it was truly like walking on the moon.

I couldn't help but be reminded of my flight with Ignacio through the desert into Mexico. The terrain was just as barren but far more dangerous because of bandits and the border patrol. Our walk now was also miles and miles shorter, although it was no walk in the park. Edward estimated it was close to two miles. I thought we could do this to reach the estate, but to come back in flight and with an infant might be significantly more difficult.

It took us almost an hour and a half to reach the point where we could see the Bovio estate ahead of us. The walking was not easy because of the rocks and small hills. We had stopped four times to drink some water and rest. Both of us were keenly aware of the danger we'd face if we disturbed a rattlesnake, too.

And after all, the most difficult part lay ahead. We couldn't afford to be tired or careless. Now that I could see the *hacienda,* I had real doubts that we could succeed. It looked too formidable.

"We won't be able to do this," I said. "I don't know why I even suggested it. I was simply fantasizing, Edward."

"Sure, we will be able to do it. You've got to think positive, Delia. Remember, I once asked you if there was anything you wouldn't do, and you said no."

"I know, but . . ."

"We can do it," Edward insisted. He squeezed my hand gently. "We can."

I took a deep breath and nodded.

"Okay, Edward."

We walked on.

As we approached the eastern boundary of the property, I saw that there was a light on in the small trailer in which Gerry Sommer lived. It was right near the stable. From the way the light and shadows played on the window, we could see that he was watching television. I had told Edward who he was and what duties he performed for Señor Bovio.

"That guy either stays up late or fell asleep in front of his television," Edward whispered.

We moved as quietly as we could, but Amigo either heard or sensed me. I heard him neigh, and then I heard the sound of his hooves against the walls of his stall in the barn. We both froze.

Then a large beam of light fell over us. I gasped and turned to see Gerry Sommer standing there with his large flashlight.

"Delia?" he asked. "Is that you?"

"Yes."

"Who's that with you?"

"My cousin Edward," I said as he drew closer to us.

He paused and stared. "What's with the blackened faces?" Before either of us could reply, he continued. "Teresa told me you were told to leave the house and property," he said, "and leave your baby behind."

"Look," Edward began, "we—"

Gerry Sommer put up his hand before Edward could try to explain anything and turned back to me.

"You walked through the canyon to get here?"

"Yes," I said.

"Sounds like Amigo knows you're here." He nodded and looked toward the *hacienda*. "Well, it's a nice night for a walk."

He turned off his flashlight and started back to his trailer.

"You think he's going to call security?" Edward asked.

"No. Amigo wouldn't let him," I said.

"Who?"

I smiled and shook my head. We walked on toward the *hacienda*. I remembered that the rear door into the pantry was never locked. Locking up the *hacienda* was never a major concern because of the security at the gate and the walls around three-quarters of the property. I hesitated at the door, half hoping it had been locked and we couldn't get into the house.

"We can do this," Edward whispered, seeing my hesitation. "We can."

I took a deep breath and turned the handle. The door was not locked. We slipped in quietly and closed the door softly. I led him through the pantry, through the kitchen, and down the hallway toward the stairway. As usual, there was some dim lighting throughout. We paused when we faced the stairway and listened. The house was very quiet.

Edward looked at me, because I stopped moving. I was frozen with fear.

"Go on, Delia. We can do this," he whispered.

I started for the stairway. We climbed so slowly that it gave me the feeling the stairway was growing longer with every step we took. When we reached the top, we stopped to listen again. I had already explained where Mrs. Newell slept and where Adan Jr. was. Señor Bovio was all the way down the other side of the hallway.

We crossed the hallway and stopped. Mrs. Newell's bedroom door was open, as was Adan Jr.'s. She could be in there with him, I thought. There was only one way to find out. Edward nodded as if he could hear my thoughts and worries, and we started down the hallway with our backs against the wall, sliding, staying as close as we could to any shadows. When we reached Mrs. Newell's door, we paused, and I slowly peered around the jamb. She slept with a night-light. I could see her in her bed, sleeping on her back. I nodded at Edward. He took his position on the other side of her doorway to watch her as I continued a few feet to Adan Jr.'s bedroom.

Then, taking a breath like someone going underwater, I entered the nursery.

My baby was moving but not crying. When I approached the crib and looked down, I saw he had his eyes open. He looked much larger and longer to me. His little arms moved excitedly. Before he could cry out, I reached in and brought him and his blanket out of the crib, cradling him softly in my arms. I knew he was about to cry, so I opened my blouse and quickly brought the nipple of my breast to his lips. While he suckled, I moved quietly out of the room.

Edward glanced at me, looked back into Mrs. Newell's bedroom, and nodded. I crossed quickly, and he followed. The three of us seemingly floated down the stairway. I had to move slower so that Adan Jr. could feed and not be upset by our movements. It was as if he knew he had to be silent. We turned at the bottom of the stairway and quickly moved down the hall back to the kitchen and out the pantry. Neither Edward nor I spoke until we were well away from the house. Then he stopped to look at Adan Jr.

"I'd say he's with the one he wants to be with," Edward told me.

We walked toward the stable as quickly as we could. It was late, and I was tired, but I was so full of excitement and happiness, I thought I could fly if it became necessary. Never once did I even consider the possible consequences for either of us.

Edward paused when I fell a little behind him. "I can help carry him if you want," he said.

"Oh, no. I'm fine," I said, and he laughed.

"I doubt that you'll ever let go of him again."

"Me, too," I said. "He's perfect."

"Well, just take it easy. You have a long way back," he warned.

I nodded, and then I smiled and shook my head. "Maybe not, Edward."

"Huh? Why not?"

"Look," I said.

He turned.

About twenty yards ahead of us, saddled and waiting, Amigo pawed the ground and nodded. Edward looked at me, astounded.

"I don't get it," he said.

"That's Amigo. He was Adan's horse. Gerry Sommer obviously saddled him for me."

"Seriously?"

"*Sí,* Edward, seriously," I said, and walked to Amigo. Edward held Adan Jr. until I mounted, and then he handed him back to me and took the reins.

Without saying another word, he started for the canyon. Amigo walked behind him quietly, smoothly. As we passed the trailer, Gerry Sommer stepped out and looked our way.

"He knows his way back," he said.

"*Gracias,* Gerry."

"*Vaya con dios,*" he called as we entered the deeper shadows and started into the canyon. Adan Jr., rocked by the movement of Amigo, soon fell asleep in my arms. The three of us moved gracefully through the darkness, silhouetted against the blazing stars. Lizards scampered in every direction. Bats circled, but nothing bothered us or interfered. It was as if the desert had always been our home.

Without my slower gait holding him back, Edward was able to make better time. In a little less than an hour, we reached the end of the canyon where we had parked my car. He took Adan Jr. in his arms so I could dismount and held him a few moments longer while I said good-bye to Amigo. The horse stood there looking at us as if he knew everything we were doing.

"He has human eyes," Edward said.

"*Sí*. Maybe Adan is looking at us through him."

"Maybe. I won't deny anything anymore," Edward said.

I took Adan Jr. back into my arms, and Edward opened the rear door for me. Then he hurried around and got into the driver's seat. When he started the engine, Amigo turned and began his trek back to the stable.

"Uncanny," Edward said, watching him go off.

"*Sí*," I said. I couldn't stop the tears of joy from streaking down my cheeks.

He handed me the washcloth for my face and cleaned his own of the shoe polish. Then he pulled onto the road, and we made our way slowly back to the small city and onto the freeway for our journey into Mexico.

Once again, I was going home, crossing over, but this time, Mexico was the promised land and not America. We stopped on the way out of the desert communities at a twenty-four-hour supermarket, where Edward went in to buy what I needed for Adan Jr. We decided that we could cross the border before we stopped to take a much-needed sleep.

We were both afraid that Edward's name and description would be with the border authorities, but no one appeared to pay much attention to us, and we had no trouble crossing into Mexico. Edward had the maps we needed, so once we entered the city of Mexicali, we continued for an hour more and then pulled into a roadside motel. It was already dawn. Adan Jr. had slept through most of the trip. I changed his diaper in the motel room and placed him beside me on the bed. Despite my own deep fatigue, I couldn't close my eyes. The wonder of him was too great. Edward, on the other hand, practically passed out. Finally, I dozed off when Adan Jr. did, and we all slept well into the mid-afternoon.

The moment Edward turned on his cell phone, it rang to indicate he had a voice message. I watched him listen to it and turn off his phone again.

"It was your aunt," he said, instead of saying "my mother."

"What?"

"She said Ray called her first thing, enraged, hysterical, but she also said she told him she doesn't know anything. She said we should just return from wherever we are hiding. Don't worry. We'll be fine. Let's just move along."

Our plan was to drive to Guadalajara, where we felt we could be less likely to be discovered. It was a little more than two more hours of driving. Edward thought we should lie low for a while before going deeper into Mexico. He said Señor Bovio would assume I'd return to my village, so it would be better to find somewhere to go where we would not stand out. He thought eventually we could settle into one of the tourist locations, perhaps Puerto Vallarta.

Most of the time, I was too occupied with Adan Jr. to think too much about all this. Holding him in my arms, seeing the Mexican landscape, reading the signs, and speaking to the people filled me with a sense of invulnerability. Nothing could interfere. This was meant to be. I was truly home with my child.

Of course, I worried about Edward. He promised that in time he would return to the United States and revive his career pursuit. He bragged that they could torture him, lock him in a dark hole, whatever, and he would never reveal where I was or that he even had anything to do with me. He believed that after a period of time, Señor Bovio would give up. Mexico, after all, was famous for swallowing up fugitives from America.

He had cleverly arranged for my funds to be transferred to a Mexican bank. The first chance we had, we withdrew them and put them into another bank. Of course, he had money of his own as well. Finances would never be a problem.

"You'll grow up with your son in pretty places," he told me. "Maybe you'll even change your name eventually. Someday, I'm sure you'll meet a new young man who will quickly fall in love with you, and you will have a good life after all. I'll make secret trips to Mexico, and we'll see each other as often as possible."

On and on he went as we drove, creating this wonderful story of my future. He even predicted that when he became an international lawyer, he would find a way to clear my name and make it possible for me to go anywhere. Nothing could stop us now.

After we settled into a small hotel in Guadalajara, I went with Adan Jr. to the beautiful cathedral and gave thanks and prayed.

Edward said he was afraid to use his cell phone now. He didn't want to be traced, so he went to a public phone to call a friend back in the Palm Springs area to see if there was any news about me. When we met afterward at a café, he said there was nothing in the papers and nothing on the television or radio news.

"Señor Bovio hasn't made this a big story. Maybe he won't. It's not the best publicity for him."

It sounded good for us, but I was still very worried.

The following day, we set out for Puerto Vallarta. The weather was perfect. Edward was enjoying the Mexican music and learning more phrases and expressions in Spanish. He thought that if he lived there a month, he would easily become fluent.

"It's in my blood, after all," he said.

It was good to see him so happy. Maybe he was right when he said I was doing him a favor by letting him help me. Maybe he needed this almost as much as I did.

We had come so far together since the day I had met him. The journey was filled with obstacles and disappointments along the way, but when I looked back at the Delia who had first arrived in America, terrified and lost, and the Delia I saw in the mirror now, I realized how much older I had become, perhaps because of those obstacles and disappointments. The same seemed true for Edward as well.

Just outside Puerto Vallarta, we stopped at a cantina

for some lunch. From the patio, we could see the ocean. I breast-fed Adan Jr. No one seemed to notice or care. Edward thought that was amusing.

"My mother," he said, "would probably pass out on the spot. We'd be scraping her off the floor here."

I laughed, and he told me some stories about things he had done when he was younger, things that embarrassed her in public. He wanted me to talk more about my mother. He was intrigued with the differences between the sisters. I realized as we ate and talked about ourselves and the family that these past days had drawn us closer than we had ever been. I couldn't remember ever feeling as optimistic as I did at that cantina table. Adan Jr. seemed just as contented, and when he smiled, Edward laughed and said, "No matter what, that makes it worth it."

Afterward, all of us feeling warm and hopeful, we continued into Puerto Vallarta. We saw the tourists coming off the cruise ships and the busy streets and shops. Edward was right, I thought. We would be less distinguishable there. We drove slowly, searching for a good place to stay. Edward had a guidebook that described some of the smaller, slightly out-of-the-way places. There was one called the Playa Iguana that he thought sounded perfect because of its small size. At one point, we had to stop so I could get directions, but we eventually reached the street where it was.

Both previous nights, I had had nightmares, some so vivid that I woke up in a sweat. I never mentioned them to Edward. When I was little and had a nightmare, Abuela Anabela would tell me, "*Los sueños sueños son.* Dreams are only dreams. Air. *Poof.*" She would clap her hands to show me how quickly they could be destroyed. No one comforted me as well as she did.

But when we drove down the side street and pulled in front of the Playa Iguana, one of my nightmares vividly came to life. It was so incredible a sight that neither Edward nor I could utter a sound.

There, standing in front of the hotel, was Señor Bovio. Beside him were two policemen.

And behind us now was a police car.

It was as if *el diablo* himself had dropped out of the sky.

17

Justice

As we were soon to discover, our biggest mistake had been to take my car instead of Edward's. Neither of us knew that the car's luxury package included a tracking system designed to find it if it was ever stolen. It had taken Señor Bovio a while to get the Mexican authorities involved, but once they were, they tracked us easily on our way to Puerto Vallarta. When we started toward the Playa Iguana, they concluded that we were headed to the hotel. Señor Bovio had been flown in and quickly brought up to date concerning the tracking. Moments before we turned into the street, he and the police had turned into it.

My heart stopped and started when I saw him, but what made the nightmare come to life even more horrendously was Mrs. Newell stepping out of the hotel to walk with him and the police toward my car. I held Adan Jr. tightly. Edward looked at the options, thinking perhaps that he might be able to pull away and escape, but another police car appeared in front of us.

"It's no use," I said. "Your mother was right. He's too powerful."

Mrs. Newell tugged on the rear door. "Open this door!" she screamed.

A policeman stood by Edward's window, glaring in at him. He tapped the window with his baton.

Edward's shoulders dropped. He flipped the switch to unlock the car, and Mrs. Newell jerked the door open.

"Please, *señor*, don't let her take my baby!" I cried.

Señor Bovio nodded at Mrs. Newell, and she leaned in.

"You'll only hurt him if you resist," she warned. "Let him go now."

As if he could sense what was happening, Adan Jr. began to cry. I thought my lungs would explode. Sobbing hard myself, I kissed him on the forehead before she took him from my arms and backed out of the car. Simultaneously, the policeman at Edward's door opened it and reached in to pull him out of the car. Señor Bovio came around the automobile.

"You can't even begin to imagine the trouble you have made for yourself and for her," Señor Bovio told him.

Another policeman ordered me out of the car as well. We were both handcuffed and put into the rear of a police car. I sat watching Señor Bovio and Mrs. Newell carrying Adan Jr. as they headed down the street to another automobile. Adan Jr. was still crying, but she didn't do anything to comfort him. I could do nothing. I could do nothing for myself, and it might even go harder for Edward, I thought, recalling that he had been prohibited from reentering Mexico.

"Don't you dare feel sorry for me," Edward told me before I could utter a word.

We were driven away, but to my surprise, we were not taken to a jail in Puerto Vallarta. Instead, we were driven to the airport, where we were turned over to a U.S. marshal. He had different sets of handcuffs to place on us.

"You two are lucky," he said. "You're not going to be held here and tried here."

But before either of us could breathe easier, he added, "You're being returned to the U.S., where you will be held and tried for kidnapping."

"It's her baby," Edward told him. "How can she be tried for kidnapping her own baby?"

He shrugged. "Hey," he said, "I'm just the deliveryman. Tell it to the judge and jury."

We were led to a plane and boarded, and soon after, we were on our way to the States. It had all happened so quickly I thought I was stuck in a dream, but that hope died as quickly as it had come.

Hours later, we were handed over to two FBI agents at the Los Angeles airport and then taken to federal court, where we were to be arraigned. Neither of us expected that Tía Isabela would do anything to help us, but we were surprised again when we arrived at the court and found Mr. Simon waiting. Tía Isabela had called him and asked him to be there.

"I might make enough off you two and not need any more clients," he joked.

Neither of us was in the mood for any humor. Maybe it wasn't so much a joke as a comment by someone quite astounded by all of these events himself, no matter how experienced he was and what he had already seen in his legal life. He explained how Tía Isabela had called him as soon as she was informed that we had been located and arrested. She immediately offered to put up the bail for us.

"First, I have to get the judge to agree to grant you bail before you are formally arraigned and charged. Your mother is on her way here to be present at this hearing," Mr. Simon said. "She gave me some helpful information, which I have given to the district attorney so he wouldn't oppose the granting of bail."

"My mother? What information?" Edward asked.

"Information relating to the custody agreement Delia signed. As you know, I'm familiar with that document. I gave you my best opinion on it before all of this occurred, but she's added some information that might have significant weight."

"What information, Mr. Simon?" Edward asked again.

"Information that might lead to the conclusion that Delia was coerced into signing," he said. "I don't want to say too much and get anyone's hopes too high. Let's take it a step at a time."

We didn't see Tía Isabela until we entered the courtroom. Of course, she looked as if she could set the place on fire with her blazing eyes. Before she could say a word to him as we were led to the front of the courtroom, Edward muttered, "Don't start, Mother."

She pulled her shoulders up and, with a face cut in stone, focused on the judge. Mr. Simon walked over to the district attorney and spoke quietly. We were taken to a table and told to sit and wait. The judge, a man who looked well into his seventies, was talking softly with the court clerk. Everyone around us seemed to be

involved with private conversations. Edward shrugged
and looked at me. I had never been in a courtroom, so
I didn't know what was happening. I was too numb to
feel anything or say anything.

After a while, we saw the district attorney and Mr.
Simon approach the judge. Their conversation took
quite a long time. Finally, everyone returned to his
seat. The judge rapped his gavel.

"Since the events of this proceeding are dependent
upon a motion being made in family court," he said, "I
will postpone the arraignment of Edward Dallas and
Delia Yebarra until a determination is made by the
family court. However, since evidence supporting the
possibility of a flight risk is strong, I am assigning bail
of one hundred fifty thousand dollars each. I understand that you will provide this bail, Mrs. Dallas?"

"Yes, Your Honor," Tía Isabela said.

I looked at Edward, but he didn't flinch. In fact, he
looked annoyed at his mother for coming to our aid.

Less than an hour later, Mr. Simon led us out of the
courtroom to Tía Isabela's limousine. Edward hesitated, but his mother came down the steps behind us
and sharply ordered us into the car.

"Where are we going?" he asked, still defiant and
unappreciative.

"To the Bovio estate," she said.

"I'll be right behind you guys," Mr. Simon told us.
"Just do as she says, Edward."

"Why are we going there?" he asked.

"You'll hear it all on the way," Mr. Simon replied.
"But it ain't over until it's over," he added as a warning. "It might all turn out to be a wild-goose chase, at
which point you two will be facing the same judge in

the same courtroom under different circumstances. So, for now, I'd advise you to do just as you're told."

Both Edward and I were very confused. We got into the limousine, and Tía Isabela followed.

"Let's not talk for a while," she said the moment she sat across from us. "I need to get my boiling blood cooled. Get us out of here, Mr. Garman," she ordered her driver, and we were on our way.

She reached into the cabinet and took out a bottle of white wine, pouring herself a glass. Stone-faced, Edward sat looking at her. I was too terrified to move a muscle. Finally, she was relaxed enough to speak.

"I can't blame Delia for actually believing you could get away with such an insane action, but how someone supposedly as intelligent as you went through with this, Edward, I'll never understand. I'm convinced now that you've lost your senses. You might very well need professional help."

Edward didn't reply. Instead, he reached into the cabinet, too, and took out a bottle of scotch, some ice cubes, and some soda to make himself a drink. He offered me a soft drink, which I took. I felt as if the sand in the desert was lining the walls of my throat.

Edward sat back and smiled at Tía Isabela. "I need professional help? I'm sure you don't remember, Mother, but when I was about twelve, you and I were having one of those very rare moments when we were by ourselves, enjoying the afternoon, having lunch on the patio. We actually resembled a mother and her child for a little while, and I asked you how you could just pick up and leave your family in Mexico, write them off like that. I don't think you appreciated my tone of voice, because you became very angry. But eventually, you calmed down, and you said, 'Sometimes you have to do something for yourself, something everyone else will think is foolish, but something that gives you a sense of self-respect. When you're older, Edward, you'll understand.' "

He leaned forward. "Well, I still don't understand you, but I'm glad I did what I did to help Delia. I never felt better about myself, Mother. It was the right thing to do, and I have my self-respect."

She sipped her wine and shook her head. "I know you don't get all of this drama and passion from your father," she said, "so I guess I'll have to take the blame."

"Your admitting blame for anything is a wonder."

"Don't be disrespectful, Edward."

He glanced at me and looked out the window for a while and then turned back to her.

"Why is Mr. Simon following us to the Bovio estate?" he asked.

"Ray understands lawyers better than any other type of professional," she replied. "You, me, and Delia don't carry enough weight."

"Well, can't we know what it's all about?"

"Of course, but first there are some questions I want answered and answered honestly." Before Edward could speak, she added, "They are all for Delia. Nothing would anger me more than going forward here on a foundation of lies and deceit. Do you understand, Delia?"

"*Sí*, Tía Isabela."

"Good. Sophia confessed to me that she has been getting this joy drug from Fani Cordova for some time now. You knew that, correct?"

"I did not know that. I told the truth, Tía Isabela. I did not see Fani give Sophia the drug this time, either."

"But you knew she had it, correct?"

"*Sí.*"

"How did you know? Did she offer any to you?"

I looked at Edward. I had never told him so.

"*Sí,*" I said. "When we were going out with the two boys and when she wanted me to stay awake for the party. I pretended to take it, but I didn't. She knew later that I didn't. I wasn't very good at pretending."

"Was that the first and only time she offered this drug to you, Delia?"

"*Sí,* Tía Isabela. The first time."

"She didn't give you this drug when you were at her house for your secret meeting with Edward or during that meeting?" she asked, nodding at him.

"No, Tía Isabela."

"And Edward didn't have any?"

"For Christ's sake, Mother," Edward protested.

"Don't put on that astonished look. I know you haven't been exactly an angel, Edward, especially the last seven or eight months."

"I would never offer Delia—"

"No, Tía Isabela. He had nothing, and he offered nothing."

She nodded. "If you're lying to me this time, I'll join the prosecution to have you put away. I promise you both."

"What is this all about, Mother?"

She stared at us a moment and shook her head. "I think for the sake of authenticity, you won't be told any more for now."

"Huh?"

"It is very important that Ray Bovio believes what we believe, and if he thinks there's a conspiracy among us, his back will go up, and he'll put on a defense that, frankly, might be impossible to pierce. The consequences after that would be severe for both of you."

She continued, "I know you don't have much faith in my intelligence, that I have not had your respect as your mother or even as a businesswoman, but you're going to have to be patient and trusting and believe that I know what I'm doing."

"I never said you weren't intelligent, Mother. You're just not . . . not a successful mother."

"Maybe not," she said. "But I'd like the chance to see if I could still be. Apparently, there was a time, like the time you described, when you loved me. Maybe you could borrow from then and have a little faith."

Edward glanced at me and looked away before I could see his eyes water. He said nothing. He sipped his drink and looked out the window. The lights from other cars going in the opposite direction streaked by. A pall of silence fell over all of us. I was sure we were all wondering the same thing. Were we on our way, rushing, to another funeral?

Anticipating our arrival, the security guard at the Bovio estate opened the gate as soon as we turned in. He stood back and watched us and Mr. Simon drive through and up to the house.

"Once we enter, neither of you is to say a word unless directly asked a question by Mr. Simon," Tía Isabela told us. "I want you as meek as mice. Is that clear, Edward?"

"Yes, Mother," he said.

Señor Garman opened the door for us. Tía Isabela got out first. Edward followed, and then I emerged. I looked toward the stables and wondered if Señor Bovio had learned that Gerry Sommer had provided Amigo for me. I hoped not. I didn't want to see someone else hurt by my actions.

"Can I ask how you got Ray to permit us to come here tonight, Mother?"

"I made him a promise," she said.

"What promise?"

"We'll talk about it later," she said. "Right now, it's not important."

Mr. Simon joined us and nodded at Edward and me. "They understand how I want to conduct this?" he asked Tía Isabela.

"Yes, they do," she said firmly. "I didn't give them any details, however. I thought it might be better if they were part of the discovery."

"Very good. Let's go do it, then," he said, and we all walked up the stairs to the front entrance.

Teresa, who had been waiting, opened the door. She avoided looking at me. "Mr. Bovio is in the library," she said. "I'll take you to him."

As we passed through the grand entryway, I looked up at the dome and said a quick prayer. I then looked up the stairway, thinking about Adan Jr. and hoping he was sleeping comfortably. There was no sign of Mrs. Newell. Señor Bovio was sitting sideways at the head of the long table, looking as if he were about to get up and walk away. I saw that he had a glass of brandy.

"I don't want this to take long," he said when we entered. "It's been an unnecessarily long enough day as it is." He focused his angry eyes on me.

"It shouldn't take us long," Mr. Simon said. "Thanks for agreeing to the meeting."

Apparently, Señor Bovio had been told who Mr. Simon was. He put his briefcase down on the table and nodded at us to sit as well. Then he opened it and pulled out the document I had signed to accept Señor Bovio's custody of Adan Jr. He slid it over the table toward Señor Bovio.

"It's not necessary to show me that," Señor Bovio said, glancing down at it but not touching it.

"Since it's the centerpiece of our discussion, I thought I should put it on the table," Mr. Simon said. "If I am right about the chronology here, you had offered and provided what you believed to be excellent medical care for Delia Yebarra during her pregnancy."

"There's no question about that," Señor Bovio said. "No matter how unappreciated it was," he added, targeting his gaze at me.

"And," Mr. Simon said, ignoring the comment, "you offered her your home for herself and her child after he was born. You offered to provide for her to attend a school for nursing, but at the time, you did not ask to have sole custody of your grandchild."

"I don't need this historic review," Señor Bovio said, and sipped some of his brandy.

"I just want us all to agree on the facts, sir."

"I agree so far," Señor Bovio said. "And?"

"And it wasn't until Delia suffered a near-miscarriage and had to have the emergency caesarean that you presented her with this document. You learned that there was the presence of a drug popularly known as Ecstasy or X in her blood and threatened to make that an issue if she refused to sign this document. Am I correct?"

"No decent grandfather would have done less," Señor Bovio said. "Especially if we consider that he had lost his son and was the sole protector of his son's child."

"No one's questioning your motives, sir."

"Then why are you here?" Señor Bovio fired back at him, "defending these . . . kidnappers?"

"Perhaps, sir, you were a bit hasty in your condemnation of Delia, either deliberately or otherwise."

"In her heart, she knows that is not so," Señor Bovio said, glaring at me. "She conspired with a fugitive in Mexico, obstructed justice, and perhaps after taking drugs or drinking too much, carelessly caused my son's death."

"Ray!" Tía Isabela cried.

"Why aren't those facts placed on this table along with my document?" he snapped back at her. He turned to Mr. Simon. "Are you here to get me to have the district attorney drop the kidnapping charges? Don't you consider what I went through when I learned my grandson was stolen? You think I should care about their pain and suffering and forget my own? My son is gone!"

"No, sir," Mr. Simon said.

"Then why did you come here?" he shouted, his face reddening and the veins in his neck straining.

"Simply to get at the truth, sir," Mr. Simon replied quietly. "Something I hope you want as much as we do."

"The truth," Señor Bovio repeated disdainfully.

Mr. Simon looked at Tía Isabela and nodded.

She rose and went to the library door, then turned back with Teresa right behind her. Apparently, she had been waiting in the hallway just outside the library.

"What is this?" Señor Bovio demanded.

"We'll know in a few minutes, Mr. Bovio," Mr. Simon said. He looked at Teresa. "Please, have a seat," he said.

Teresa glanced at Señor Bovio and then sat. She kept her gaze down.

"Your full name is Teresa Donald?" Mr. Simon began.

"Yes, sir," she said.

"And you've been working for Mr. Bovio for a long time, Teresa?"

"Nearly thirty-two years," she replied.

"That's dedication," Mr. Simon said.

"Teresa is practically a member of my family," Señor Bovio said. "So?"

"I'm happy you feel that way about her. Apparently, she feels the same way about you," Mr. Simon said. "Teresa, I know this is difficult for you. You made that clear to Mrs. Dallas, but you see where it's all taken us. Please, tell Mr. Bovio what you have told Mrs. Dallas."

Teresa looked up at Señor Bovio.

"What is it, Teresa?" he asked.

"It's Mrs. Newell, sir," she said. "She was the one who put the drug into Delia's body."

It was as if thunder had clapped in the library.

Señor Bovio stared at her, and then he smiled and shook his head. "No, Teresa. You're mistaken, I'm sure."

"I'm not, sir. I'm sorry. I saw her on a few occasions add some tiny portions to the nutritional drink she prepared for Delia right before she suffered the near-miscarriage."

"It was probably one of those nutrients she said Delia needed," Señor Bovio told her. "You wouldn't know, Teresa. I'm—"

"No, sir. Normally, I wouldn't know, but I thought she was keeping this stuff in an odd place." She looked at Mr. Simon. "I clean her room as well as Adan Jr.'s, you see. I was making her bed, changing the sheets, when I lifted the mattress a bit, and the packet fell out of the bedsprings. I wouldn't have noticed it, but I always dust under the bed after I remake it. Naturally, it frightened me to see it hidden like that. I recalled seeing her sprinkle powder from a packet just like it, and as you said, sir, I assumed it was something to do with the special concoction she made for Delia. Who was I to question that?"

"What did you do with it?" Mr. Simon asked.

"I was very frightened. I put it back where it was, squeezed in the bedsprings."

Señor Bovio just stared at her and then shook his head slightly. "Why didn't you come to me with this story?" he asked.

"I thought about that, sir, but you were so . . . dependent on Mrs. Newell. You thought so highly of her, and I saw how having Adan Jr. here had given you a new lease on life, as they say. I didn't have the heart to destroy your happiness and . . ." She paused. "I didn't think you'd take my word for anything against her."

"Why would she do such a thing?" Señor Bovio asked, pulling his head back, still very skeptical.

I thought Teresa would retreat in the face of Señor Bovio's determination to discredit her report and keep his faith in Mrs. Newell, but she held her ground and even strengthened it.

"For one thing, she's still here, sir. She wouldn't have been if Delia was looking after her son, now, would she?"

"That's—"

"I've seen some other things that bothered me from time to time," she quickly added, and looked down again as if she were the one who should be ashamed.

"What other things?" Señor Bovio demanded, pressing his palms against the table so hard I thought he would snap his own wrists. "What other things, Teresa?"

"There were times I caught her trying on Delia's maternity clothes."

No one spoke. Señor Bovio's mouth opened slightly.

"I wouldn't have thought much about it, but I had heard some stories about her. Even so, I wouldn't dare be the one to spread new rumors, and I didn't know how to tell you about such a thing, Mr. Bovio."

He shook his head. "This is blatantly ridiculous. Why would you come forward now with this, Teresa?"

"I can't say I'm proud of myself for not coming to you sooner, sir, especially after you sent Delia away like that. I know Mrs. Newell was pleased, and you looked very pleased as well."

She continued, looking to me now, "I never had a child of my own, but I could only imagine what it was like having your baby literally ripped out of your body and then your arms. It got so I couldn't sleep at night thinking about it, and then, when this happened . . . well, I can't say I wasn't rooting for you, Delia. As soon as I heard you and your cousin were arrested, I went to Mrs. Dallas."

She told Señor Bovio, "I was still afraid to go to you, sir. You were so angry now, I didn't know what you'd do or say. I didn't want to lose my position here, but it was like swallowing something sour, sir. I couldn't hold it down anymore. I'm sorry. I truly am." She said that more to me than to him.

"This has got to be some sort of misunderstanding," Señor Bovio insisted.

"Then you're telling us you know nothing about this?" Mr. Simon asked.

I had no idea why or how he could ask Señor Bovio such a thing, but he had his lawyer's motives and sounded stronger and more like a prosecutor now. I also understood what Tía Isabela had meant when she explained why she wanted a lawyer at the table.

"What? Giving her drugs? Are you a total idiot? Do you think I would endanger my grandson like that?"

"I hope not. I don't imagine most people would believe it, but in a courtroom—"

"What courtroom?"

"Well, you can plainly see that these events change things, Mr. Bovio. There was, whether you were aware of it or not, obvious coercion here. This young woman was maneuvered into signing over custody of her child." He pointed to the document on the table. "Following that injustice, she came here as any mother might and took her baby back, and now she's about to be charged with kidnapping. If she was coerced into signing over her child, there's no kidnapping charge. She might have grounds for her own lawsuit, and I'm sure the district attorney would have interest in all of this."

Señor Bovio was quiet for a moment. He looked at all of us and then at Teresa before addressing Mr.

Simon. "I still don't believe any of this. Just because you have a maid's impressions of some ingredient . . . the girl was just involved in a drug incident in Los Angeles, wasn't she?" he snapped back, now sounding more like someone grasping at straws.

"Fani Cordova will admit to providing the drug to my daughter, and my daughter will admit to getting it from her," Tía Isabela said. "She will testify that Delia knew absolutely nothing about it. In fact, she realizes she's alive today because of Delia's quick thinking. I guess Edward would say his sister's begun to grow up."

"This is all just confusing the situation," Señor Bovio insisted.

Mr. Simon turned to Teresa. "When was the last time you changed Mrs. Newell's bedding and dusted under that bed, Teresa?"

"Today, sir. This morning."

"And can you tell us anything about the item you found and put back in the bedsprings?"

"It's still there, sir. Last I looked."

"Well, we have no search warrant, Mr. Bovio, but I would think you would want to get to the bottom of this as quickly as we do," Mr. Simon said. "It would also go far to prove you weren't part of this."

Señor Bovio looked at us and at Teresa. We were all staring intently at him.

I held my breath. Would he tell us all to get out, or would he do what Mr. Simon asked? Was Mrs. Newell's grip on him and his happiness so strong that he would blot out the truth?

He saw a tear escape my eye. I wiped it away quickly, but he nodded and stood.

We all rose and followed him out slowly. Our march

to the stairway and the slow climb up was so somber I could feel the weight of all of the darkness I had gone through on my shoulders. In my heart of hearts, however, I believed Adan was walking up those stairs beside me.

Mrs. Newell heard us coming and stepped out of Adan Jr.'s room. She held him in her arms. He was asleep. "And what's this?" she asked.

Señor Bovio paused. "Maybe nothing," he said. "Maybe everything."

He nodded at her bedroom, and Teresa opened the door.

"What are you doing?" Mrs. Newell asked, stepping forward.

Adan Jr. squirmed in her arms but didn't awaken.

We entered her bedroom. The lights were on. She came in behind us. I stood beside her, watching Adan Jr., dying inside to reach out and take him from her arms but deathly afraid to do anything to interrupt.

Teresa went to the bed and got to her knees. She looked under the bed and then up at Mr. Simon and nodded.

"What is this?" Mrs. Newell demanded now. "This is my bedroom!"

"For the moment," Señor Bovio said, nodding at her, "let Delia hold Adan Jr."

"What?"

"Just do what I ask, Mrs. Newell."

She turned to me, but I didn't think she was going to relinquish my baby. I moved forward and reached for him. She hesitated, tightened her grip, and then relinquished him. I held him closely.

Edward moved forward and lifted the mattress. Mr.

Simon shook the bedsprings, and then Teresa reached under and brought out the packet.

Mrs. Newell seemed to freeze. Even her eyes turned to ice. She didn't move. "I don't know what that is," she quickly said.

Señor Bovio looked at her and took the packet from Teresa. He stared at it a moment.

He didn't look up at Mrs. Newell when he spoke. "I would like you to pack up your things immediately and be out of this house and off my property as quickly as humanly possible."

"What? I tell you I don't—"

"As quickly as humanly possible," Señor Bovio repeated, looking at her coldly this time.

"You are making a big mistake, Mr. Bovio. Why, if your son was alive—"

His lips trembled. "He would be smiling," Señor Bovio said. He looked at me and Adan Jr. "He's smiling now, I am sure," he said.

My tears fell on Adan Jr.'s face.

He opened his eyes and looked up at me.

And I would swear until the day I die that he smiled.

Epilogue

One day in early April, *mi tía* Isabela's head house-keeper, Señora Rosario, came to Adan Jr.'s nursery to tell me I had a visitor. He was waiting outside. She said he wouldn't come into the *hacienda*. I had just finished feeding and changing Adan Jr. and set him in his crib, contented and ready for his nap.

"*Quién es?*" I asked. The days of no Spanish permitted in the house were gone. I thought Señora Rosario appreciated that more than anyone.

"*No sé. Él no diría.*"

Why wouldn't he tell her his name? I wondered. For a moment, I thought about the boy with whom I had gone on that dreadful double date when I was with Fani in Los Angeles. I don't blame him for not giving his name, I thought, and marched to the front entrance. I had no patience for this.

It had been months since I had returned to live with

Adan Jr. in Tía Isabela's *hacienda*. Edward had returned to college, and Sophia was attending a college-preparatory school in San Diego. Her near-death experience had matured her in ways Tía Isabela had lost faith in ever seeing. I had put off nursing school until the fall and now would attend the one in San Bernardino, which meant I could commute and not be away from Adan Jr. too long. With Inez and Señora Rosario assisting, I felt comfortable about all of it.

Señor Bovio was a frequent visitor, never arriving without gifts for Adan Jr. and me but sometimes bringing something for Tía Isabela as well. They were starting to see each other socially again, and he was even talking seriously about returning to politics. He had finally gotten to the point where he could look at me without tons of guilt darkening his eyes and lowering his gaze. It was Adan Jr. who, with his wondrous smile, tied us together in ways that would bring us to forgive.

I opened the front door and stood for a moment looking out with a mixture of surprise and happiness but also some fear.

Ignacio stood by his father's truck, his arms folded across his chest. He looked even bigger than the last time and still had that military-style short hair. I walked down to him slowly.

"I thought if I sent in my name, you would not come out," he said.

"What a foolish idea," I told him, and he smiled.

"Someone with some influence managed to get me out early."

"I'm happy for you and for your family, Ignacio."

"*Sí, gracias,*" he said, and then he looked away and confessed that he had been out for almost a month.

"A month? I did not know."

"I was afraid to come see you. I was afraid you hated me now or wouldn't want to have anything to do with me."

"Another foolish idea," I told him.

"My parents knew all about you, about your returning to live with your aunt. Do you still want to be a nurse?"

"*Sí.* I'm going to school in the fall."

"That's good. I'm sure you will be a very good nurse."

"Are you working again with your father?"

"For now. He keeps pressuring me to go to school, too. While I was in prison, I worked in the warden's garden. I changed a lot, and he liked it very much. My father thinks I should study landscaping and become a fancy gardener."

"That would be wonderful, Ignacio."

"He says it's a holy thing to bring beauty into the world."

"*Él es un hombre sabio.*"

"*Sí.* I should only be as wise at his age."

"You will."

"Maybe. How is your son?"

"He is very well, *gracias.* He's sleeping now; otherwise, he would be in my arms."

Ignacio laughed. "I'm sure you don't let go of him often."

"That time comes soon enough."

"You sound as if you've become very wise, maybe too wise for me," he said.

"I can afford to share it," I said, and he laughed. Then he nodded. "It's been a while since I really laughed. I'm glad I stopped by."

"Then you'll have to return often. It's better to laugh than to cry."

"Another saying of your grandmother's?"

"No. This is my own."

"Now I know you're a fully grown woman. You have your own sayings to pass on."

"Then you'll be back?"

"*Sí,*" he said. "We've both come too far, made too many crossings, to turn and walk away."

"I'll be waiting," I said.

He unfroze his arms and embraced me. In that long moment as we held on to each other, all of the pain and suffering we had endured seemed to fall away, dropping to our feet like old, dead leaves. He pressed his lips to one of my tears.

"The salt of your body is now the salt of mine," he whispered, and then he got into his truck, smiled, waved, and drove off.

I watched until he was gone.

I didn't know that Tía Isabela was watching from a window. She was waiting when I entered the *hacienda.*

"That was a surprise for you," she said. I studied her face and saw an impish smile.

"Maybe not so much for you," I told her.

She laughed. "Ray did whisper in my ear a while back, but I did not want to say anything for fear Ignacio would not contact you. No more disappointments are permitted in this house," she declared.

"That's good," I said.

We were both in a good mood, anyway. Edward was coming home to spend the weekend with us.

Later, we had a nice dinner together. Edward was very excited about his decision to go to law school and talked so much that neither Tía Isabela nor I had a chance to tell him anything. It made us laugh even harder. Finally, toward the end of our dinner, he put down his coffee cup and leaned toward his mother.

"I have been meaning to ask you something," he said. "I didn't want to bring it up, because I didn't want to spoil everything."

"What is it, Edward?" Tía Isabela groaned, throwing me a look of feigned agony.

"When we were on our way to Señor Bovio's home that night, you told us you had gotten him to grant the meeting by making him a promise. You never told us what that promise was. What was it?"

She looked down at her coffee cup and fiddled with her spoon, a slight smile on her lips. "I promised him I would marry him," she said. "Who knows? Maybe I will keep it."

"I thought you always wanted to marry him," Edward said.

"Not while he was living with a ghost. If I had married him then, I'd probably be doing what Delia had to do, wearing his dead wife's clothes, maybe even her wigs."

"That was quite a chance you took, then," Edward said.

She looked at me and nodded. "I thought it was time to take one."

None of us spoke. I took a deep breath.

"I think it's time to do one more thing," she said.

"What?"

"Let it be a surprise."

We didn't pursue her. When Sophia's spring holiday began, and Edward's as well, she revealed it.

Two days after we were all together, she presented us each with a plane ticket.

The following morning, we were all on our way to the airport. The flight and the drive took most of the day, but we arrived in our village in Mexico before the sun had gone down. Sophia was all eyes as we navigated the broken streets and passed the cantinas to the square, where the people had gathered to eat and sing. For her, it was truly like visiting another planet. It was even a little like that for me. I had been in such a different world.

It wasn't until we reached the cemetery and got out to stand before the family graves that I felt I had truly come home again.

And when I looked at Tía Isabela, I could see she finally felt something similar.

She smiled and talked about her parents. She knelt at their graves and my parents' graves and said her prayers.

"I'm sure my father is still angry at me," she told us.

"Not anymore," I said. "You've returned and won't let him die the third death."

She smiled and put her arm around my shoulder. "*Gracias,* Delia, *gracias* for bringing us all here."

We joined hands, the four of us, and walked to the car to go to the square, where we would find the Mexico that was in us, that would not die, that would take us farther than we had ever dreamed, that would help us to cross over any obstacle.

And where the spirits of our family waited to embrace us and help us light the candles to guide us forever through the darkness.

Family Storms
Virginia Andrews

Coming soon . . . the first in a
compelling new series

Living on the streets and selling knickknacks with her destitute
mother, Sasha Porter dreams of someday having a normal
life, with a real house and family. But she never thought a
devastating tragedy would bring her those very things:
one stormy night, a speeding car veers out of control,
killing her mother and badly injuring Sasha.

While in hospital, Sasha is whisked off to a fancy private
suite courtesy of the wealthy Mrs Jordan March, a complete
stranger who insists that Sasha come to live at her family's
luxurious mansion. With nowhere to go, Sasha accepts;
however she soon learns that Mrs March has never gotten
over the death of her daughter Alena. Before she knows it,
Sasha is using Alena's old room, sleeping in her bed and
wearing her clothes. But someone will make sure that
Sasha never takes Alena's place: a jealous sister
dead set on making Sasha's life a living hell.

ISBN 978-0-85720-785-2

Daughter of Darkness
Virginia Andrews

One night, woken by the sound of a young man's scream,
teenager Lorelei Patio discovers that her stern but loving
father, who adopted her and her sisters as infants, is no
ordinary man. He has raised his beautiful girls
for one purpose only: to lure young men
into their world of shadows.

Like her sisters, Lorelei has been trained in the art of seduction
and warned never to fall in love, as every man she attracts
is destined to fall victim to her father -
a two-hundred-year-old vampire.

But when she meets a handsome and charming classmate,
Lorelei is torn. Should she lose her father's love and follow
her own heart, or will the duty she has been brought up to
fulfil force her to sacrifice the love of her life?

ISBN 978-1-84983-359-2

Delia's Heart
Virginia Andrews

**Torn between two worlds - and two loves –
will Delia be able to follow her heart?**

Enticed by the glamour and privilege of life in Palm Springs,
California, Delia Yebarra is convinced by her cousin Edward
to leave her Mexican village and begin a new life in America.
But in a world where ruthless ambition and cruel lies are the
norm, will Delia be able to handle the pressures of this high-
powered lifestyle?

As Delia quickly gains a large group of friends and admirers
at her exclusive private high school, her spiteful cousin Sophia
becomes jealous of her beauty and popularity. Seething with
envy, she sets out to destroy Delia by spreading malicious
rumours. And when tragedy strikes back in Mexico as well,
will Delia find herself caught between her old and new lives
with nowhere to call home?

ISBN 978-1-84739-473-6

This book and other Virginia Andrews titles are available from your local bookshop or can be ordered direct from the publisher.

| 978-1-84983-359-2 | Daughter of Darkness | £6.99 |
| 978-1-84983-786-6 | Into the Darkness | £6.99 |

The Family Storms Series

| 978-0-85720-785-2 | Family Storms | £12.99 |

The Delia Series

978-1-84739-472-9	Delia's Crossing	£6.99
978-1-84739-473-6	Delia's Heart	£6.99
978-1-84739-474-3	Delia's Gift	£6.99

The Secret Series

| 978-1-84739-225-1 | Secrets in the Attic | £6.99 |

Free post and packing within the UK
Overseas customers please add £2 per paperback
Telephone Simon & Schuster Cash Sales at Bookpost
on 01624 677237 with your credit or debit card number
or send a cheque payable to Simon & Schuster Cash Sales to
PO Box 29, Douglas Isle of Man, IM99 1BQ
Fax: 01624 670923
Email: bookshop@enterprise.net
www.bookpost.co.uk

Please allow 14 days for delivery. Prices and availability
are subject to change without notice.